THEODOSIA
and the
EYES *of* HORUS

THEODOSIA

—— and the ——

EYES of HORUS

R. L. LaFevers

illustrated by Yoko Tanaka

HOUGHTON MIFFLIN BOOKS FOR CHILDREN
HOUGHTON MIFFLIN HARCOURT
BOSTON   NEW YORK   2010

Houghton Mifflin Books for Children is an imprint of
Houghton Mifflin Harcourt Publishing Company.

www.hmhbooks.com

The text of this book is set in Minister Book.
The illustrations are acrylic on board.
Map of 1905 London used courtesy of the Harvard Map Collection.

Library of Congress Cataloging-in-Publication Number 2009049709

ISBN 978-0-547-22592-0

Manufactured in the United States of America
DOC 10 9 8 7 6 5 4 3 2 1
4500219270

To true blue friends who stand by you through thick and thin.
In other words, to Mary Hershey,
a most excellent friend.

CHAPTER ONE

THE GREAT AWI BUBU

MARCH 23, 1907

I HATE BEING FOLLOWED. I especially hate being followed by a bunch of lunatic adults playing at being occultists. Unfortunately, the Black Sunners were out in full force today. I'd spotted the first one on High Street, and by the time I'd reached the Alcazar Theater, there were two more on my tail.

I glanced at the sparse crowd waiting outside the rundown theater, my heart sinking when I saw that Sticky Will wasn't there yet. Not knowing what else to do, I got in line for the ticket window, then checked to see if the men would follow. One leaned against the building across the street, and another one lounged against a lamppost, pretending to read the paper.

"If you aren't going to purchase a ticket, get out of the way," a coarse voice said.

I pulled my gaze away from my pursuers to find the woman in the ticket booth glaring at me. While my attention had been focused elsewhere, the line had moved forward, and it was now my turn. "Sorry," I muttered, setting my coin on the counter.

She snatched it up and shoved a green paper ticket at me. "Next?" she called out.

As I left the ticket booth, Will was still nowhere in sight. Keeping a close eye on the Black Sunners for any sudden moves, I ventured over to the playbill pasted to the crumbling brick wall.

INTRODUCING
THE GREAT AWI BUBU!
PERFORMING
REAL EGYPTIAN MAGIC!

The lurid picture showed a man in traditional Egyptian garb raising a mummy.

I was relatively sure that whatever the Great Awi Bubu did, it was *not* Egyptian magic. He was most likely some charlatan taking advantage of London's heightened interest in all things Egyptian.

Not that I'd had anything to do with that—well, not intentionally anyway. All those mummies running loose in London hadn't really been my fault. How was I to know that there was such a thing as a staff that could raise the dead? Or that it would be lurking in the Museum of Legends and Antiquities' basement? It could have happened to anyone.

Sticky Will had been instrumental in fixing the situation, and in the process he'd learned a little more about my unique relationship with the artifacts in my father's museum. Rather too much, if you asked me. But it couldn't be helped.

Oh, he didn't know I was the only one who could sense the vile curses and black magic still clinging to the artifacts. Or the true extent of my knowledge of the ancient Egyptian rituals and practices that I'd used to remove the curses. But he had seen some of the magic in action. And he'd seen what unscrupulous people were willing to do to get their hands on it. Consequently, Will now spent a large portion of his time scouring London in search of even more Egyptian magic, determined to prove that he was ready, willing, and able to take on the dark forces that surrounded us.

Which was why I now stood in front of the Alcazar Theater, ticket clutched in my hand, after everyone else had gone inside. The Black Sunners across the street—they called themselves scorpions, in honor of an old Egyptian myth—also seemed to realize that the crowd had thinned. With no one else about, one of the scorpions—Gerton, I believe—decided to make his move. Stepping away from the building, he headed across the street.

Will or no Will, I had to get inside. As I turned for the door, I heard a loud, wet, snuffling sound from behind the ticket booth. I perked up. There was only one person I knew who could turn a runny nose into a calling card: Snuffles.

I hurried around the corner, nearly bumping into one of Will's younger brothers. He wore a loud, plaid morning coat that was so large it nearly dragged on the ground. His sleeves had been rolled up several times, and he peered up at me from under an enormous bowler hat that was held in place by his rather remarkable ears. "Yer late," he said.

"No, I'm not. I've been waiting here for ages. Where's Will?"

"'E's inside already. Sixth row from the stage, center section, aisle seat. And 'e says to 'urry. The show's about to start."

"Aren't you coming?"

"I'll meet you inside," he said, then disappeared back down the street.

With one final glance in Gerton's direction, I proceeded to the theater entrance, gave my ticket to the porter, and went inside.

The lobby was empty and I could hear the feeble music of an out-of-tune piano. I opened the door that led to the auditorium and found that the lights had already been turned down. I let my eyes adjust to the dark, relieved when I finally recognized Will in the sixth row. He was easy to spot, actually, as he kept turning in his seat and looking around.

For me, no doubt.

He spotted me, then waved. I hurried to the empty seat next to him.

"Wot took you so long?" he asked.

"I've been waiting out front for ages," I said. "Where were you?"

Before I could answer, Snuffles and another boy appeared in the aisle. "Let us in," Snuffles said, a bit urgently. I turned my knees to the side so he could work past me. The second boy removed his tweed cap as he scooted by and I recognized the thin, pinched features of another one of Will's brothers—Ratsy. We had met briefly aboard the *Dreadnought* during a rather distracting set of circumstances. Nevertheless, he gave me a nod of greeting.

"How did you get in here?" I whispered to Snuffles.

He looked at Will, who pointedly wouldn't meet my gaze. "We used a side entrance, miss. Now 'ush. It's about to start."

Just then, the piano music became louder, more jangling.

The curtain opened. I settled back in the lumpy, threadbare seat and resolved to enjoy myself.

The stage held two fake palm trees, a pyramid that looked as if it was made of papier-mâché, and half a dozen burning torches. A sarcophagus sat in the middle of the stage. The music stopped, and the theater was so quiet you could hear the hiss of the gas lamps. Slowly, the lid to the sarcophagus began to open. It fell against the side with a thud, then a figure rose up from its depths.

"The Great Awi Bubu," a loud voice intoned from somewhere offstage, "will now perform amazing feats of Egyptian magic. This magic is old and dangerous, and the audience is advised to do exactly as the magician says in order to avoid any misfortune."

The magician was a skinny, wizened man who did indeed look to be of Egyptian descent. His head was bald and rather large. He wore a pair of wire spectacles perched on his beakish nose; it gave him the air of a very old baby bird. He wore a tunic of white linen with a colorful collar that looked vaguely like ancient Egyptian dress.

He stepped toward a basket near the front of the stage. Will elbowed me in the ribs. "Watch this now," he whispered.

"I *am* watching," I whispered back. What did he think, that I was sitting here with my eyes closed?

Awi Bubu pulled a flutelike instrument from the folds of

his robe and began to play a strange, haunting melody. Slowly, he sat down in front of the basket and crossed his legs. After another moment of music playing, the lid of the basket began to rise. It swayed gently, then fell to the side.

"You must all be very quiet," the announcer told us in a hushed voice. "Any sudden noise could be disastrous."

A moment later a small, dark form appeared at the lip of the basket. It hesitated for a moment, then darted free and scurried over to the magician. Several more forms followed. Scorpions—scores of them. I shivered as they scuttled their way up Awi Bubu's legs, onto his chest, and across his arms. One even climbed up his neck to rest on his bald head, like a macabre hat. Throughout it all, other than playing his flute, the magician did not so much as twitch a muscle.

As the audience held its breath, there was a disturbance at the back of the theater. "Hey! You can't go in there without a ticket!"

I craned my neck around to see two heavily cloaked men walking down the aisles, searching the faces in the theater. More scorpions! Only this time, of the human variety.

I scrunched down low in my seat, grabbed Snuffles's hat, and plopped it down on my own head, trying not to think of lice. I held my breath, hoping Gerton and Fell wouldn't spot me.

The strange music chose that moment to clatter to a stop.

The two human scorpions came to a halt in the aisle, giving the porters a chance to catch up with them. As they were escorted out of the theater, Awi Bubu opened his eyes and, with surprising grace, rose to his feet, the scorpions still clinging to him. The audience gasped.

Next to me, Will shuddered violently. "That's disgusting, that is."

"There must be a trick to it," I whispered back to him. "Scorpions are deadly poisonous. Perhaps he's had all their stingers removed."

Will cut a glance my way. "Do you always try to ruin the suspense, miss?"

Before I could reply, there was a nudge in my ribs. "Can I 'ave me 'at back, miss?"

"Sorry," I said, handing it to Snuffles.

"Shh!" someone behind us hissed.

I scowled, but was saved from answering when the music began again, coming in short staccato bursts. The scorpions changed their direction and began to crawl off the magician. However, instead of heading back to the basket, they scuttled to the edge of the stage. A woman screamed, and the audience reared back in their seats.

"Quiet now," the announcer reminded us. "You don't want to provoke the magician's beasties."

The entire audience (myself included) held its breath as

the scorpions hovered at the edge of the stage. Finally, they gave one last wave of their claws and swarmed back into the basket.

The audience relaxed a bit as the magician went over to secure the scorpions in the basket. Before he had finished, there was a loud thumping from within the pyramid. After two more thumps, something crashed right through and onto the stage. We all gasped in surprise as a mummy lumbered out. I glanced at Will, whose eyes were as big and round as guineas. Honestly. It was clearly a man wrapped up in linen; how could anyone be fooled by this? They wouldn't be if they had ever seen a real mummy. Especially if they'd been unfortunate enough to see a real mummy on the move, as I had. I stifled a shudder.

"It's right creepy, ain't it, miss?" Will whispered, mistaking my shudder as having to do with the mummy onstage. Not wanting to ruin his enjoyment, I simply said, "Fascinating." (*Fascinating* is such a lovely word—it covers so many possibilities.)

The mummy shuffled around onstage a bit while the audience oohed and aahed. Then the mummy paused, as if noticing the audience for the first time. Slowly and with great theatrics, he began to lurch toward the audience as if he planned to come right off the stage and into our midst.

"Awi Bubu seems to have lost control of the mummy," the

9

announcer said in a breathless voice. "Quick now, before it's too late, toss coins at him. Coins are the only thing that will stop him."

Oh, for heaven's sake. What kind of operation was this anyway? There was a halfhearted smattering of coins onto the stage. From the corner of my eye, I saw Will, Ratsy, and Snuffles all toss something toward the mummy. That's when I began to get angry. Will and his brothers had so little, as did most of the other people in this rundown joke of a theater. How dare the management try to milk even more of their hard-earned money from them?

Finally, as if beaten back by the coins, the mummy retreated into the pyramid. The audience settled down, and I shifted in my seat.

The torches dimmed and two stagehands dressed as Egyptian slaves hurried out onto the stage. While they laid bricks down on the floor, Awi Bubu went to one of the fake palm trees and lifted a bronze dish from behind it.

"For Awi Bubu's next amazing feat of magic, we need a volunteer from the audience. Who will volunteer?"

Like deranged jack-in-the-boxes, Will, Snuffles, and Ratsy leaped to their feet, their hands thrust high into the air. Awi Bubu studied the audience carefully before raising a long skinny arm and pointing at Ratsy.

He gave a hoot of glee, and Will and Snuffles groaned in

disappointment. An usher arrived at the end of the row to escort Ratsy up onto the stage. Once Ratsy was there, Awi Bubu positioned him on the bricks, face-down, then set the vessel on the floor by his head. One of the stagehands lit some incense, and Awi Bubu poured a few drops from a flask into the bronze dish.

A jolt of recognition shot through me. The Great Awi Bubu was reenacting an ancient Egyptian oracular ceremony, the very same one Aloysius Trawley had forced me to perform a few short weeks ago! Whoever this magician was, he clearly knew something about real ancient Egyptian practices. Which made him very interesting indeed.

"Remove all thoughts from your mind," the magician instructed Ratsy in a low, singsongy voice. "Let it become a blank slate by which the gods can communicate." Then he began to chant. "Horus, we call upon your power and strength. Open this child's eyes to your wisdom."

I sat bolt upright in my seat. Those were the exact words that Trawley had used. Did this Awi Bubu belong to Trawley's Arcane Order of the Black Sun—a secret society dedicated to matters of the occult? Is that why Trawley's men had been so comfortable barging into the theater?

As the smell of incense in the theater began to overpower the smell of gin, Awi Bubu asked Ratsy a question. "What is your name?"

11

"Ratsy."

"What is your occupation?"

"A rat catcher." I was suddenly very glad Will hadn't been picked; he'd have been forced to confess he was a pickpocket in front of this rough crowd.

"Where do you live?"

"Nottingham Court, off Drury Lane."

The magician turned to the audience. "Who has a question they'd like to ask the oracle?"

Hands shot into the air. How could people be so gullible? How could they not tell this was all a hoax? But no one seemed to suspect a thing. They were all waving their arms in the air, hoping Awi Bubu would pick them.

"Will me old man's ship come in soon?" a young clerk clutching his hat in his hand called out.

"No. He will be in debtors' prison by the end of the year," Ratsy intoned in a hollow voice.

A woman sprang to her feet. "Will my son get better?"

"'E'll be right as rain come next Tuesday."

She closed her eyes in relief.

"What 'orse should I bet on this Saturday?" a man shouted.

"Pride o' the Morning," Ratsy said. The man—along with half the occupants of the theater—hastily scribbled the name down on a scrap of paper.

"Will there be any more funny business like them mummies?" an old man asked, his question causing the others to quiet down.

There was a pause, then: "The Black Sun shall rise up in a red sky before falling to earth, where a great serpent will swallow it."

I gasped. Those were the very words I had uttered to Trawley! How did Ratsy know? Had Awi Bubu slipped him a note? Whispered in his ear? Surely this proved the magician was one of Trawley's men.

"It is time to come back to earth, my child," Awi Bubu said gently.

Ratsy blinked, then scrambled to his feet and looked sheepish. "Will I 'ave a chance to do magic?" he asked.

"You *have* done magic," Awi Bubu informed him kindly. Then he bowed. The audience applauded, and Ratsy flushed bright red all the way to his ears. Awi Bubu motioned to Ratsy, and the audience applauded even louder. As Ratsy made his way back to his seat, the magician bowed one last time, and then the curtains closed.

People began leaving their seats and heading up to the exits, but there was one determined man coming down the aisle. Gerton had got past the porter somehow.

I quickly turned to Will. "Do you think you could get us backstage? I'd like to meet this magician of yours."

Will's face brightened. "'E's something, ain't 'e, miss! I told you I could be more than just an errand boy. I've got a nose for this stuff, I 'ave."

"Er, yes, you do," I agreed. "Can we hurry?" I asked, glancing once more at the approaching Gerton.

"I'm sure Ratsy can get ye back there. Let's ask 'im."

We went toward the stage and caught up with Ratsy just as he was coming down the steps. He still looked a bit dazed and sheepish. "Did I really do magic?" he asked.

"Sure did, bucko! Spouted out all sorts of stuff. Ratsy's small pinched face glowed with pleasure. "D'you fink you could get us backstage? You knows the way, don't you, Rats?"

Ratsy nodded. "Sure."

Will turned to Snuffles. "You guard the exit so it don't get locked before we're done 'ere."

With a quick look around, Ratsy led me and Will toward a small door to the left of the main stage. I glanced over my shoulder. Gerton was still searching through the seats, trying to find me.

Almost as if he'd felt my gaze on him, he lifted his head and looked my way.

I quickly darted through the door, hoping he hadn't seen me.

CHAPTER TWO
CURIOUSER AND CURIOUSER

THE SPACE WAS DARK AND SMALL and smelled of mice. Once he'd gotten his bearings, Ratsy led us through a twisting set of hallways.

"How does he know his way around so well?" I asked Will.

"'E's worked 'ere before, miss. When you're a rat catcher, you get to know your way around a lot of places."

Will's words filled me with unease. I risked a glance behind me, afraid giant rats might be following us even now, but I could see nothing in the gloom.

Will came to an abrupt stop, and since my attention had been behind me, I bumped into him with an *oof.*

"Careful, miss. There's people about now."

Indeed, I could hear voices and the sound of steps hurrying back and forth.

Backstage was a confusing collection of small rooms and closets opening off a crooked hallway. To make matters worse, the entire floor listed sharply to the right. A faint odor of old sweat and pipe smoke hung in the air.

Ratsy held his finger to his lips, then pointed to a door that was slightly ajar.

"Take's dropping off," said a voice. If I wasn't mistaken—and I rarely was—it was the announcer's voice. It had the same flat vowels and oratory quality.

"Some days are better than others, are they not?" This voice was softer and had a lilting accent. Awi Bubu's? "And the daytime shows, they are never as good as those at night."

"Mebbe. But that's the whole point of keeping a foreigner around, to pump up the profits. If you can't do that, I'll get someone else in here."

"You have had three weeks of very good profits."

"And I want three more. Now keep the money coming in or you and that mummy of yours are out on your ear."

"You don't really mean that."

I flinched, certain the other man would begin yelling that he certainly did too mean it. Instead, there was a long pause, and then he spoke again. "You're right. I don't. Just try to bring in more than you did today."

Before the three of us eavesdroppers could react, the announcer came barreling out of the small room directly into us.

We stared at each other in surprised shock before my instincts kicked in. "Is this where the Great Awi Bubu is?" I asked in a breathless voice. "Do you think it would be all right if we spoke to him?" I clasped my hands together as if in adoration.

The announcer looked nonplussed for a moment, then shrugged. "I don't care what you kids do as long as you're out of here in five minutes." He pushed past us, and we were left staring at the door.

"Go on, then." Will nudged me. "You 'eard the man. We only got five minutes."

I suddenly felt shy. What was I going to say to the magician anyway? *Ho there, were you using real Egyptian magic? Are you by any chance a member of the Arcane Order of the Black Sun?*

"Do come in and quit hovering at my door," the magician called out.

We all froze, then shuffled into the room like a small herd of sheep.

"'Ow'd you know we was out there, guv'nor?" Will asked, his eyes round again. They were going to pop out of his head if he kept this up.

"Did you use yer Egyptian magic on us?" Ratsy asked eagerly.

"Nothing as exciting as all that, I'm afraid. I heard the stage manager talking to you."

As the magician spoke, his eyes drifted to me. He blinked twice, then asked, "How can the humble Awi Bubu serve you?"

"Whoa," Ratsy said, ignoring the man's question. His eyes were glued to the cloth-wrapped figure propped against the wall. "Is this the mummy you use on stage?"

It was so clearly a fake that I couldn't help but snort. Awi Bubu cocked his head to the side and studied me. "You do not believe in mummies, miss?"

"Of course I do, but real ones, not fakes like this." I turned to Ratsy. "It really is a fake. Go ahead and poke it. With your permission, of course," I hastily added.

Awi Bubu nodded, his glittering black eyes still sharply focused on me. "But of course."

Will grabbed Ratsy and pulled him back. "'E ain't touchin' that thing. No way, miss. It'd curse him, it would. You should know that better'n anyone."

I felt Awi Bubu's glance sharpen even more.

"But that is the point, Will. I do know more than most, and it is clearly a fake. Here." I sighed in exasperation, stepped over to the wall, and poked the wrapped figure (I refused to call it a mummy) in the stomach.

It grunted, which startled Will and Ratsy so bad that they squealed and leaped backwards.

"See?" I told them. "Real mummies don't grunt. And they aren't soft, like this one is. It's a man wrapped up in linen, just like I told you."

"Let me introduce you to my assistant, Kimosiri," Awi Bubu said.

The tall figure reached up and unwound the wrappings from his head, revealing a large lumpy face with weathered skin and small black eyes.

"Very pleased to meet you," I said.

He nodded solemnly at me.

"So Little Miss is a skeptic?" Awi Bubu said. "How does she come to be such an expert on mummies, I wonder."

The room grew a little warmer and for a brief moment, I found myself wanting to tell him just how very much I knew about mummies and Egyptian magic. Instead, I said, "That's funny, sir. That's exactly what I wanted to ask you. Some of the tricks you performed were very authentic reenactments of ancient Egyptian rituals. I wondered how you came to know of such things."

"Ah, but I asked you first, did I not? Shall we agree to a trade of information?"

"Very well," I said, intending to tell him as little as possible. "My parents run a museum with Egyptian exhibits. Since I spend a lot of time there, I've picked up a few things about ancient Egypt. Now it's your turn."

"I'm afraid I've nothing as interesting as a museum in my past. I am but an exile from my own country, Egypt, as you rightly guessed. When I found myself alone in a strange land with no means of support . . . well, one must make a living however one can." He glanced pointedly at Ratsy and Will, and I was suddenly afraid that he somehow knew that Will was, or had been, a pickpocket. Then I realized I was being silly. He was most likely referring to Ratsy's profession.

"Which of my tricks most impressed Little Miss?" He smiled at me, revealing a gold tooth. "Clearly not my mummy act."

"Er, no." For some reason, I was reluctant to let him know what exactly had alerted me. "It was the oracle trick. The one where you used Ratsy here."

"Ah." Was it my imagination or did his face relax slightly?

"In fact, I wanted to ask if by any chance you know Aloysius Trawley? I've seen him perform the very same trick."

"Alas, I do not know this Mr. Trawley, and I am crushed to hear I am not the first to perform this act in London.

However, I am curious as to how Little Miss comes to know so much about ancient Egyptian rituals?"

Bother. That was the problem with asking questions. Sometimes one revealed more than was wise. "I told you, my parents run a museum."

"Yes, but museums do not generally offer insight into the actual rituals performed by ancient Egyptian priests."

I ignored that for the moment. "That thing you had Ratsy say, about the black sun and red sky. Is that something you have all your volunteers say?"

Awi Bubu turned to Ratsy. "Did I tell you to say that?"

Ratsy shook his head.

The magician spread his hands wide. "I said nothing other than what you and the audience heard. Do his words mean something to you?"

"Of course not," I lied. "They were just odd, that's all."

"Exactly which museum do Little Miss's parents run? Perhaps I may come visit next time I am feeling homesick."

"The British Museum." The lie popped out of my mouth like an eager toad. Startled, Will turned and looked at me. Before more questions could follow, I bobbed a quick curtsy. "Thank you very much for letting us chat with you. It's been lovely, but your manager said we only had five minutes and we don't want to keep you." I grabbed Will's arm and we headed for the door, Ratsy right behind us.

"Goodbye, Little Miss! Thank you for honoring me with your visit." Awi Bubu's mocking voice followed us out into the hall.

As Ratsy led us to the nearest exit, I realized the conversation hadn't been as informative as I'd hoped. I had no choice but to chalk up the similarities between Ratsy's prediction and mine to coincidence. The only problem was, I wasn't very fond of coincidences.

We met up with Snuffles, and when we were outside, I asked Ratsy about it again, hoping that with Awi Bubu nowhere in sight, he'd feel free to tell me the truth.

"No, miss. 'E didn't whisper nothing in me ear or slip me a note."

"Ratsy couldn't read a note, even if Awi Bubu had given him one. 'E doesn't know 'ow to read."

"Oh." I didn't know what to say to that.

Will motioned his brothers on ahead, then pulled me aside. "So, wot'd you fink?"

"About what?"

"About the magician, o' course!"

"Oh. He was fascinating."

"So don't you fink that proves I have a nose fer Egyptian magic? Don't you fink I could 'ave a future in the Brotherhood as somefink more than a errand boy?"

"I would certainly think so," I said. Unfortunately, it

wasn't my decision. It was up to Lord Wigmere, head of the Brotherhood of the Chosen Keepers.

"Then you'll put in a good word wif Wiggy next time you see 'im, won't you?"

Somehow, I didn't think a group of men dedicated to protecting their country from the influence of ancient magic and curses would give two figs about the Alcazar Theater or penny-show magicians. However, I promised that I would talk to Wigmere, then left Will to his brothers and began walking back to the museum.

My mind whirred frantically, trying to puzzle out just who exactly Awi Bubu was. I suppose it was possible that ancient Egyptian rituals were common knowledge among Egyptians. Except that was one of the things that were so exciting about archaeology; it unlocked the secrets to the past, secrets that even the Egyptians themselves had forgotten about their history, so that explanation didn't really work. It seemed more likely that he was simply unwilling to confess that he was a member of the Black Sun. Or, I thought, my steps slowing, perhaps he was a plant for the Serpents of Chaos. They also knew quite a lot about Egyptian magic. And were dedicated to using it to plunge our world into, well, chaos.

As I turned the corner off Phoenix Road, I detected a flicker of movement nearby, and then a man fell into step behind me. I thought it was Gerton, but I couldn't be sure. Either way, it wasn't good news.

Half a block later, another man stepped out of a recessed doorway as I passed. I kept my eyes in front of me and pretended I hadn't seen him. If I ignored them, perhaps I'd make it back to the museum without a confrontation.

However, when Basil Whiting, Trawley's second in command, stepped out of an alley and leaned up against a lamppost, effectively cutting off that avenue of escape, it became clear that not only had the scorpions found me, but they weren't about to let me pretend otherwise.

CHAPTER THREE

SCORPIONS ON THE LOOSE

BOTHER. I had hoped to avoid another meeting with the supreme master of the Arcane Order of the Black Sun for a while longer. Say, a lifetime. In fact, that's why it had taken so long for Will to coax me out to the Alcazar to see Awi Bubu; I'd been trying to avoid Trawley. He was mad as a hatter and convinced I was a reincarnation of Isis and had mystical powers. Of course, that was all nonsense, but even so, he had a nasty habit of snatching me off the street.

Whiting stepped away from the lamppost and sauntered in my direction. He hesitated as a black carriage turned down the street and then drove past. Just as he started to move again, the carriage pulled sharply against the curb, merely a few feet in front of Whiting.

Oh dear, not reinforcements, I thought. Surely three grown men against one eleven-year-old girl were good enough odds for them. Wait a minute. I knew that carriage. It was spotlessly clean and shiny, unmarked black; it belonged to the Brotherhood of the Chosen Keepers. The door opened, and a worn, familiar face with a thick white mustache and solemn blue eyes looked out at me. "Theodosia?"

"Lord Wigmere!" My voice caught on a faint sob of relief as I hightailed it over to the carriage, giving Whiting a wide berth.

"What on earth are you doing in this part of town, child?"

"Attending a magic show," I explained, looking longingly inside the carriage.

"Here, get in. This isn't a safe neighborhood for a young girl to be wandering alone. Danger seems to find you easily enough without compounding the problem by being careless."

"It's not my fault, sir. Trouble does seem inclined to follow me around," I said as I hopped into the carriage, settled myself on the opposite seat, and smoothed my skirts to hide the trembling in my hands. That had been close. "Thank you, sir."

I thought briefly of mentioning the scorpions following me, but I didn't want to bring on another scolding. Besides, he had told me a while ago that they were harmless. Annoying, but harmless.

Wigmere rapped on the ceiling with his cane, and the carriage lurched forward. Although he was impeccably dressed in his frock coat and top hat, he looked older than he had the last time I'd seen him. More careworn. "I wouldn't have thought you were interested in parlor tricks and magic," he said.

In for a penny, in for a pound. "It was because of Will, sir. He'd located a rather suspicious Egyptian magic show and wanted to see what I thought of it."

Wigmere snorted through his mustache. "That boy! He has no idea what we're up against. He thinks he's landed in a penny dreadful and is having a grand adventure."

"It *was* an unusual magic show, sir."

"Bah!"

"And Will *was* extraordinarily helpful with the *Dreadnought* situation," I reminded him. "I could never have pulled it off without his aid."

"Nevertheless," Wigmere said. "This isn't a game, and I won't have him treating it as such. Too much is at stake. Your safety included."

"Yes, sir." Well, I'd tried.

"Speaking of the *Dreadnought* . . . did Fagenbush give you the news about Bollingsworth and the others?"

"No, sir, he didn't," I said.

Wigmere cleared his throat. "Well, the good news is our doctors from Level Six were able to stabilize Bollingsworth's condition. It will take a while, but he will recover from the curse he got from that rope of yours."

"And then what will happen to him?"

"Then we'll toss him into our deepest, darkest prison and throw away the key."

"What's the bad news?" I have learned that when someone starts out with the good news, bad news is certain to follow.

"Unfortunately, there has been no sign of the men who escaped the *Dreadnought*. The Brotherhood has searched high and low, to no avail. I'm afraid they have gotten clean away."

My heart sank. "It would be so lovely if just once they could all get locked up," I said.

"I agree. But having them on the loose is just one more reason it is so important for you to be careful. You and Will are children, and as such, I feel an extra responsibility to keep you safe. All the operatives that I can spare are out searching for the Serpents of Chaos. Even so, one of their agents could easily follow Will to your arranged meeting place and nab you both. It is even more important than ever that you put aside your dislike of Fagenbush and begin following instructions. Speaking of which, he has yet to bring me a report from you."

I squirmed, wretchedly uncomfortable. "Well, you see, sir, he really doesn't care to deal with me—"

"Nonsense. He'll deal with whom he's instructed to deal. There is no room for personal animosity within the Brotherhood, Theodosia. Our mission is too critical for such petty concerns." His piercing blue eyes bored into me, as if searching out any flaw or selfishness.

"Yes, sir," I murmured, relieved that the Museum of Legends and Antiquities had just come into view.

"Excellent." Wigmere nodded, his face relaxing. "Then I'll expect to receive regular reports on your progress from Fagenbush."

The carriage rolled to a stop across the street from the museum. It wouldn't do to have anyone see Wigmere and me together.

"Thank you for the lift, sir."

"You're most welcome, and do try to stay out of unsavory neighborhoods, would you?"

"Yes, sir." I hopped out of the carriage and made my way across the street. While I was most grateful for the rescue from the Black Sunners, I really could have done without the sharp reminder to work with Fagenbush. Even though I had recently discovered he was one of the Chosen Keepers (what had they been thinking?), I still tried to ignore him whenever possible.

Once back in the museum, I decided to search out my parents and see if they'd wondered where I'd got to. They weren't in the private family withdrawing room we kept here at the museum or in the staff withdrawing room. Their offices were empty too, so I went up to their workroom on the third floor. I paused at the door, listening.

"I don't know why you think it's hopeless," Mother was saying. "I'm sure we can appeal to Maspero and get a second hearing. Surely Davis isn't the last word on the subject."

My ears perked up. They were talking about their work in the Valley of the Kings.

"You put more faith in the workings of the Cairo Antiquities Service than I do, Henrietta. I doubt we'll get help from that quarter."

"But it was our discovery . . ." Mum muttered, then fell silent.

The good news was that they hadn't noticed I was gone. The bad news was, well, they hadn't even missed me. Their lack of attention used to bother me, but I'd learned to accept it as something of a blessing. It allowed me to take care of business without having to answer all sorts of awkward questions.

And there was quite a lot of business to take care of.

There were at least two curses, possibly three, down in Receiving. I had to get them removed before the new exhibit opened. We couldn't risk cursing untold numbers of museum visitors. It would be bad for business!

Having located my parents, I went to my own little room in the museum. It was actually more like a rather large closet, but it made me feel better to think of it as a room. Once there, I slipped out of my coat and put on a pinafore, then tugged off my dress gloves and replaced them with a pair of sturdier ones. Next I checked to be sure all three amulets were still safely around my neck. Satisfied that I was as protected as could be, I fetched my curse-removing kit from the cupboard and made my way to Receiving.

Luckily, it was Sunday, so neither Dolge nor Sweeny, the museum's two hired hands, were about and I had the entire receiving area to myself. I quickly got to work.

There had been a shocking number of cursed artifacts among the antiquities Mum had brought back with her a few short months ago. I didn't remember ever seeing so many in one batch.

The first object on my list was a basketful of black rocks carved to look like grain. I had discovered this curse by accident one day when I'd gone into the staff room to fix myself a jam sandwich and had found the loaf of bread full of bugs. When I looked closely, I saw that they weren't ordinary bugs but teensy-tiny scarab beetles. I followed the thin trail of them all the way back to the staging area. Honestly! It was hard enough to get any food around here with my parents as preoccupied as they were with their work; I did not need curses mucking up what little food there was.

This particular curse had required oodles of research, and I had found only one similar curse listed in T. R. Nectanebus's *Hidden Egypt: Magic, Alchemy, and the Occult.* I'd had to adjust the recipe to suit my needs.

I set my carpetbag down and rifled through my supplies until I found my mortar and pestle, a jar of honey, a small sack of dirt, and a pillbox Grandmother had tossed in the rubbish bin. The primary ingredient of the recipe was honey, because one of the principles in Egyptian magic is that demons abhor things that we humans love, such as sweets. It was a common method of driving demonic spirits and black magic away, using sweets.

I poured the honey into the mortar, then added the measure of dirt. There was a tickling sensation at the back of my neck, as if someone had blown on it. I whirled around. "Who's there?" My voice wavered as the fine hairs at my nape still tingled.

Even though there was no one in sight, I was certain I was being watched. I peered into the shadowy corners of the room, but nothing moved.

With my shoulder blades itching, I held my nose and opened the pillbox. Nectanebus's recipe called for swallow droppings, but I hadn't been able to find any of those. However, there was a large flock of pigeons that often roosted near the museum, so I'd scraped their droppings into the pillbox. (Yet another reason it is so important to wear heavy-duty gloves when conducting magic!)

Using a bit of stick, I scraped all the droppings into the mortar, then ground everything together with the pestle. Last, I took a piece of bread and crumbled it into the honey-and-dropping mixture. Nectanebus claimed that using the honey, bread crumbs, and dung together would redirect the cursed miniature scarabs from the bread to the dung. One could only hope.

I dumped the grain-shaped rocks out onto the table and smeared the mixture in the bottom of the basket, as instructed. Then I put all the grain back in the basket, and that was that. I had only to wait for three days, and the curse would be permanently removed. Either that or Receiving would stink to high heaven.

I felt a chill on my shoulders and turned around again, thinking Mum or Dad had wandered down to check on me. But there was still no one there, and no open door to account for a draft. Uneasy, I quickly carried the grain basket to where it had been and then put the empty jars and bags back into the satchel, pausing when I heard a faint rustling sound.

I strained to hear better. It had come from the northwest corner of the room. I peered up into the shadows. Something dark lurked up there. It rustled again, and in one sweeping movement I knocked the rest of the supplies off the worktable and into my bag.

As I headed toward the door, the rustling grew louder. Out of the corner of my eye I saw the shadow detach itself from the ceiling and begin oozing in my direction.

I picked up my pace and fled. Clearly, I had more work to do.

CHAPTER FOUR

THE ARCANE ORDER OF THE BLACK SUN CALLS A MEETING

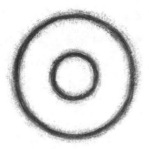

MY PARENTS NEVER DID REALIZE I'd been gone, and Monday morning arrived without incident. Well, except for being rushed through my breakfast, as Father wanted to get to the museum bright and early. We were in the process of preparing our newest exhibit—Thutmose III: The Napoleon of Ancient Egypt—and my parents were eager to get started. They were certain this would be an important exhibit for the Museum of Legends and Antiquities; it might even put us on the same footing as the British Museum.

Father called a staff meeting first thing.

"Very well," he said, clapping his hands together awkwardly to get everyone's attention. Father was brilliant but not at his best when directing people. "Two weeks," he said. "That's how much time we have to finish putting this exhibit together, the finest exhibit of the decade, I might add. The board has allowed us to close for two weeks so we may devote our full attention to this matter, so let's make the most of it, shall we? Weems?"

The priggish first Assistant Curator pranced forward, his feeble little mustache twitching as he said, "Yes, sir?"

Vicary Weems is the sort of grownup who believes children should not be seen and not heard. At all. He also dresses rather above his station, always wearing loud patterned vests that make my eyes ache and—of all the ridiculous things—spats. I don't care if King Edward himself wears them, they are still ridiculous looking, like bibs for one's feet.

"You have the floor plans I gave you for the new display cases, correct?"

Weems patted the pocket of his scarlet and gold vest. "Right here, sir."

"Good. You'll direct Dolge and Sweeny with the placement of the cases." He paused a moment, then turned to Dolge. "They have been delivered, haven't they?"

"Aye, sir."

"Fagenbush?" Father continued.

The loathsome Second Assistant Curator stepped forward, bringing a small cloud of boiled-cabbage-and-pickled-onion fumes with him. His thick black eyebrows were drawn together in a V. Whatever did Lord Wigmere see in him?

"We'll need you up in the workroom so you can start packing the artifacts for transport down here."

Fagenbush nodded.

"Stilton?"

My favorite curator, Edgar Stilton, sprang to attention, a faint tic beginning in his left cheek. "Right here, sir."

Father consulted his list. "Let's see, you're to . . ."

"I'm to visit the draper this morning and approve the material for the display backing," Stilton said, then blinked rapidly, as if surprised by his own boldness.

"Oh, that's right. Very well, then. I guess that's it. Any questions? Let's get to it." The others began to trickle away, and he turned to me. "Theodosia?"

"Yes, Father?"

"How's that inventory coming along down in long-term storage?"

"Nearly done," I said cheerfully, waving my ledger book.

"Excellent." He turned to go, but I stopped him.

"Are you sure there's nothing I can do to assist you and Mother with the upcoming exhibit?"

"Not right at the moment, no. Perhaps later . . ."

I sighed. "Very well." It was beastly unfair, if you asked

me, especially since it had been my discovery of the annex to Thutmose III's tomb that had given them this idea for the exhibit in the first place. It seemed as if I should at least be able to help. However, I am sad to say, that I have found there to be little justice in the world.

Feeling somewhat sorry for myself, I cast one last longing glance at all the commotion going on in the foyer then, resigned to my fate, headed for the catacombs.

Of course, they weren't really catacombs, merely long-term storage space for the museum, but it felt as creepy as catacombs. I clutched the three amulets around my neck and reached for the door.

A shadow loomed in front of me and I jumped. "Stilton!" I said, rather louder than I'd intended. "What are you doing here? You gave me quite a start."

The entire left side of the Third Assistant Curator's body twitched as he held his finger to his lips. "Shh." His eyes were bright, his cheeks slightly flushed.

"What is it?" I whispered.

"The grand master wants to see you."

My sense of victory at having evaded him yesterday evaporated. "Now?"

"Yes, miss. He's called a meeting of the Black Sun. Everyone will be there."

That was Stilton's one glaring fault. He belonged to the Arcane Order of the Black Sun. "Well, I'm very busy. I'm afraid it's not a good time."

Stilton blinked twice and looked apologetic. "Everyone's preoccupied with the exhibit just now, Miss Theo. And you're supposed to be down in the long-term storage. No one will miss you for hours."

Well, he had that part right. I'd be lucky if they remembered me when it was time to go home. "But what about you? Aren't you supposed to be visiting the draper's?"

Stilton looked a bit smug. "I took care of that on my way home last night."

"Oh. But I already gave Trawley his magical favor. What does he want with me now?"

A hatchet-faced man stepped out of the hallway behind Stilton. "I thought you said she was coming?"

Stilton flinched at the sound of Basil Whiting's voice. Sent reinforcements, had they? This didn't look good.

"S-she is. In just a moment," Stilton said. "Aren't you, Miss Theo?" His weak tea–colored eyes pleaded with me.

Since Trawley had sent his second in command as backup, it was clear I had no choice. "Of course, Stilton. I'd love to." If he caught my sarcasm, he made no sign.

"Very well, miss. This way." He motioned toward the east

entrance. With a sigh, I headed down the corridor. "I thought you scorpions were supposed to *serve* me," I muttered, feeling quite put out.

"We're to see to your safety, miss," Whiting said, falling into step behind me.

"Yes, but that's not quite the same thing, is it?"

He looked over my head at Stilton as if to say *You deal with her.* Stilton shrugged. Or twitched. I couldn't be sure which.

Once we were outside, he opened the carriage door for me, then followed me inside it. Much to my relief, Whiting joined Ned Gerton up on the driver's box. Stilton cleared his throat and held up a black silk blindfold.

I stared at it with distaste. "Is that really necessary?"

"The supreme master says so, miss. I'm just following orders."

"Like nice little sheep," I murmured.

"What was that?" he asked, a startled look on his face.

"I think I'll have a nice little sleep. On the ride over," I added. "Do wake me when we're there." I wedged myself in the farthest corner, leaned my head back, and closed my eyes. There. Stilton would have to manhandle me to get that wretched blindfold on. Let's see if he would go that far.

I waited, nerves on edge, but after a long tense moment, I heard him sigh and settle back into his seat. Excellent.

Fifteen minutes later, I felt the carriage draw to a stop.

"Please, miss," Stilton whispered. "You must let me put the blindfold on now or we'll both be in trouble."

I opened my eyes. "Very well." I had, after all, won a small victory. It would be easy to allow him to save face.

He slipped the blindfold on and tied it very gently, making sure not to get my hair tangled up in the knot. "Do you have sisters, Stilton?"

"Why, yes, miss. How'd you know?" There was a touch of awe in his voice, as if he thought I'd divined it somehow. I hated to lose that advantage by explaining that only a man with sisters would be so good at dealing with hair, so I simply said, "Just a lucky hunch."

There was a low whistle from outside the carriage. "All right then, the coast is clear," Stilton said. I heard him open the door; he took my hand and carefully led me down the steps. We shuffled along until he told me to stop. He knocked out the signal on the door, which opened immediately. "'E's waiting in the chamber. Right impatient, 'e is. Wants to know wot took you so long."

"The girl resisted at first," Basil Whiting said from just behind us.

"I thought Tefen here said he could control 'er," the unidentified porter said.

"I can." Stilton sounded a bit testy as he guided me through the doorway.

Once again I was led down a dark and twisting corridor before we came to a stop. The silk was removed from my eyes and I found myself in the familiar dark chamber, lit only with black candles in sconces against the wall. Half a dozen cloaked, hooded figures knelt before me. Only Aloysius Trawley remained standing, his eyes glittering, black and wild in the dim light. It was quite unsettling really, having a half-dozen grown men in hoods watching you while you have no idea who they are.

"You're late," he said to Stilton.

"There was some trouble getting away, I'm afraid."

Trawley turned his crazed eyes on me. "I thought you said you could handle her."

"I can." Stilton's gaze shifted to Whiting, as if daring him to contradict. "It's just that Throckmorton called an unexpected staff meeting, so we were running late."

Accepting this excuse, Trawley jerked his head toward the kneeling men. "Go ahead and join the others. We've had to start without you."

Stilton and Whiting took their places on the floor, and Trawley turned back to me.

"Welcome, O Light Giver of Heaven."

Oh, for goodness sake. Not that again. "Mr. Trawley," I said, forgoing his favored title of supreme master. "Why have I been brought here against my will?"

"Against your will, O Maker of Morning? Have you no wish to see your loyal servants? It has been over two weeks since we last spoke. I thought you had agreed to share your wisdom and magic with us. With you as Isis, and me as Osiris, we will usher in the new age of Horus."

Age of Horus? What did he mean by that? Horus was the son of Isis and Osiris, and the slayer of Set, but I'd never heard of an age of Horus before. The man was clearly a lunatic. "No. I agreed to do you one magic favor, which I've done."

"Are you referring to your prophecy, by chance? The one that hasn't yet come true?" His voice grew annoyed as he spoke.

He was going to hold me responsible for that, was he? "Surely you realize I can only repeat what the gods tell me. I have no power as to whether or not it comes to pass."

He took a step closer, his wild eyes growing angry. "Is that really so? The Queen of all Gods, who can raise the dead and give men vile curses and command the jackal Anubis, cannot order a prophecy to come to pass?"

I shot a hot glance Stilton's way. *Someone* had been reporting my activities back to Trawley. As if understanding my accusation, Stilton gave a quick, tiny shake of his head. I returned my attention to the fuming man in front of me. "First of all, as I told you last time, I am not the queen of all gods. I'm simply a girl who's learned to remove curses. That's all."

Trawley glowered at me. "How then did you raise the mouse back to life?"

"He was just stunned," I lied.

"And how then did you cause the man at the docks to be covered in boils? And don't deny it. One of the scorpions heard him lay the blame at your feet."

Who had been tattling? "It wasn't *me*. He simply managed to get a hold of a cursed object and that's what caused the boils."

Trawley took another step closer and I resisted the urge to back up. "If you are not the Queen of the Gods, why then does the jackal Anubis do your bidding?"

No choice but to just bluff this one out. "Jackal? What jackal?"

Trawley jerked his head, and Basil Whiting stepped forward, the flickering light glancing off his razor-sharp cheekbones.

"Please tell the Rosy Light of Morning what you saw down on the Prince Albert Docks two weeks ago," Trawley ordered.

"I was in position, keeping an eye on the man she'd cursed, who was cooling his heels in the river. After about half an hour, a commotion broke out on the deck of the boat they was on—"

"Ship," I corrected.

Startled, Whiting stared at me. "What?"

"It's a ship, not a boat," I explained.

"Quiet!" Trawley ordered. Then to Whiting, he said, "Continue."

"A jackal appeared, carrying a long stick or cane of some kind in his mouth. I decided to follow, and he led me back to her museum, where he went inside through a broken window. I tried to go in too, but the watchman stopped me and said the museum was closed."

This was not good. Not good at all. I had so hoped no one had seen Anubis as he ran through London. Or at least, no one who could connect him with me. "Er . . . ," I fumbled.

"Sir?" Stilton interrupted gently.

Trawley turned on him. "What?"

Stilton tugged at the cloak around his neck. "We really do have only a short time."

Trawley stared at Stilton intently, as if trying to bend the younger man's will to his own, then finally looked away. "If time is short," he said, "let's begin the ceremony."

I was so relieved by this reprieve that I didn't even mind that I was stuck spending the next half-hour watching a number of grown men wander around in ancient Egyptian dress and wave flowering branches in the air. They looked beyond ridiculous. Their chanting was equally nonsensical, blathering on about the fruits of the great mysteries and whatnot. At the very end, they all laid their flowering staffs at my feet and then Trawley cast himself upon them.

I was horrified. "Get up!" I snapped.

"You must raise me up, O Isis. Raise me up, so like the sun rising in the sky, the Age of Horus can begin."

Oh, for heaven's sake! I reached down, grabbed hold of his meaty arm, and yanked—none too gently. He lurched to his feet and then straightened his robes.

"The Age of Horus is born," he declared. "All hail!"

The rest of the men shouted out, "Hail the Age of Horus!" then fell silent.

"Are we done?" I asked hopefully.

Trawley closed his eyes for a long moment. Stilton stepped forward. "Her parents will miss her before too long," he said apologetically.

His words, while not exactly true, gave Trawley pause. "Very well. We are done for the moment anyway." He took a step in my direction, using his superior height to try to intimidate me. "But the next time you come," he said, "I want you to bring the staff Whiting spoke of. I would like to see it for myself, even if it cannot raise the dead."

I bobbed a small curtsy. "I will do my best to arrange it," I lied. The problem was, I no longer had it. Wigmere had taken it for safekeeping. "But it's hard enough to sneak away as it is without carrying a five-foot-long stick," I pointed out.

Trawley sighed. "Remove her," he told Stilton.

Oh dear, he sounded angry, and I really didn't want to provoke someone as unstable as he was. "I'm terribly sorry, sir. It's just very difficult to move about freely when one is a child. And if my movements were further curtailed, we'd never have a chance to have our little talks."

"Very well," Trawley said, sounding somewhat appeased. "But you and I shall meet again." His frantic eyes zeroed in on mine. "Soon."

"Of course, Mr. Trawley!" I bobbed another curtsy. "It would be my pleasure."

"Tefen." Trawley jerked his head in Edgar's direction. "See her home."

"Very well, sir. Come along, Rosy Light." His lips twitched ever so slightly as he said this, and I resisted the urge to slug him. Instead, I high-stepped it over to his side, then followed him down the corridor. Walking quickly, we made our way to the front door, where he paused and began patting his pockets, looking for a blindfold.

I took advantage of his distraction and opened the door and marched straight outside without waiting for the blindfold.

"Miss Theo!" he said, scandalized.

"Too late," I chirped at him. "I've seen it. Now quit dawdling and let's get back to the museum." As we moved to the carriage, I took stock of my surroundings. It was a quiet, well-to-do neighborhood. Near Fitzroy Square, if I wasn't mistaken. Who knew a temple of the Black Sun would lurk in such normal surroundings?

Stilton looked about nervously, anxious that none of the Black Sunners see my unblindfolded state. "In you go," he whispered, opening the carriage door. "Before the driver sees you."

I climbed into the carriage while he gave the address of the museum to the driver. As Stilton settled into his seat, he looked serious. "I know that I'm the one who introduced you to the Black Sun," he said, picking his words carefully. "But I think it best that you don't visit them when I'm not there."

"Visit them! I *don't* visit them! They jolly well kidnapped me right off the street."

Stilton looked even more worried. "Trawley seems very focused on that staff, doesn't he?" His foot began tapping out a rapid tattoo on the carriage floor until he quickly reached out with his hand and stopped it.

"You're the one that told him about the mouse." I didn't even try to keep the accusing tone out of my voice.

"I know, and I'm sorry for it. I'd hate to think I'd gotten you mixed up in something unhealthy, Theo."

"Shouldn't you have thought of that before you introduced us?"

"I was trying to rescue you at the time," he pointed out, a bit defensively. "I didn't have many resources available."

"True. I'd forgotten about that." If not for Edgar, who knows what would have happened to me when the Serpents of Chaos had commandeered my carriage.

When we arrived back at the museum, there was a grand carriage parked outside. Grandmother Throckmorton! My heart sank. Suddenly, Aloysius Trawley didn't seem so bad.

CHAPTER FIVE

HENRY MAKES AN UNEXPECTED DISCOVERY

STILTON HAD THE DRIVER DROP ME at the corner of the square then take him around to the back of the building so we wouldn't be seen together and raise any suspicions.

I opened the front door of the museum and peered cautiously inside. The foyer was a jumbled mess, partially assembled display cases were scattered throughout and half-unpacked crates littered the floor. At first glance, it appeared empty. Then I spied Clive Fagenbush coming down the stairs, carrying an enormous crate.

Like a hound on a scent, he quickly found me.

"Where have you been? Your parents and grandmother have been looking all over for you." He seemed oddly pleased, as if he hoped I'd be getting in trouble for it.

"I was out for a walk," I told him. It felt as if I'd been gone for days, but it hadn't been more than two hours.

His look of disbelief told me what he thought of that excuse. Fagenbush managed to be more aware of my clandestine activities than anyone else, so he had good reason to be suspicious. He set the crate down and came over to where I stood. He confirmed we were alone, then lowered his voice. "Do you have a message for me to give to Wigmere?"

"Nope. Not a thing." I stepped around the crate to make my way to the family withdrawing room, but he moved to cut me off.

"You're supposed to report to Wigmere every day. Through me," he pointed out, his long nose quivering in frustration. "Have you come across anything else of note down in long-term storage? Anything else that Augustus Munk might have had hidden there?"

"Nothing more," I said. "You can tell Wigmere I'm still looking."

"Since you're not having any luck, perhaps someone with more experience ought to have a look. You might be missing something."

I arched an eyebrow, like I'd seen Mum do. "Wigmere seems to trust me with the task."

His lip curled in disdain. "Not everyone is as easily fooled by you as he is. Besides, if you're so very trustworthy, why did you sneak out today?"

Keeping tabs on me now, was he? "I don't see how that's any of your business."

"Wigmere has made you my business. And in spite of what I think of you, I have no intention of failing in my duties." Fagenbush sharpened his gaze, and I resisted a shudder. "I *will* have your reports for Wigmere. I will not let an eleven-year-old girl derail my career with the Brotherhood. Do you understand me? You can make this easy on us both, or you can make it quite difficult."

"We'll have to see about that," I muttered.

He recoiled in surprise. "What did you say?"

"I said, Have you seen my cat? I can't seem to find her this morning."

Before he could say anything further, an imperious voice came from the nearby hallway.

"But where *is* the gel?"

Grandmother! While I was rarely glad of her visits, I had to admit that today she'd timed it perfectly. Fagenbush shot me a dark look, then scuttled back up the stairs to retrieve another crate.

Grandmother's voice continued. "She's usually always un-derfoot, and now when I have need of her, she can't be found. How very contrary of her."

A horrible thought occurred to me. What if she had another one of those beastly governesses in tow? Just as I was considering hiding, she barreled into the room with Father trailing behind her. He looked quite put out.

"I don't know where she is, Mother, but perhaps next time if you'd let us know ahead that you planned to visit, we could be sure she was here to greet you."

Grandmother paused and surveyed the mess around her. "Really, Alistair. Is this any way to run a museum? It's a pigsty. It's bad enough you chose to work; the least you could do is keep your museum tidy."

"We're preparing a new exhibit, Mother. And we're closed for preparations, so no one will have to see the mess. Except for those who drop by unannounced," he said pointedly.

"Theodosia! There you are," Grandmother said, sailing toward me. "Where have you been, child? We've nearly turned this place upside down looking for you. It was most inconsiderate of you to disappear."

I opened my eyes wide and tried to look innocent. "I've been in the basement all day, cataloging the items down there."

"Really?" Father frowned. "That was the first place I looked."

"Well," I demurred. "I did have to come upstairs to use the facilities. Perhaps you just missed me?"

Grandmother thumped her cane. "Do not be vulgar."

"What would you prefer I call it, Grandmother? The water closet?"

"I would prefer you didn't call it anything at all. It's not spoken of in polite company. Now, Sopcoate seemed rather fond of you. I thought perhaps you'd have some ideas."

Oh no! I did not want to discuss Admiral Sopcoate with Grandmother Throckmorton! She'd been rather sweet on him, which, as disgusting as it was, wasn't nearly so bad as him turning out to be an agent of Chaos. She thought he'd died a hero's death when really he'd simply escaped with his fellow Serpents of Chaos. "Ideas for what?" I asked cautiously.

Father clapped his hands together. "Well, now that you've found her, I think I'll be off to the workroom."

Honestly. He was such a coward sometimes!

Grandmother waved him away. "Very well. I'll see myself out once Theodosia and I have finished. Come, gel. I don't want to stand in this mess. Let's go to the withdrawing room. I only have a few minutes before I must leave for the admiralty."

Thank heaven for small favors, I thought as I meekly followed her into the room our family used as a refuge from museum business.

"Sit down," she said, taking a seat on the small red-velvet settee.

I perched myself on the edge of a chair. It doesn't do to get too comfortable around Grandmother.

"So." She glanced at me briefly, then turned to study the clock on the mantel. "There's been no more word on Admiral Sopcoate."

"I'm very sorry, Grandmother," I murmured.

"Yes, well. It can't be helped. However, I've decided that something must be done to commemorate his courage and patriotism." She speared me with a gaze. "It's the least we can do, don't you think?"

"Er, yes, Grandmother."

She gave a small satisfied nod, pleased that, for once, she and I were in accord. If only she knew! But I'd been forbidden to tell her. Not to mention, I wasn't certain how she'd take the news. She was a devout Conservative and it might do her in if she realized she'd been consorting with an enemy, however unknowingly. "What did you have in mind?"

She stood up and went over to the fireplace. "Something grand, I should think. With lots of pomp and ceremony. A big brass band and dress uniforms. Maybe even a forty-one-gun salute. It seems appropriate for a hero such as Sopcoate."

"But Grandmother . . ." I had to step carefully here.

"There are many heroes who don't receive a forty-one-gun salute, aren't there? Otherwise, we'd hear the guns going off constantly. I imagine there must be regulations for who gets that sort of fanfare, don't you think?"

She scowled at me. "You sound just like the admiralty."

"I beg your pardon?"

She sighed and turned back to the fireplace. "The admiralty has finally agreed to allow me to hold a memorial service for Sopcoate. However, they stopped short of letting me use Westminster Abbey or have his coffin paraded through London on a gun carriage. They were strangely reluctant to honor him in the proper manner, which made me just that much more determined. I will not have him snubbed or forgotten."

How Grandmother had managed to convince the admiralty to allow a memorial service, I'd never know. I could only assume it was approved by someone who wasn't cleared to know the true reason for Sopcoate's disappearance. Since I had vowed to be tactful, all I said was "Perhaps it had less to do with his status as a hero and more to do with the fact that there isn't a body?"

"Either way, it is unforgivable. Now, I have selected a mahogany coffin, lined with a tufted mattress made of silk. I decided Sopcoate would not want ruffles. I've ordered an inscribed brass plate and brass handles, and, for the pall, I've chosen silk, not velvet, since it is nearly spring. Don't you agree?"

It seemed pointless to mention—yet again—that there was no body to put in this fancy coffin, so I merely nodded my head.

"I've also hired a carriage with six horses. They tried to talk me into only four, but I think Sopcoate deserves at least six. I've also arranged for black crepe scarves, black gloves, and black hatbands to be distributed to all those attending the service. Oh, and black ostrich plumes as well. I do think they add so much dignity to a funeral, don't you?"

"Actually, Grandmother, I've never been to a funeral," I pointed out.

She turned around to face me. "But of course! You weren't even born yet when my dear husband passed on." She paused for a moment, dreamy-eyed. "Now *that* was a funeral." Grandmother clucked her tongue. "If you've never attended a funeral before, you'll need to be fitted for proper mourning clothes."

"Mourning clothes?"

"Of course. You cannot attend in anything but unrelieved black." She thumped her cane. "I'll be back in a day or two with a seamstress so we can get you fitted." Before she could elaborate, the sound of the front door crashing against the wall made us both jump.

"What on earth—" Grandmother began.

"Is anybody in this moldy old place?"

I leaped to my feet. "Henry?" Horrified, I ran to the front door. There my brother stood, hands on his hips, glaring into the foyer.

"I say, what's all that racket?" Father appeared on the top step.

"It's Henry, Father," I told him. "He's home for Easter holidays."

"I would have been here loads sooner," Henry said, fixing his glare on me, "if *someone* hadn't neglected to come fetch me. Which reminds me. I need cab fare to pay for the hansom."

Father came down the stairs in a hurry. "Why didn't you tell us, Theodosia? We would have gone to pick him up ourselves."

I squelched a bubble of irritation. While it was true that I was usually the one to remember such things, it didn't seem fair that I should get in trouble when I forgot.

The cabby stuck his head in the door. "Where's me blunt, mate? You said someone 'ere would pay me. You'd best not be messin' wif ol' Bert here."

"I'm not," Henry said, then turned to me. "I need cab fare," he repeated.

"Well, I certainly don't have it," I told him. "Father? We need to pay for Henry's cab."

"A young child taking a cab, all by himself?" Grandmother sounded scandalized. She had followed me into the foyer and now stood in the doorway looking down her long nose at us.

Father stepped outside to pay the cabby. As Grandmother made a path through the crates and artifacts in our direction, Henry sidled up to me. "I had thought things were different between us, but I can see that I was wrong. You're still up to your old ways."

"No, Henry. Honestly. I just simply forgot—"

"You? Miss Know-it-all? Forget? Ha. You've always threatened to forget to remind Mum and Dad, but why this time?"

"No, really. I did. You see—" How was I to explain it to him? Where to even begin?

"See? It's like I said. You forgot."

I hate it when Henry is right. I especially hate it when he is right and I am wrong. The truth is, I would *not* have remembered even if Grandmother hadn't been waiting. Or even if the wretched scorpions hadn't ambushed me.

Before we could continue our conversation, Grandmother reached us and began fussing over Henry, who lapped it up like Isis with a bowl of cream. At least now I could make my escape.

I edged toward one of the pillars, hoping to slip out of sight unnoticed. I wanted to head for the reading room and research the oracle ritual Awi Bubu and Trawley had used. Maybe there were clues that might explain how both Ratsy and I had managed to have the same prediction.

I had nearly made it to the hall when I had to hop out of the way as Vicary Weems strode by. He held his nose so high in the air he didn't even realize he'd nearly bowled me over. Beast. I waited to see what he was up to.

Father had returned, and Weems pranced toward him, throwing a glance at Henry as if he were something nasty my cat had dragged in. Weems cleared his throat. "Excuse me, sir?"

Father, who had just managed to get Grandmother out the door, looked annoyed. "What is it, Weems?"

He cleared his throat again and tried to look as if what he was about to say pained him. However, the relish in his eyes belied that. "We've had a note from Lord Chudleigh, sir. He reminds us that the board of directors is still waiting for the museum's inventory, which was due Friday."

After the recent fiasco with all of London's mummies ending up on our doorstep and suspicion landing, however briefly, on Father, the museum directors had decided they wanted a detailed inventory of all our artifacts, something that hadn't been done in years—if ever. Presumably, the board members wanted a head count in case one of our artifacts decided to wander off. They completely missed the point that all the other artifacts had migrated *here.*

Father sighed and stabbed his fingers through his hair in frustration. "Yes, Weems. But as you can see, I'm a little busy at the moment trying to get this new exhibit ready for the opening."

"Yes, sir. I understand. But the opening is two weeks away, while the inventory was due three days ago. I find that it is all a question of managing one's time proper—"

"Thank you, Weems," Father interrupted, not sounding the least bit thankful. "I'll have it to him directly."

Weems quivered in righteous indignation as he gave a crisp "Very well, sir," then high-stepped it out of there. Honestly, how does he not trip over his own feet like that?

"Theodosia?"

Oops. "Yes, Father?"

"Have you finished inventorying the basement yet?"

"Almost done, Father. Just one more shelf, really."

"Well then, get to it. I need it by the end of business today so I can get it to Chudleigh first thing in the morning."

"Yes, Father." Assigning me to inventory the basement had been a combination treat/punishment. (Yes, only my father would try to combine those two!) It was also an attempt to keep me occupied, since Grandmother had been unsuccessful in finding a governess who'd stick.

My research on the oracle rituals would have to wait. I changed direction and hurried to my small closet to fetch my ledger.

A miasma of cursed magic had hung over the basement for some time, but I hadn't been able to pinpoint it to a particular artifact. Since I was running out of time, I decided to just grab every last bit of wax I owned and conduct a mass Second Level Test on everything at once.

I reached my closet and fetched the ledger from the washstand, where I'd carelessly set it. Next I went to the large satchel where I kept all my curse-removing supplies and rummaged around until I had a handful of wax bits—candle stubs, mostly. Thus equipped, I headed for the catacombs.

On my way, I called softly for Isis, wondering where she'd gotten to. She normally came to greet visitors, so I was surprised she hadn't turned up in the foyer when Henry had.

Unfortunately, she didn't turn up on my way to the basement either. Which was too bad, as I always preferred a bit of company down there.

The problem with the catacombs was that so many forgotten relics had been stacked on top of one another, it was nearly impossible to tell which ones were responsible for the vile magic and dark curses that swirled about. What made matters even worse was that the Staff of Osiris hadn't even *felt* cursed, and I had no idea how to distinguish a power-laden artifact from an uncursed one.

I opened the door, turned up the gaslights, and then paused as the force of the dark magic hit me. I shuddered once and gripped the three amulets I wore around my neck. Just as I lifted my foot to head down, a voice behind me said, "Can I come too?"

My pulse slowed a bit at this reprieve. "Henry!" Heartened considerably by the idea of a companion—even if it was only Henry—I said, "Why, of course you can come down. If you want to. But I didn't think this sort of thing interested you all that much."

Henry shrugged. "It's not like there's anything else to do in this stuffy old place."

"Very well, then. Come along. But you need to wear this." I lifted one of the amulets from my neck and held it out to him.

He recoiled as if I had offered him a plate of boiled suet. "I'm not wearing one of your stupid necklaces."

"It's not a necklace, Henry. It's protection. Remember? I gave one to Stokes when he was injured in St. Paul's churchyard."

He shook his head at me. "Quit pretending to be all

magical and mystical," he said. "You're not fooling anyone, and you just look stupid." Then, before I could stop him, he shoved past me and raced down the stairs. His words stung, and I had half a mind to leave him to the mercies of whatever magic he might find. Then we would see who was pretending. However, just the thought of that had me hurrying down the stairs after him. At the bottom step, instead of stopping, I kept right on going until I bumped smack into him.

"Watch it!" he said, pushing me away.

"Sorry," I murmured·as I slipped the amulet into his coat pocket under the guise of steadying myself. Once that important business had been taken care of, I turned my attention to the catacombs.

The gaslights barely penetrated the shadowed corners of the room, mostly because they weren't run-of-the-mill shadows. I suppressed a shudder at the thought of an unprotected Henry. In front of me, Henry sniffed. "It smells like wet dog."

My eyes flew to the Anubis statue sitting atop the Canopic shrine. He was sleek black stone, not a twitch of a whisker or tail, thank goodness. He hadn't come to life again, not since I'd returned the Orb of Ra to his shrine. But I'd been alone every other time I'd come down here. I wasn't sure if a second person's *ka* would have an effect on him.

Some curses remained dormant for centuries until they were exposed to a person's life force, which activated the magic in much the same way that the sun caused a flower to bloom.

"What's your cat doing down here?" Henry pointed to where Isis lay, curled up between the statue's front paws.

"What on earth *are* you doing here, Isis?"

She raised her head and blinked her golden eyes at me, then gave a meow of greeting.

Henry whistled, pulling my attention from the cat. His eyes were big and round as he stared at the mummies against the wall. "All right," he finally said. "Now I see why you call it the catacombs. This place *is* creepy."

I found it heartening that he finally felt a niggle of discomfort. He'd never admitted to that. "You should have seen it before I straightened it up some," I told him as I headed for the shelves in the far corner, the very place I'd found the Staff of Osiris. Ever since I'd learned that the staff had come to us as part of an entire warehouse of artifacts of unknown provenance, I'd been trying to identify the rest of the batch. That was why I'd been dragging my feet on this inventory. If there were other powerful artifacts that wielded the power of the gods, I wasn't sure I wanted to record them for all the world to see. Best to let them hide until I could get them to the Brotherhood of the Chosen Keepers and let them take it from there.

I glanced over my shoulder at Henry, who was still examining the row of mummies, paying particular attention to the mummy formerly known as Tetley. "I say, this fellow is rather odd-looking compared to the others."

"You're correct, Henry. He *is* from a much more recent time period than the others are." Would Henry recognize him? He had seen him once before, when Tetley was alive and we had been following him. As Henry continued to stare at the mummy, my worries grew.

"Here." I took a blank page out of my ledger and handed it to him. "Could you go write down the names of all those weapons over in the corner? I haven't had a chance to do it yet." Actually, I had, but I knew that Henry had a keen interest in weaponry and it seemed like a good place to sit him.

"Weapons?" Henry's whole face brightened. He took the sheet I held out and went over to the corner.

When he was safely occupied with that task, I proceeded toward the last shelf. As I'd inventoried the basement, I'd also done a bit of organizing, and this shelf was where all the stone tablets had ended up, along with a few nearly unidentifiable odds and ends.

Hoping for a hint of latent power, I picked up the first stone tablet and held it tight. The stele featured a pharaoh offering wine to the god Amen-Ra and looked to be from the

New Kingdom. However, there was no hint of power or magical energy. Of course, there hadn't been a trickle of power when I'd first held the staff either. However, there had been a distinct flicker when I had accidentally activated it by setting the Orb of Ra into the jackal's jaws. I stared at the stele in my hands. How on earth would one activate a stele? I wondered. I shook it slightly, but nothing happened. I turned it over and over in my hands, looking for a small aperture such as a key might fit in, but there was nothing. If there was a way to activate this particular stele, it was a mystery to me.

After a quick glance at Henry to be sure he was well occupied (he was feinting and jabbing with a late Bronze Age ceremonial knife), I went on to the next stele. This one showed a pharaoh wearing the crown of Upper Egypt. The ibis-headed god of wisdom, Thoth, stood on one side while the falcon-headed god Horus stood on the other and appeared to be almost embracing him. Again, there was no visible means of activating it . . . but of course! It could be a much more subtle means of activation than a mechanical method. It might respond to *ba* or *ka* or something ethereal of that nature.

Once, I had accidentally breathed too close to a bronze vessel, and my breath had activated the curse hidden in inscribed hieroglyphs, causing the vessel to fill with a revolting substance reminiscent of frog slime. Leaning in close now, I breathed on the stele, then waited.

But that wasn't the key this time. Not quite willing to give up, I carried the artifact closer to one of the gas lamps. Perhaps the flame would mimic the energy of the sun and bring any dormant curses or power to life.

"En garde!" Henry's voice erupted in the silence, startling me. I turned toward him in time to see the point of a lance coming at my head. Without thinking, I held up the stele to ward off the blow. The lance connected with the stone tablet and sent it crashing to the floor.

CHAPTER SIX
THE EMERALD TABLET

"HENRY!" I YELLED. "What on earth are you doing? These aren't toys, you know."

Henry stared in horror at the tip of the lance blade, which was now slightly crumpled. "How was I to know you were going to bash it with a stone tablet?"

"What do you expect me to do when you come at me with a lance? Besides, I didn't mean to. It was just instinct to get something between me and the point of the blade."

I knelt down to examine the stele. Sure enough, a huge crack ran right through the middle. "Oh, Henry, you've destroyed it!"

"Have not." He replaced the lance in the corner and came to kneel beside me. "Maybe we could glue it?" he suggested.

"And hope that no one would notice? I don't think so."

"Well, it can't be very important if it's been moldering down here for ages."

"All artifacts are important, Henry." I reached out and picked up the stele, horrified when the top right corner fell onto the floor. The damage was much worse than I'd thought.

"I say! Look!" Henry pointed. Under the corner that had fallen off, a dull green stone peeked out.

I frowned in puzzlement and brought the stele closer so I could examine it more thoroughly. Henry leaned in to see better too. I glared at him. "You're breathing on me."

"Sorry. But what is that underneath, do you think?"

"I'm not sure. It almost looks as if the stele was covering something else."

"Well, then, this isn't a disaster, it's a find," he was quick to point out.

I wasn't ready to let him off the hook that easily. "I'm not so sure . . ."

"It is. Look!" He grabbed the stele out of my hands, set it on the floor, and began breaking off the rest of the outer layer.

"Henry! Stop! That's not how you do it."

But I was too late. In less than ten seconds he had completely peeled off the outer layer. It came away as easily as the skin of an orange, revealing a dull green stone of some sort.

I couldn't tell what kind of stone it was. Even more intriguing, there were symbols carved into its surface. They were unlike any I'd ever seen and were certainly not Egyptian hieroglyphs. Which was odd, because there were also figures of Egyptian gods carved into the surface. I recognized the ibis-headed Thoth, who was handing something to the falcon-headed Horus. They stood in front of three mountain peaks with light from Ra shining down upon them.

"This is an important discovery, isn't it, Theo?" Henry said, his chest puffing up a bit.

"Well, it was completely the wrong way to go about it, but yes," I finally admitted. "This would definitely qualify as a discovery. Of some sort."

Just then, a creak on the stairs had Henry and me jumping to our feet. Instinctively, I stepped in front of the green tablet, hoping to hide it from view.

Edgar Stilton hovered on the second stair from the bottom. I was relieved to see he wasn't looking at us but instead staring rather uneasily at the mummies against the wall. Specifically, at Tetley.

"Stilton, what are you doing down here?" My question

came out rather harsh, but I hadn't forgotten that his snooping on my activities was what had led Aloysius Trawley to suspect I had magic powers to begin with.

"Your parents asked me to come find you and tell you they are ready to leave for—I say! What have you got there?" Eyes fixed on the green stone tablet, he came over to where Henry and I stood.

Without thinking, I reached down and grabbed the heavy stone from the floor and clutched it tightly in both hands. "I'm not sure," I said with a warning glance at Henry. "It's just one of the steles from the shelf." I tried to turn away as if to put it back, but Stilton reached out and stopped me.

"Can I have a look?" His face was shining and eager. And, I reminded myself, he was almost as good as I was at picking up odd threads of power and magic. Of course, he didn't know it, but I could tell. He always twitched and shuddered like a bug on the end of a pin when there were vile curses about. Rather handy, that. Especially in our museum.

He took the green stele from my hands, and I had to resist an urge to grab it back. I watched his face as he studied it, his academic interest quickly giving way to something else—awe. He looked at me, his face glowing eerily in the faint green reflection of the stele. "Do you realize what you've found, Theo?"

"Actually, it was me that found it," Henry said with a bit of a swagger.

"No, I don't," I said, elbowing Henry. "Do you?"

He returned his eyes to the stele and stared at it reverently. "I believe I do. If I'm not mistaken, you've just found the Tabula Smaragdina, otherwise known as the Emerald Tablet, which magicians and alchemists have been searching for for centuries."

"Oh," I said, uneasy. If my experience with the Arcane Order of the Black Sun was any indication, when magicians are interested in something, it usually means it holds dangerous and questionable properties.

"Does it do anyhing?" Henry asked.

Hearing Henry's voice seemed to remind Stilton that he and I were not free to talk openly. He blinked, focused his gaze on Henry, then smiled. "It is said to contain the alchemical formula that turns metal into gold."

"Gold," Henry breathed.

I frowned at Stilton. "But alchemy is all bunk, isn't it? Just an old misguided scientific theory that turned out to be wishful thinking, right?"

"I don't know, Miss Theo. Some people think there is much truth to be found in the ancient science." I cleared my throat and caught Stilton's eye.

"Er, right," he said. "Historical nonsense, really. From a more ignorant time."

"Thank you, Stilton." I did not need him planting such rot into Henry's head.

Henry's face fell. "But even if the formula was just wishful thinking, wouldn't a tablet made of emerald be worth a fortune?"

"Well, yes. There is that," Stilton conceded. Honestly. The man was not helping a bit!

"Did you say our parents were getting ready to leave?" I asked.

"Yes. Yes, I did. They were about to walk out the door when I came down here."

"We'd best hurry then, Henry. We don't want to get left behind." I turned back to Stilton. "Thank you, Stilton. Could you tell them we'll be right along? Oh, and do me a favor, if you would. Let's not tell anyone—*anyone*—about this find just yet. I'd like to surprise my parents with it."

"Of course, Miss Theo," Stilton said. "I won't breathe a word." Then he winked. Or twitched, I couldn't be sure.

"Henry, come put these weapons away," I said as Stilton disappeared up the stairs.

With a sigh and a sullen shuffle of his feet, Henry slumped back to the corner and replaced the weapons he'd been playing with. While his back was turned, I slipped the tablet under an old wooden shield on the shelf. While I *thought* Stilton was mostly trustworthy—at least, more so than the others—I felt it best to hide the tablet, just to be on the safe side.

When Henry continued to dawdle, I gave him a little nudge (more of a push, really). I glanced around for Isis, but she had disappeared again. I worried briefly about locking her down in the catacombs for the night, then realized that since she'd gotten down there on her own, she could get out as well.

We reached the top of the stairs but found the hallway empty. "Maybe they're waiting in the foyer," I suggested. They weren't, so we hurried to the sitting room, hoping to find them there.

"Tell me again why we can't spend the night working here?" Father was saying as he shrugged into his coat. "We have over six weeks' worth of work we need to accomplish in only two."

"But darling," Mother said, wrapping his scarf around his neck. "This is Henry's first night home since Christmas."

"Blast! I forgot again!"

Well, at least I wasn't the only child he forgot about.

"That's because you've been working too hard," Mum said. "It would do you good to have a night off. Now, come along. Let's go find the children."

Not wanting to be caught eavesdropping, I stepped into the room, pulling Henry behind me. "Here we are!" I said brightly.

"Like bad pennies, you two are," Father said. Even though his words were gruff, he ruffled Henry's hair in a playful manner. I found myself wishing for a much shorter haircut, like a boy's. It's hideously unfair that boys get to have their hair mussed as a sign of affection whereas girls aren't allowed to get mussed at all. Just as I was beginning to feel sorry for myself, Father put his arm around my shoulders. "Let's go find some dinner, shall we?"

CHAPTER SEVEN

An Unexpected Visitor

WHEN WE RETURNED TO THE MUSEUM the following morning, we found a small gathering of constables loitering in the foyer talking to Flimp, the night watchman.

"Oh no, not this again," Mother muttered.

When Father saw Inspector Turnbull, his face grew bright red. Before Father could charge at him like a raging bull, the inspector stepped forward and greeted us pleasantly. "Morning, Throckmorton. Mrs. Throckmorton. Your night watchman sent for us. He caught someone wandering around uninvited last night. Normally, I'd leave it to the constables, but with the problems you had just a few weeks ago, I thought it best if I checked it out myself."

An intruder! My gaze went immediately to the wall, but there were no mummies lined up there like the last time Inspector Turnbull had come calling.

Father decided to accept Turnbull's pleasant greeting as a peace offering. His color returned to normal and he asked, "Where is he?"

"Right this way, sir." Turnbull led us down the hallway to a utility closet. Two constables stood at attention at either side of the door. My thoughts flew to the Emerald Tablet. Had Stilton broken his word and told Trawley about it? Had the supreme master himself come last night to take it?

"Well, open it up," Turnbull told them.

The constables hurried to open the door, then stood back. I gasped. There, sitting cross-legged on the floor among the mops and pails, was none other than—

"Awi Bubu?" I blurted out.

Six pairs of adult eyes zoomed in on me. "You know this man, miss?" Turnbull asked at the same time as Father said, "How the devil do you know *him*, Theodosia?"

I glanced from one outraged face to another. "He's a magician. He performs in a show at the Alcazar Theater. I saw a picture of him on a playbill once."

"What were you doing in that part of town, young lady?" Mother asked.

Sometimes she picked the absolutely worst moments to

turn into a concerned parent. "Isn't it rather more important to ask what he is doing here?" I countered, trying to divert their attention back to where it belonged.

"Yes," Father said, turning to the old Egyptian in the closet. "What *are* you doing here?"

Slowly, Awi Bubu rose to his feet. One of the constables reached for his billy club as if he expected the shriveled little man to attack him. Instead, the magician gave a deep, respectful bow. "I am sorry to have intruded. I was merely looking for a place to spend the night."

Turnbull looked sharply at Flimp. "Is that true? Did he have anything on him when you found him?"

"No, sir. But what person in their right mind would spend the night in a museum, of all places?"

It seemed impolite to point out that Flimp himself did just that every night.

"Well," Turnbull barked, "answer the man's question."

Awi—or would it be Mr. Bubu?—bowed again. "I was planning to spend the night in the park—"

"Vagrancy is vagrancy, man. Sleeping in the park isn't allowed either," Turnbull said.

"Even so, as I had no place to spend the night, I was going to try there, but before I reached it, I was set upon by thugs who did not like my foreign appearance. Wishing to escape them before I suffered too much harm, I sought refuge behind the museum. I found one of the doors ajar and slipped in, hoping to evade my pursuers. When they did not follow me, I fear I was lulled into a sense of security and fell asleep."

Turnbull glared at Father. "Can't you keep this museum of yours locked?"

Father turned on Flimp. "Which door was it?"

"The entrance door back by the receiving dock, sir. I suppose it's possible that Dolge or Sweeny left it open." He scratched his head. "But I would have sworn I checked it last night, sir, like I always do."

Of course he had. And I had no doubt that it had been locked. I looked at Awi Bubu, only to find him staring directly at me.

I grew warm and flustered and looked away, not wanting any of the adults to realize Awi Bubu and I knew each other well enough to have had an actual conversation.

"Perhaps they forgot," the Egyptian magician said. "For I would never have entered had the door not already been open." He turned to Mother. "And may I compliment you on your excellent collection? It is one of the finest I have seen since I left Cairo."

"Even so," Turnbull said, "I can take you in on vagrancy charges. Constable!" One of the men stepped forward to grab Awi Bubu, but Mother stopped him.

"Cairo, you said?"

Awi bowed deeply. "Yes, ma'am. I am far from my native land."

"Indeed you are. And have you no place to stay?"

He spread his hands. "I have been evicted from my lodgings, ma'am. While Egyptian magic is much in fashion in London, I am afraid actual Egyptians are not."

Mother's face softened. "And how do you come to know so much about museum collections, Mr. Bubu?"

"I had occasion to work for Gaston Maspero at the Antiquities Service in Cairo."

Mother's face brightened as if someone had just dropped a prettily wrapped gift into her lap. "Really, Mr. Bubu?"

"Oh no, Henrietta!" Father grabbed her arm and walked her a few paces down the hall. I inched after them. "Whatever you are thinking, forget about it," he whispered.

"But Alistair! He's worked for the Antiquities Service in Cairo. Just how often does a professional acquaintance of the director's land on our doorstep? It's a wonderful opportunity. He may have suggestions that would help us present our case to them!" Mother's eyes were bright, her cheeks pink. I risked another glance at the Egyptian; he was staring intently at Mother, his lips moving silently. A ticklish sensation ran up my back. Not quite as strong as when I was in the presence of a curse, but strong enough to let me know that some form of magic was being worked.

"Stop!" I shouted. Awi Bubu's mouth snapped shut and he turned to look at me. So did everyone else.

"Stop what, Theodosia?" Father asked, annoyed at the interruption.

How was I to explain? Glancing around frantically, I spied Henry. "It was Henry. He was pinching me."

"Was not!" Henry said, outraged.

"Were too," I replied, desperate to create a diversion from my inexplicable behavior.

"Silence!" Father barked.

I bowed my head, shame heating my cheeks. But Awi Bubu was no longer muttering his chant.

"Not to worry, guv'nor," one of the constables said. "Young'uns will be young'uns."

"Now," Turnbull said, "I suggest you allow us to press charges against this vagrant and be on our way."

"No, Inspector," Mother said. "That will not be necessary. I think we can all agree that there were extenuating circumstances in his situation. After all, one cannot expect a man to willingly subject himself to a beating when there is an open door at hand."

Inspector Turnbull was clearly not happy with this. "But ma'am . . ."

Awi Bubu bowed again. "Thank you, madam. I only hope I can return the kindness someday."

"Well, actually . . . ," Mum replied. "If you wouldn't mind, I would like to talk to you sometime about your work at the Antiquities Service in Cairo."

"But of course. Whatever madam wishes."

"Perhaps you could come tomorrow at two o'clock?"

Awi Bubu bowed yet again. "As you wish. Until tomorrow then." With that, Awi Bubu gave one last bow and walked toward the door. We all stared after him until he disappeared. Then Inspector Turnbull said to my parents, "I'd be careful of that one, I would. Who knows what someone of his kind might be up to."

"Someone of what kind?" Mother asked frostily.

Turnbull blinked. "Someone who spends his nights in parks and museums, madam," he replied, just as icily.

"We'll take all due care, Inspector," Father interjected before we all got frostbite. "And thank you for your quick response."

While the adults exchanged goodbyes, I slipped away down the hall. As soon as I was out of their sight, I burst into a run, determined to catch up to Awi Bubu. When I stepped outside the museum, he was already half a block away. "Wait!" I called out, doubling my speed in an effort to reach him before he disappeared.

CHAPTER EIGHT

FAGENBUSH ISSUES A CHALLENGE

AWI BUBU SLOWLY TURNED AROUND, folded his arms together, and gave a precise little bow. "Little Miss has need
of me?"

"No, I don't have need of you," I huffed out, trying to
catch my breath. "But I want to know what you were doing
snooping around our museum last night."

"I believe Little Miss was there when I explained it to your
constabibbles. I was headed to the park—"

"I don't believe that for a minute! Two days after we first
meet, you just happen to walk by our museum?"

"Ah, but Little Miss told me her parents worked at the

British Museum, did she not? How was I to know she had lied to me?"

Bother. He had me there. Well, as Father always says, the best defense is a good offense. "What about that utter bunk you told Mother about working at the Antiquities Service in Cairo?"

"But it is not, as you call it, bunk. It is the truth. I worked there before I was exiled from my country."

I studied the wiry little man. It was hard to believe that a performing street magician had once worked in one of the most important archaeological organizations in the world. But then, it was also hard to believe that grown men wore black robes and hoods and belonged to secret societies.

"Will I have the pleasure of seeing Little Miss when I return tomorrow?" Awi Bubu asked, as if we were having a polite chat.

I glared at him. "You can bet on it. I know you're up to something, and I will not let you trick my parents with any of your shenanigans."

"Little Miss is a most devout skeptic," he said, then gave one of his infernal bows and took his leave. Before I could so much as turn toward the museum, Henry's voice accosted me. "Why were you talking to that man?"

"Henry!" I whirled around, wondering how much he'd heard. "What are you doing out here?"

He shoved his hands in his trouser pockets. "What did he mean when he said you told him your parents worked for the British Museum? Father isn't going to be very happy about that, you know."

"No, Henry, you mustn't tell him!"

"I don't see why not. Seems I owe you one for making up such tommyrot about me. As if I'd pinch a girl!" he said, clearly still furious with me.

I stepped forward. "Henry, I didn't have any choice. Really."

He snorted and turned back toward the museum. "Wait!" I hurried to catch up to him.

He stopped and scowled at me. "Why should I listen to a word you say? First you leave me twiddling my thumbs at the train station, then you make up lies to get me in trouble with Father. In front of strangers, no less! Any truce we might have reached last time I was home is long over."

"No, no, Henry. Let me explain. There are perfectly good reasons for everything." My mind raced as I wondered just how much I should—or could—tell him. "There is so much that isn't what it seems."

He kicked at a pebble. "Go on. I'm listening. And it had better be good." He folded his arms across his chest.

"Not here." I looked around the square, uncertain if any

of the scorpions might be lurking nearby. "Down in the catacombs, where no one else can hear us."

He rolled his eyes. "Quit playing at being so mysterious."

"I'm not. You'll understand once I explain."

Luckily the foyer was empty when we returned to the museum. Neither the constables nor Flimp nor my parents
were in sight. We even managed to miss Fagenbush as we
hurried down to the catacombs.

Henry reached the bottom of the stairs first. "Hey!
Where's that Emerald Tablet?"

My heart lurched in my chest at his words until I remembered that Henry didn't know I'd hidden it last night. I
sailed past him to the shelf and lifted the wooden shield. "I
hid it under this. Just in case."

"Just in case of what?" Henry scoffed.

"Intruders in the museum," I told him.

He stared at me blankly for a moment before the penny
dropped. "You mean you *knew* that old Egyptian guy would
come looking for it?"

"Well, not him exactly," I admitted. "But it did occur to
me that someone might come after it."

"But only you and I and Stilton knew—oh! You thought

Stilton might come after it?" He frowned, puzzled. "I always liked Stilton."

"Me too, Henry, but there are many strange things afoot these days." Still uncertain how much to tell him, I took a deep breath. He had to know some of it, if only so he could stay safe. And really, a second set of eyes keeping a lookout for odd goings-on couldn't hurt. Surely it was all right for him to know as much as Sticky Will did. That seemed reasonable. "You remember how I told you I'd gone to Egypt on Wigmere's orders?"

Henry stopped fidgeting.

"There's rather more to it than that." I paused, trying to get my thoughts in order.

"Go on," he said.

"I'm still keeping an eye on things for Wigmere. But there are others involved too. Remember von Braggenschnott?"

"I'm not likely to forget him, given that he nearly killed Sticky Will."

"Yes, well, it turned out that Nigel Bollingsworth had been working with him."

Henry's eyes nearly popped out of his head. "Our old Assistant Curator? The one you always made cow eyes at?"

"I never did," I said.

"He was a traitor?"

"Exactly. And Wigmere wanted me to keep an eye out for any other traitors."

Henry leaned forward. "It's that Fagenbush fellow, isn't it? He's always seemed fishy to me."

I sighed. "I'm afraid not. Wigmere claims to have checked him out rather thoroughly."

"Maybe he's wrong."

"Yes, my thoughts exactly."

"What about Stilton?"

"Stilton doesn't work for the Serpents of Chaos, but he does belong to a secret organization—"

"Like a club?"

"Yes, like a club. It's called the Arcane Order of the Black Sun, and they are wildly attracted to all sorts of magic. Especially Egyptian magic. So while Stilton means well, I don't necessarily trust the others in his organization."

Henry whistled.

"But wait," I said. "It gets better. Remember when you and I went into the Seven Dials last time you were home? And we followed that gentleman from the British Museum?"

Henry nodded. "Tetley, you said his name was."

"Shhh!" I glanced over my shoulder, afraid that the mummy formerly known as Tetley would somehow respond to hearing his name.

"What?" Henry whispered.

"That's him." I pointed to the mummy up against the wall.

"Quit pulling my leg . . ."

"No, Henry, really! Von Braggenschnott got mad at him for failing when we were in Egypt and he had him mummified as a punishment. These are extremely dangerous people, which is why I'm telling you all this. So you will be on your guard and watchful at all times."

"You mean I get to work for Wigmere too?"

"Well, not Wigmere exactly. But me. You can help me in my duties for Wigmere, and that will be just like working for him," I rushed to explain.

He wasn't fooled. "No, it won't. It will be like working for *you*." He sighed, clearly put out. Then he frowned. "How does that old Egyptian fellow fit into this? Does he work for Wigmere too? Or the Caning Order for Blackson—what did you call it?"

"The Arcane Order of the Black Sun. And I don't know yet how he fits in, but that's what I intend to find out."

"Find out what?"

I jerked my head up at the sound of Clive Fagenbush's voice. He stood on the bottom step. How on earth had he gotten all the way down those creaky stairs without my hearing him? "What are you doing here?" I asked, none too politely.

He came fully into the basement; his gaze slowly took in the mad jumble of long-forgotten artifacts before finally settling on the row of mummies on the far wall. He crossed over to them and began studying them with interest. "I see you're keeping Tetley down here."

"Not by choice. Chudleigh wants nothing to do with him now that he knows that it's a fake. He clearly doesn't belong in the museum, but there's not much else to be done. Unless you have a suggestion," I said sweetly. Actually, what I longed to do was give the poor man a proper burial; I just hadn't figured out how to go about it yet.

Fagenbush sauntered over to the Canopic shrine on which the statue of Anubis rested. "Ah, yes. Your jackal."

Oh, do be quiet, I thought. *You're going to spill all my secrets.* I glanced at Henry, who was watching Fagenbush with narrowed eyes. "Amazingly lifelike, isn't it?" I said.

Fagenbush looked over his shoulder at me, then down at Henry. "Amazing," he drawled.

"What are you doing down here?" I demanded again, my nerves stretched thin by his examination.

"Now, Theo, you can't blame me if I wanted to check out where you've been keeping yourself for the last few weeks. You can't hog all the choicest artifacts, you know. I'll have to be sure and come down here more often. In fact, you might say I'll be dogging you." He glanced at the Anubis statue, then laughed at his own joke. But I knew a threat when I heard it. He was going to follow me around if need be—whatever was required for him to make those wretched reports to Wigmere.

He continued his perusal of the room, sauntering ever nearer to the shelves. As Fagenbush worked his way closer and closer to the tablet, I realized I had to divert him—but how? I glanced around, and my eyes fell on a Canopic jar that held a length of rope ensorcelled with a particularly nasty curse. Hmm. I could use that, except it was a rather vile piece of magic, and while I wanted Fagenbush out of the way, I didn't wish him any permanent damage. Well, not often, anyway.

When Fagenbush reached out and picked up a funerary mask from the shelf just above the hidden tablet, my gaze settled on a stool from the New Kingdom that was nestled up against the base of the shelves. Carefully, as if I didn't want him to see me, I lifted my foot and gently pushed the stool behind the Canopic shrine.

Fagenbush's head snapped up, his nose quivering like that of a hound on point. "What was that?"

"What was what?" I asked innocently.

He dropped the now forgotten mask back on the shelf and strode toward me. "What are you trying to hide from me?"

"I'm not trying to hide anything from you."

"You little liar." He pushed past me and reached behind the Canopic shrine, then smiled in triumph as he pulled out the stool. "See! I knew you were trying to conceal something." He examined it. The leather seat had rotted away centuries ago, but the legs were inlaid with small pieces of ivory and ebony, so it didn't take long for Fagenbush to figure out it had belonged to an important individual. His gaze turned speculative. "Now, why didn't you want me to see this? I wonder."

Actually, I *had* wanted him to see it. That was the whole point and the basis of the new strategy I had just devised on the fly: redirect Fagenbush's nosiness to harmless artifacts. Well, relatively harmless. The stool had a mild curse on it, one that roughly translated to "May the sands of the desert settle in your knickers until the next new moon."

I scowled, as if I were upset he'd found the stool. "I'm sorry, did you say what you were doing down here?"

He gripped the stool and closed the gap between us. "I have actually been sent down here by your father and Weems to see if you've finished their precious inventory yet. If not, I am to assist you until it is done. I have, in essence, been sent to clean up after you."

"Hardly," I said, thrusting the ledger at him. "The inventory was completed last night. Here. It's all yours." Of course, it wasn't complete. There were a number of questionable artifacts I hadn't included, such as the tablet and the Orb of Ra, but I wasn't about to confide that to Fagenbush.

He snatched the ledger from me, then thumbed through the pages, reading what I'd written. "Well, it looks complete, anyway."

"It *is* complete. I am very thorough." *And you would do well to remember that,* I thought. "Now, since you have what you need, perhaps you should get back to work."

He leaned forward and I was enveloped in a small cloud of pickled-onion-and-boiled-cabbage fumes. "Watch yourself, Theo" was all he said. Then he snapped the ledger closed and began climbing the stairs. I breathed a sigh of relief and looked at Henry.

"What a beast!" Henry said. I winced, sure that Fagenbush hadn't made it to the top of the stairs yet.

My suspicions were confirmed when the entire basement suddenly went black. I froze as Fagenbush's soft laughter floated down the stairway, followed by the click of the door closing. I waited to see if he would lock it, but no. He seemed satisfied to simply turn off the gaslights and leave us to fumble about in the dark.

"I say, why is Fagenbush so mean?" Henry asked.

I sighed. "I don't know, Henry. Perhaps he doesn't think

he should have to work with a young girl? Whatever the reason, it is most tiresome. I honestly don't trust him a bit."

"Can't say that I blame you. You know, it's not as dark in here as I thought it would be," he added.

"You're right." A faint sickly green light kept the room from being pitch-black. We quickly found the source of the light. It came from the shelf. From the Emerald Tablet under the wooden shield, to be precise.

"Is it supposed to glow like that?" Henry sounded a bit awed.

"Maybe. If it's as powerful as Stilton was telling us."

"Does it mean something, do you think?"

"That's what I intend to find out."

"How?"

I turned to look at him. "Research," I announced. "Piles and piles of it."

Henry groaned, then moped his way up the stairs. I started to follow, pausing when I thought I saw a small patch of shadow dribble down from the ceiling behind the mummies. I blinked to clear my eyes, and when I looked again, it was gone. Clearly, the strange light was playing tricks with my vision.

Thinking of green light reminded me that I'd yet to conduct a Second Level Test on the Emerald Tablet. I quickly slipped a few wax bits from my pocket onto the shelf next to it. It wouldn't hurt to find out if it was cursed before we handled it much more. Then, because I realized I'd been distracted from my mass Second Level Test the day before, I took another moment and scattered more than a dozen wax blobs throughout the catacombs. It really was time to get a handle on the curses down here.

"Are you coming or what?" Henry shouted down the stairs at me.

"I'm right behind you," I called back.

CHAPTER NINE
All Roads Lead to ... Chaldea

"ARE YOU DONE YET?" Henry asked for the third time even though we'd been in the reading room less than ten minutes.

"No, Henry. I'm not done. I'm just getting started." The truth was, I hadn't even cracked open a book yet, just managed to pull them from the shelves. Honestly. Did he think I could absorb the words through my hands? "This will take a while, so you might as well get comfortable."

He sighed, then trudged over to an open space on the floor, sat down, and pulled some marbles from his pocket. Satisfied that he would entertain himself for at least five minutes, I returned to my books.

Since Stilton had said the tablet was revered by those who

studied alchemy and the occult, the best place to begin my research was with the grimoires, the ancient books alchemists and magicians of old had used to record their experiments and working knowledge of magic. One in particular, written by Silvus Moribundus, seemed like a good place to start. Much of his information came from Nectanebo II's head priest and magician. The problem was, the book was written in Latin in an old-fashioned script and there were a number of handwritten notes scribbled in the margins, all of which made it painfully slow to translate. Research is not for the easily discouraged.

I thumbed through the old, worn pages looking for the words *Tabula Smaragdina* and felt victorious when I actually found them.

Moribundus wrote that the tablet had been handed down from Hermes Trismegistus, who was thought to be a combination of the Greek god Hermes and the Egyptian god Thoth. Many considered the two gods to be one and the same, and hence the book was credited with being the source of all Western occult knowledge and lore.

Perhaps Stilton was correct and the tablet was simply a record of the failed recipes for turning lead into gold.

"Now are you done?" Henry's voice at my shoulder made me jump.

"No," I said, rather more crossly than I intended.

"All right, already, you don't have to bite my head off."

I took a deep breath and tried to hold on to my patience. "I'm sorry, Henry, but being startled makes me a bit grumpy." He looked so bored and miserable that I took pity on him. "I have an idea. Why don't you go spy on Fagenbush? See what he's up to this morning. find out if he tries to go down into the catacombs again, that sort of thing."

Henry's face brightened. "Truly? You'd let me do that?" Then his face fell. "This isn't like the pinching thing, is it, where you're setting me up to take the punishment?"

I felt my cheeks pinken slightly at this reminder of my unfair behavior. "No, Henry. It's nothing like that. I truly think it's a good idea to know what one's adversaries are up to. I don't know how angry people will be if you get caught, so just be good enough at it that you don't get caught."

"Prime!" he said, then headed for the door. "When should I report back?"

I checked my watch. "After luncheon, perhaps? That way if Fagenbush meets anyone for lunch, you'll be there to see it." Henry looked positively thrilled at this possibility and hurried out. I settled back into my grimoire, determined to make some headway.

Moribundus called the tabula the bible of all alchemical knowledge. It had formed the basis for generations of alchemical experiments and magical theories, which confirmed that Stilton did indeed know what he was talking about. Moribundus also claimed that the tablet had been inscribed by the god Thoth himself. If that were the case, then the tablet could be much more valuable—and dangerous—than Stilton, or Moribundus, knew. It would have been much easier to believe this claim if the symbols on the tablet had been Egyptian hieroglyphs, but they weren't. They were distinctly different.

Frustrated by that puzzle, I continued reading. Moribundus went on to say that the tablet, along with the Book of Thoth, a thirty-six-volume work that contained the entire Egyptian philosophy and magical doctrines, had been stored in the Alexandria Library and destroyed in the great fire. I sighed in disappointment. It's hard to describe just how much ancient knowledge was lost in that wretched fire.

But wait a moment! If the Emerald Tablet had been lost in the fire, then it couldn't be hidden in our basement! Hoping for more clues, I turned the page. There was yet another handwritten note in the margin, this one in a different hand. *It is rumored that some of these books survived the fire and were secreted away in the nearby desert, where they are carefully hidden and only initiates of the* wedjadeen *can know their location.*

Most interesting. Unfortunately, I was a bit unsure as to

what a *wedjadeen* was, so I had no hope of learning the location. There was a sound at the door. "Henry," I said, without looking up. "It's not even lunchtime yet."

"Actually," said Stilton, clearing his throat. "It's not Henry, and it *is*, in fact, lunchtime."

"Oh, sorry, Stilton. I lost track of time."

"You always do, Miss Theodosia, when you're researching something. Find anything on the Emerald Tablet?"

I winced as he said the name out loud. "Shh! No, not yet. But I don't want everyone to know that I've found it, either."

"Of course!"

"What can I do for you, Stilton?"

His left hand twitched convulsively as he came fully into the room. "Actually, miss, I was wondering if you could tell me what all the excitement was about this morning. I'm afraid I missed it."

I leaned back in my chair, glad of the break. "A vagrant broke into the museum and spent the night in the broom closet," I explained.

"But what was that I heard about him being Egyptian? Quite a coincidence, that."

"True," I said, not sure how much I should tell him. He *did* work for Trawley, after all.

A rapid tic began in Stilton's left cheek and continued

until he finally bit down to get it to stop. "Was that the Egyptian fellow you were outside talking to this morning?"

"Who told you that?" I asked sharply.

"N-no one, Miss Theo. I happened to arrive just then and saw you."

"Oh. Yes, well. He was one and the same."

"Odd, that you and he would have something to talk about."

I narrowed my eyes. Why was Stilton pumping me for information? "Not so odd," I said. "It turns out he used to work for the Antiquities Service in Cairo. Mum invited him back to visit tomorrow. I was merely curious as to his duties there."

Stilton leaned forward, practically quivering in anticipation. "And that's all you talked about?"

"Why, yes, Stilton. What else would we talk about?"

"N-nothing. I was just curious."

Tired of his crypticness, I rubbed my eyes and changed the subject. "Stilton, you seem to know quite a lot about this Emerald Tablet. How do you think people are aware of it if it's been hidden inside a false stele all these years?"

"It was housed in the Alexandria Library for some time and was one of the most copied documents of its day."

"But how was it deciphered? I didn't recognize the glyphs on it, did you?"

"Ah!" Stilton's face lit up. "That's because they're Chaldean cuneiform, miss, not Egyptian."

"Chaldean?"

"From Chaldea, what the Greeks called Babylonia. More specifically, from the eleventh dynasty of Babylonia, during the sixth century B.C."

"But if the tablet was fashioned by Thoth, or even Hermes Trismegistus, why would they use Chaldean script rather than Egyptian?"

"That's an excellent question, Miss Theo. Our current translations of the tablet were all taken from medieval Latin or Arabic copies of the original."

"Does anyone even know how to read Chaldean?" I asked.

"A handful of scholars," Stilton said. "But they only managed to decipher the cuneiform a few decades ago, so no one who is actually able to read the cuneiform has ever seen the original inscription on the tablet."

"Which would make it quite valuable from a scholarly standpoint," I said thoughtfully.

"There are many who feel the reason the formula never worked was that there was an incorrect translation. Who knows what a true, accurate translation would produce?" His eyes gleamed, as if he were imagining piles of gold.

"Stilton," I began, then stopped when Henry called out, "Theo!"

Stilton bade me a quick goodbye as Henry appeared. Honestly. There were as many comings and goings here as there were at Charing Cross Station! When Stilton was gone, Henry began hopping about as if he were going to burst.

"What? What is it, Henry?"

"You're right, Theo! Fagenbush is definitely up to something."

"Really?" What luck to have finally caught him at it. "What exactly did you observe?"

"Well, he was restless and nervous. Kept jumping out of his chair then standing and pacing for a while."

"Oh." My excitement left me. Those actions were more in keeping with sand in the knickers rather than with traitorous activity. However, I told Henry he'd done a good job so as not to discourage him early on. I glanced at the clock ticking on the wall. "Goodness! It's nearly time to meet Will."

"We're meeting Will?" Henry perked up considerably at this announcement.

"Yes, we arranged to meet in the park today." Of course, we'd arranged that before Wigmere's rebuke. Even so, I couldn't leave him hanging. I needed to explain what had happened.

Henry hurried over to the area where he'd been waiting for me to finish up my research and began hunting around on the floor.

"What are you doing? We need to go."

"I want to take my marbles to the park with me, but they're not here. Where'd you put them?"

"Me? I didn't put them anywhere. I never touched them."

"But I left them here," he insisted.

"Maybe you just thought you did." Then, before he could continue to argue, I said, "I'm leaving right this minute. Are you coming or not?"

He stood up, shoved his hands in his pockets, and kicked at the floor. "I'm coming."

CHAPTER TEN

A WALK IN THE PARK

LUCKILY FOR US, it was one of those rare spring days when the weather was lovely. We could even see the sky for a change, which was a rarity. As we walked to the park, I tried to assemble my thoughts so I could send a coherent message to Wigmere. It was difficult, however, because Henry kept skipping along and asking questions such as "Do you think Will is going to remember me?" (Of course, Henry), "Do you think he'd teach me how to pick pockets?" (I sincerely hope not, Henry), and so on, so by the time we reached the park, I still had no idea of the actual message I would send.

Because of the nice weather, there was a small crowd and

quite a lot of boys running around. Excellent. That should keep Henry entertained.

I searched the crowd, not sure what—if any—disguise Will would be wearing. There was one chimney sweep, but he was too small and too young. Besides, his hair was bright red. Just then, an older boy headed our way. I immediately recognized Will's bright blue eyes under the brim of his slightly grimy cap.

"'Ello, miss!"

"Will! You made it. Did you have any trouble getting here?"

"Nah, simple it was."

"Good. You remember my brother, Henry?"

"Course I do! 'Ow could I forget them whirligigs 'e came up with last time?"

Henry positively beamed. Will could not have said anything that would have pleased him more. Glancing around, I couldn't help but notice that all the other children had stopped their playing and were watching us. I lowered my voice. "We seem to have a bit of an audience," I said.

Will gave me a queer look. "Them's no audience, miss. Them's me brothers."

"All"—I made a quick count—"six of them?"

"Aye. You know Snuffles and Ratsy already." Indeed I did know Snuffles, but I'd never seen him without his enormous bowler hat on. And Ratsy I'd seen only in the dim light of the Alcazar Theater or covered in coal dust on board the *Dreadnought.*

"Ratsy's easy to remember because 'e kind of looks like a rat, don't 'e, miss?"

I had to admit, Ratsy's face was small and pinched and he had a rather long nose. However, even though Will had said it first, I thought it impolite to agree, so I simply pointed to the small chimney sweep who was trying to climb a tree. "Who's that?"

"Oh, that's Sparky, miss. There's no work for 'im today, so 'e's wif us."

"Is that why he's named Sparky? Because he works with chimneys?"

"Oh no, miss. 'E's named Sparky because 'e's right fond o' fire. Can light one using just about anything too."

"Fascinating," I said.

"Then that little blighter over there by the big bush is Pincher."

"Does he pinch then?" I asked, feeling somewhat leery after my experience with Miss Sharpe, one of my former governesses.

"Only wallets, miss. 'E's nearly as good as I am," Will said with a great deal of pride.

"What *is* he doing to that shrub?" I asked.

Will turned to have a look. "Oh, 'e's practicing. Seeing if 'e can pinch a leaf off wifout 'aving the other branches quiver. It's 'arder than it looks."

"So I would think," I said faintly.

"Then the two young'uns are Soggers and the Gob. Me mam isn't feeling well today so she gave 'em to me to take care of."

"Soggers? The Gob?" Honestly. Didn't anyone in his family have a real name?

Will leaned forward and in a stage whisper said, "Soggers still wets 'imself at night, miss, and the Gob, well, there 'e goes, see?" The toddler had picked up what looked to be an old cigar stub and was bringing it toward his mouth. "No, Gob! Put it down," Will shouted, then grabbed the stub from the toddler, who promptly began to cry. Will stuffed the cigar stub into his pocket—"There's a few good puffs left on this one," he explained—then picked up the wailing child and began jiggling the unhappy Gob on his hip. "So, miss, you got a message fer me to get to Wigmere?" His eyes shone with anticipation.

"I'm afraid there's been a change of plans. Wigmere's reminded me that I'm not to use you for messages anymore."

Will looked crestfallen. "Yer not going to use Fagenbush, are you?"

"No, no. If I can't send messages through you, I'll just deliver them myself."

Horrified, Will said, "No, you can't, miss! That neighbor'ood isn't safe for the likes of you. Besides"—a determined look settled over his face—"if that old goat finks I'm not trustworthy enough to deliver 'is messages, well, I'll show 'im. I can be just as reliable as any of 'is other agents."

"Wigmere won't be happy with us."

Will snorted, and the Gob stopped crying, fascinated by the sound his brother had just made. "I ain't afraid, miss."

"Very well. If you're sure."

"I'm sure." He turned and hollered across the park. "Sparky! Get over 'ere and take the Gob, will you?"

The redheaded boy leaped off the tree and jogged over to us. Will handed the Gob to him. "'Ush up, Gobby," Sparky said, then turned to Henry. "You going to stay and listen to them jaw or d'you want to come wif us?"

Henry looked at me. "Go on," I told him. "You already know what I'm going to tell Will."

A broad smile split his face. "Is it true you can make anything burn?" he asked as he followed Sparky to the far end of the park.

I rolled my eyes and tried not to think of what new skills Henry might learn.

"So, miss, what 'ave ye got?"

"Well, I think I've found another special artifact, sort of like the Staff of Osiris."

Will's eyebrows flew up. "One that can raise the dead?"

"No, no. At least, not that I know of. But one that seems more powerful than normal. Tell Wigmere I think I've found the Emerald Tablet—"

Sticky Will whistled. "Is it made of emeralds, miss?"

"I'm not sure. If so, it's one enormous emerald. But tell Wig—"

"Must be worth a fortune then."

I waved that assessment away. "Its value is in the carvings and its history. They're supposed to convey the alchemical secrets or some such. Wigmere will know. Ask him if he thinks this might belong to the same lot as the staff and what he'd like me to do with it. According to my research, people have been hunting for it for centuries."

"Very well, miss. You found the Emerald Tablet and want to know what 'e'd like you to do with it."

"Roughly, yes." I was distracted right then by the smell of smoke. Startled, I saw Sparky, Henry, Snuffles, and the Gob all squatting around a small pile of smoldering rubbish. "Henry! No!" I shouted.

"It's all right, miss. Sparky knows what 'e's doing," Will assured me.

"Yes, but Henry doesn't!" I hurried over to the group of

boys, reached down, grabbed Henry's arm, and pulled him to his feet.

"Ow. What'd you go and do that for?"

"Henry, you can't start fires in the park!"

"Sparky was just showing me how to—"

"I don't care, Henry! And you—" I turned to Sparky. "You should know better than to start fires. What kind of example does that set for the Gob here? Plus," I said, eyeing two nannies who were beginning to watch us, "it's a good way to call the wrong sort of attention to yourself."

Sparky stood up and began stomping on the small fire. "She's about as much fun as a wet blanket," he complained to Will.

Will reached out and knocked Sparky's cap from his head, exposing more wiry red hair. "'Ush yer mouth now. Sorry, miss," he said to me.

Just then, one of the nannies—or perhaps she was a governess—rose up from her bench and headed our way. "Oh dear," I said to Will out of the side of my mouth. "Here comes trouble."

Indeed, she was starched and pressed to within an inch of her life and held herself with a distinctly military bearing. She stopped a few feet away from us, as if she were afraid she'd catch something if she ventured too close. "Excuse me." Her words were clipped and brisk. "I don't believe this park is intended for your use. It is specifically for those who live in Hartford Square. If you do not remove yourselves immediately, I shall go for the constable."

"We was just leavin' anyway, you old cow," Will said. "Come on, boys," he bellowed, then tipped his cap to me. "Later, miss."

I watched them go, furious that the woman had been so heartless. Before I could tell her so, she spoke. "I meant *all* of you," she said, pointing the way to the street.

Embarrassment, hot and sharp, flooded me. She thought I was an urchin just like Will! Furious, I tried to think of something to say, but Henry grabbed my hand and tugged. "Yeah, we were just going, too, you old bat."

When we arrived back at the museum, my cheeks were still stinging from the wretched governess at the park. I decided to go to ground for a bit. Henry was starving and went in search of food (*Good luck,* I thought to myself). Determined to make my quest for solitude productive, I decided to go see if the results from the Second Level Test had come in yet.

Luckily, the hallways were empty; all the curators were no doubt busy in the foyer setting up the display cases and making them ready to receive the collection. As I descended the stairs, I couldn't help but wonder what I'd find. Even if the wax bits had turned foul, could I be certain it was the tablet and not a curse from something else close by?

However, what I did find was even more puzzling than that. The wax that I'd placed right next to the tablet was still white and untainted, even though all the rest of the wax I had scattered throughout the basement was indeed a foul green-black color. How odd. It was almost as if the space around the tablet were the only part of the basement that wasn't cursed. Did that mean it held a protective charm? Or merely that everything else down here was thick with evil magic, and the tablet was the only thing that wasn't? I sighed as my head began to ache. Why couldn't Egyptian magic ever be simple and straightforward?

CHAPTER ELEVEN

FIVE IMPOSSIBLE THINGS BEFORE SUPPER

THE NEXT MORNING when we arrived at the museum I put Henry on sentry duty and went immediately to the reading room. I liked having someone keep an eye on the curators and report on their whereabouts, as it helped cut down on the number of surprise visits I received. Since the tablet had passed the Level-Two Test with flying colors, I was feeling optimistic that it was important most likely only to those who studied occult lore. Of course, to be thorough, I would have to conduct a Level-Three Test, but I needed moonlight for that, and who knew when we'd spend the night at the museum again? That happened much less often when Henry was home.

After my conversation with Stilton, I wanted to spend some time researching the Chaldeans. According to the book he'd given me, the Chaldeans had ruled Babylonia until it was conquered by the Achaemenid Empire, in 539 B.C.

The interesting thing was that the Achaemenids had also ruled Egypt for a time. I fetched *A History of Ancient Egypt* by Sir Bilious Pudge from the shelf. Yes! Here it was! The Persian emperor Cambyses II had taken Egypt in 526 B.C.

Which meant that the Chaldeans and the Egyptians had both been conquered people under the same ruler. Was that when the Chaldeans became interested in Egyptian gods? Or when the Egyptians decided to use Chaldean cuneiform to make the tablet more difficult to decipher? Nothing united two distinct factions like a common enemy. For example, just look at me and Fagenbush.

Speaking of which, it had been awfully quiet all morning. I paused in my reading and looked at my watch. Deciding I needed to stretch my legs, I went to check on Henry. I found him nestled next to a suit of armor in an alcove near the foyer. "Excellent cover, Henry! What's your report this morning?"

He squeezed out of his hiding spot, being quite careful of the armor, I was glad to note.

"Rather boring, really. Everyone's been working on the exhibit this morning. Well, except for Fagenbush. He's hiding out in his office and keeps squirming and fidgeting as if he had ants in his pants."

Er, try desert sand, I thought, but all I said was "Excellent work."

"The stuff you do around here is pretty boring," he complained. "I don't understand how you find it so exciting."

With luck, he never would. "If you'd rather, you can go play marbles or read in the family room for a while."

He perked up. "Did you find my marbles then?"

I winced, regretting bringing up the subject. "No, Henry. I didn't. I'm sorry."

His face fell. "They were my favorite ones," he said sulkily.

"I guess you'll just have to read then, won't you?"

He sighed in frustration and went down the hall. Before I could head back to the reading room, a "Pssst!" emanated from behind one of the pillars. There was only one person I knew who announced his presence in that manner.

"Will?" I poked my head around the pillar, making him jump.

"Oy, miss. You startled me."

"Sorry about that. Have you got a message for me from Wigmere?"

At the mention of Wigmere's name, Sticky Will scowled. "I 'ave, miss. 'E says we is not to keep sending messages through me. You is to use your other contact. 'E says, 'If you wish to be a part of this organization, you must follow the proper channels.'"

Oh dear. It was just as I'd feared. "I'm so sorr—"

"Aren't I good enough to carry messages for 'is Nibs?" Will's fists were clenched, but he looked at me with a question in his eyes. A glimmer of hurt lurked behind all that bluster.

"Maybe it has less to do with us," I said slowly, feeling my way, "and more to do with Fagenbush? Maybe this is Wigmere's way of getting his training's worth out of him or doing a trial run before sending him out on real missions? He's only a Chosen Keeper in training, after all."

Will's face cleared and returned to his normal cheerful countenance. "Oy, then. That's all right. So wot are we goin' to do now, miss?"

"Did he say anything about the Emerald Tablet?"

"No, miss."

Bother. I'd been so hoping he'd have a recommendation. "We'll lie low for a day or two and see what develops," I said at last. After that, we agreed that Will would come around again on Friday morning, and he took his leave.

And just in time! No sooner had he disappeared down the west hall than Grandmother's voice rang out from the foyer. "Theodosia?"

As I was rushing forward to greet her, Grandmother spotted me. "There you are, child."

"Hello, Grandmother," I said, using my best manners.

Grandmother sniffed. "Took you long enough. It's not as if we have all day, you know." She motioned with her cane to the long-nosed sallow-faced woman trailing behind her. "This is Madame Wilkie, the seamstress who will measure you for your mourning gown."

Oh no! I'd completely forgotten about the mourning clothes.

"Come along." Grandmother strode forward, grabbed my arm, and began dragging me toward the family room. "We can't get you fitted out here."

There are few things I hate more than being measured and fitted for gowns. For one thing, it is beyond tedious, nothing to do but stand there as some sour-lipped missus pokes and prods with her bony fingers, trying to measure every last inch of you. To make matters even worse, you're never allowed any say in the design or fabric of the frock being made. All the really lovely stuff is too loud or too garish or completely unsuitable (whatever *that* means!).

Ignoring the tussle between Madame Wilkie and me, Grandmother turned to her favorite subject. "I'm trying to decide if the mourners should wear weeper veils," she said.

Honestly. Did I look like an undertaker? How was I to know if they should wear veils? Luckily, I was saved from replying when Madame Wilkie looked up from poking me with her vicious pins and said, "Weeper veils haven't been used for quite some time, madam." She spoke with some hesitation, as if not sure Grandmother would welcome her advice.

She didn't. Grandmother thumped her cane. "That's because people have no notion of how to organize a proper funeral anymore."

Madame Wilkie blinked at this onslaught, murmured, "Of course, ma'am," and retreated into her work.

Hoping to distract Grandmother, I asked, "May I see the pattern for the dress you've chosen?"

She sniffed. "Don't be vain. The dress isn't to make you look good but to show proper respect for the dead."

Which no doubt meant it would be about as becoming as a turnip sack. I sighed and said, "Yes, ma'am," then jumped as Madame Wilkie poked the measuring tape into my armpit.

"Hold still now," she admonished. Small beads of perspiration had gathered on her upper lip, and she smelled faintly of currants.

"But you're tickling," I protested. I glanced up at the clock and wondered how much longer I had to endure this torture. It was nearly two o'clock! Awi Bubu was due any moment. I could only guess how Grandmother would react to seeing someone of his nature calling on Mother. "Are we almost done?" I asked Madame Wilkie.

"This is the last one." She slipped the tape around my chest, pulled it tight, and noted the measurement, all before I had a chance to so much as blush in embarrassment.

Then she stepped away. "I have everything that I need, madam."

"About time." Grandmother sniffed.

Madame Wilkie looked as if she'd just been forced to swallow worms, but she held her tongue.

"Very well," I said brightly, trying to herd them to the door. "You probably have to get back to your funeral planning. Which reminds me, Grandmother—is there a date yet for the service?" They were nearly at the door now. Three more steps and they'd be gone and the coast would be clear for Awi Bubu's visit.

"I've already told you, it's Tuesday. Do be sure and tell your parents. I insist that they be there. If it hadn't been for Sopcoate's intervention, your father might even now be sitting in jail."

Well, not entirely. I'd had a little something to do with getting him out. "Of course, Grandmother. I'll let them know."

She opened the front door and let herself out, Madame Wilkie right behind. I sighed in relief as they both headed straight for the carriage, Grandmother's nose held so high in the air she never saw Awi Bubu approaching.

Not wanting to arouse the suspicion of the curators working in the foyer—especially Stilton, who had already asked far too many questions about the Egyptian magician—I waited until Awi Bubu knocked on the door before opening it.

"Hello?" I inquired politely, as if he and I had never met before.

His glitter-black eyes studied me. "I am Awi Bubu, and I believe I have an appointment with Madame Throckmorton."

At his announcement, Stilton, who had been in the process of setting the basket filled with grain-shaped stone in place, twitched violently. A clatter echoed all through the room as the miniature stones scattered on the cold marble floor.

Fagenbush looked up from the pieces of Thutmose III's war chariot he was attempting to reassemble. "Well done," he said, causing Stilton to blush beet red all the way to the roots of his hair. Luckily, just then Mother appeared on the top step.

"Mr. Bubu," she said, sailing forward with a smile of greeting. "I'm so glad you were able to join us today."

I produced a very quiet snort, one that only Awi Bubu

could hear, but it let him know that I was onto him. However, the Egyptian simply ignored me and bowed at Mum. "I am honored to receive such a kind invitation as yours, madam."

"Come, let us go have our little chat. Theodosia? Would you mind preparing some tea? I lost track of the time and didn't get to it."

Seething in frustration—how was I to eavesdrop when I had to go for the tea?—I hurried to the staff room and put the kettle on to boil.

I opened a cupboard and rummaged around until I found a teapot and two cups that were barely chipped at all, and I slammed them on the tea tray. I hurried over to the kettle, which wasn't boiling yet. Could water take any longer to boil? My imagination ran wild with the sorts of information Awi might be revealing to Mother that I was missing. In frustration, I finally decided that the water was close enough to a boil, grabbed the kettle, and poured water over the tea leaves in the teapot. That would have to do. We didn't have any milk or lemon, so I stuck the sugar bowl on the tray and grabbed two teaspoons, and I was done. I snatched the tray by the handles and began carefully making my way to the staff room.

Only to find that Mum had closed the door. Honestly! I glanced around, but there was no place to set the tray down so I could free up my hands. Finally, in desperation, I knocked with the toe of my boot.

"Come in," Mother called out.

Gritting my teeth in embarrassment, I called back, "I can't. My hands are full." There was a low murmur of voices, and then Mum was at the door, apologizing. "I'm so sorry, darling! I forgot that you'd be carrying the tea. Here. Set it down on the table there in front of Mr. Bubu."

Carefully avoiding Awi's eyes, I set the tray down and tried my hardest not to feel like a scullery maid. However, if I had to play servant in order to stay and hear what they said, then so be it. I lifted the teapot and turned to ask Awi Bubu if he'd like sugar in his tea when Mother appeared at my side. "I'll pour, dear. You've already been helpful enough. You can run along and play now."

Play! When have I ever played, I'd like to know? My cheeks went hot with embarrassment at being dismissed like a child in front of Awi Bubu, but I ducked my head so Mother wouldn't see my annoyance, bobbed a curtsy, and said, "Yes, ma'am." I walked as slowly as I could in case they started to talk before I left the room.

They didn't, except to discuss how Awi Bubu would like his tea. Then I closed the door, and their voices were reduced to indistinguishable murmurs. Checking quickly to be sure no one was in the hallway, I hurried into the next room, crossed over to the wall, and put my ear to it, hoping I would be able to hear something.

"A glass works better."

I jumped at the voice behind me and turned to find Henry sitting on the couch reading a book. He closed it and stood up. "Who is it and why are you listening?"

"It's Mother talking to that strange magician. I wanted to hear what they said."

Henry nodded, went to the cupboard, and got down two glasses, then came to stand next to me. He handed me one of the glasses and put the open end of the other one to the wall. He leaned close so that his ear rested on the bottom part of the glass. "Go on," he said. "Try it. This is how we stay two steps ahead of the bullies at school."

Marveling at Henry's previously unknown skills, I put my ear to the glass on the wall, relieved when I could clearly hear Mum's and Awi's voices. "It works," I whispered to Henry.

"Told you," he whispered back, looking awfully pleased with himself. I ignored his smugness and settled in to listen.

". . . said you worked at the Antiquities Service, Mr. Bubu?"

"That is so, madam. I trained under Auguste Mariette, then had occasion to work as an aide to Gaston Maspero when he took over."

"Excellent!" Mum said. "We were hoping you might be able to . . . enlighten us on how best to persuade Maspero to grant additional firmins in the Valley of the Kings. He's given one fellow an exclusive commission to dig there and shut the rest of us out. Most frustrating."

"What does she want vermin for?" Henry whispered.

"Not vermin, *firmins*," I told him. "It's when permission is granted to excavate an archaeological site. Now, shh! I can't hear."

Awi Bubu murmured something sympathetic, then said, "Well, it has been a long time since he and I have worked together," he demurred.

"Yes, but since you did work for him, surely you have some insight to offer?"

"Perhaps if madam told me more about the work being done there, I could help devise a request that would carry some weight with Monsieur Maspero?"

"But of course." There was a pause, then a faint clink as she set down her teacup. "Very well. Back in 1898, when Monsieur Loretti was in charge of the Antiquities Service, we obtained permission to dig in the Valley. My husband and I discovered the tomb of Thutmose III. Unfortunately, as you no doubt know, Loretti took credit for many digs he never even visited."

"That has been said of him, yes," Awi agreed.

126

"Even so, we did manage to acquire a great deal of knowledge as well as several artifacts. Using that knowledge, Mr. Throckmorton developed a few additional theories, which I had occasion to test last year when I returned to the Valley."

"But didn't Mr. Davis still have the exclusive firmin for the Valley, even last year?"

"My, you do stay current on things, don't you? Yes. He did. But after a series of disappointing seasons, he had begun to feel that there was nothing left to be found and so agreed I could continue the work we'd started years ago."

"And were you successful?"

"Yes, beyond our wildest dreams." There was a pause, as if she were weighing her words. "We even found the Heart of Egypt."

There was a clunk as someone—Awi Bubu?—set down a teacup in a hurry. "The Heart of Egypt, madam? That was a find, indeed. And Maspero let you take it out of the country?"

"Yes, after some persuading from a very helpful colleague, a Count von Braggenschnott, of Germany. He stepped in and used his considerable influence to persuade Maspero to let me take it."

"May I see this Heart of Egypt?" There was an odd note in Awi Bubu's voice, something I couldn't quite pin down but that made me very uneasy, nevertheless.

"I'm afraid not. You see, it was stolen soon after we returned."

There was a long moment of silence before Awi Bubu continued. "That is a true tragedy, madam."

"Yes, well. In January, we made a quick trip back to Egypt when we heard that someone was trying to take over our tomb. However, we didn't have time to pursue the matter, as our son became quite ill and we had to return home at once. Our daughter, however—"

"The one I just met?"

"Yes, Theodosia. She was with us—it's rather a long story. But suffice it to say she was desperate to see where we'd been working and she sneaked into the Valley. Incredibly enough, during her explorations, she discovered a secret annex that we had missed."

"She has the makings of a good archaeologist already, then."

"Yes, she does, doesn't she? Anyway, we wish to go back and explore this annex in more depth, especially now that we've had a chance to decipher some of the tomb's writing. Their revelations are most . . . interesting and we'd love to pursue the research further. However, Davis is refusing to let us back in now that we've actually found something worthwhile. I thought perhaps Maspero could be persuaded to step in and allow us to continue our excavations, since we had originally discovered the tomb."

There was another long silence. "This is a most—how do you British say? Sticky wicket? I shall have to think on it and see what approach would be the best for you."

Mother clapped her hands together. "Then you will help us? Oh, lovely; I told Alistair you might be able to," Mother said.

"I shall do all that is in my power to help you, dear madam, not least because of your kindness when the police would have arrested me."

I felt a nudge in my ribs and looked away from the wall to find Henry smiling at me. "So that's what you did when you stowed away!"

"Shh! And yes, I . . . I had to see what Mother had been working on." That was the best excuse I could give him, even though it was far from the truth.

I put my ear back to the glass in time to hear Mother and Awi exchanging goodbyes. They were in the hallway now, and I heard Awi say, "I will see myself out, madam."

"Thank you, Mr. Bubu. I cannot wait to tell my husband you've agreed to assist us. He will be most grateful. As am I." There was the faint rapid click of Mother's heels along the hall, then silence.

Should I follow the Egyptian? I would so love to know why he'd zeroed in on our museum, but I wasn't sure if it were wise to put myself in his path.

"Little Miss." Awi Bubu's voice at the door had me jumping away from the wall in surprise.

"I-I thought you were going to show yourself out," I stammered.

"I will. Once I have a word with you."

I glanced over at Henry, who was staring at the magician with his mouth agape.

"You would like to go get some fresh air outside," Awi Bubu gently suggested to Henry.

A look of surprise appeared on Henry's face. "Yes. I would, actually." He set his glass down, grabbed his jacket from the back of the couch, and disappeared out the door.

"Stop that!" I hissed in annoyance.

Awi Bubu held his arms out to his sides. "Stop what, Little Miss?"

I narrowed my eyes. "Are you a mesmerist? Is that how you get people to do what you want them to do?"

"Surely Little Miss is just imagining—"

"Little Miss is *not* imagining. Do not play me for a fool. I can tell when you do that trick."

"Really?" Awi cocked his head like a curious bird. "And how can Little Miss tell?"

How *could* I tell actually? I wasn't sure. I just . . . could. Just as I could tell when an object was cursed. "I-I can feel it. Somehow."

Awi's eyebrows shot up. "Little Miss has the power to detect mesmerism? That is unusual indeed. Do her parents know she has this talent? I wonder."

Blast him! "No. They don't. Not that they'd care," I lied. "And quit talking *about* me instead of *to* me."

Awi Bubu folded his hands together and bowed, then he came more fully into the room, closed the door, and waved his hand over the knob in a strange gesture. "I will make Little Miss—you—a deal. If you will tell me why you ran away to visit your parents' excavation in the Valley of the Kings and how you came to find the new annex your mother spoke of, then I will *not* tell them you are having hallucinations about my powers, and yours."

I couldn't tell him that! Wigmere had sworn me to secrecy, and rightfully so. I would have to make something up. "I-I just wanted to see where my mother spent so much of her time." I threw a grain of truth his way to make my lie more believable. "Wh-what was so wretchedly interesting that it took her away from us for months on end."

Awi Bubu studied me, his face impassive. "Or could it be because Little Miss was returning the Heart of Egypt?"

I gasped. I shouldn't have, because it let him know he'd

guessed the truth, but I couldn't help it. "How—no! I was just—what makes you think the Heart of Egypt has been returned to the Valley of the Kings? Mum just said it had been stolen." The more time I spent with this Egyptian magician, the more confused I became. Who was he, and how did he know so beastly much?

"Even exiles have their ways of staying current on events in their native land."

"Yes, but it's not as if this sort of thing is reported in the newspaper, for heaven's sake."

"So you did return the heart to its tomb. Very commendable, Little Miss. But how, I wonder, did you know to do that?"

This man was dangerous. Oh, it wasn't his mesmerist tricks but the fact that he kept me so thoroughly off balance that I was unintentionally giving away vital secrets. "I have to go. I have lessons I must attend to."

"No one pays attention to your comings and goings, miss. No one is watching to see whether or not you do your lessons or wash your face or have proper supervision."

I gaped at him.

"Or else you wouldn't have been allowed to see my show with your companions," he said in answer to my unasked question.

I pressed my lips tightly together, vowing that no other

words would slip out and confirm or deny his eerily accurate guesses. I lifted my arm and pointed to the door, indicating that he should leave. Now.

"Oh, no. Not yet." He shook his big bald head at me. "Not until I've gotten what I came for."

"And what is that?" I asked, curious in spite of my best intentions.

He met my eyes with his own depthless black ones. "The Emerald Tablet."

CHAPTER TWELVE
AWI BUBU SHOWS HIS HAND

"TH-THE WHAT?" I repeated, stalling for time. How had he even *known* about that?

"Do not play stupid with me, Little Miss. I know you to be quite smart indeed."

"But what makes you think it's here? Have you seen it in a display that I've missed?"

Awi Bubu stepped closer, and in spite of being such a small man, he looked quite menacing. "That tablet does not belong to you. It belongs in Egypt, and it shall be returned."

"Why not take all the artifacts back to Egypt then?"

Awi shrugged. "Because some things we are willing to lose through the stupidity of our administrators, and others are too precious and must be returned at all costs." His eyes glittered feverishly. "Like the Heart of Egypt."

What was he saying? Was the tablet cursed like the heart had been? But it had passed the first two tests with flying colors. "And this tablet is too precious?"

"Yes, among other things. Now. Hand it over, please." I felt his will bumping along my skin, urging me to do exactly as he asked. Fortunately, I was too angry to pay it any heed.

"I'm sorry, but I think you are sorely mistaken. And off your nut if you think we'd hand any artifact over to you, let alone something as valuable as an emerald tablet. If we had one." I frowned as a thought occurred to me. "Are you working with Trawley and the Arcane Order of the Black Sun, by any chance?"

"Who?" The Egyptian looked truly puzzled at the name.

"But Theo, we *do* have the Emerald Tablet," I heard someone say. I whirled around to find Henry had returned and stood just behind me, his glazed eyes fixed on Awi Bubu.

"Hush!" I said, clamping my hand over his lips.

Awi Bubu laughed softly. "Out of the mouths of babes . . ."

I took my hand away from Henry's face and glared at him. "Do not say another word, do you hear me? Not. One. Word." I turned back to face Awi Bubu. "And just because we do have the tablet does not mean we'll give it to you, so you can just be off now, thank you very much."

Awi shook his head patiently, as if he were dealing with a stubborn child. Which he was, come to think of it. "I shall not rest until I have it in my possession. I will be back two days hence. You will hand over the tablet or suffer the consequences."

The word *will* bumped up against me like an insistent dog, and Henry actually spun on his heel as if he were ready to march off to the catacombs, get the tablet, and hand it over. I grabbed Henry's arm and held on tight. "We'll just have to see about that," I said.

As I spoke, Awi Bubu's eyes drifted from me to the doorway behind me, his face growing almost reverent. He made a formal little bow. I turned, expecting to see Mother, and instead found my cat, Isis. Then Awi Bubu said something in either Egyptian or Arabic (I haven't much experience hearing the languages spoken, so I wasn't sure). Isis listened carefully, then twitched her tail. The old magician finally looked away from my cat and met my gaze. "Little Miss has very powerful friends. Nevertheless, I will be back in two days."

And with that he took his leave. Henry would have followed Awi Bubu if I hadn't had a firm grip on his collar.

I steered Henry over to the table and sat him down on one of the chairs, my mind reeling. How could Awi have known about the tablet? Did he find it the night he broke in? And if so, how? And why hadn't he just taken it then?

"You're choking me!" Henry squawked.

I glanced down at him. His eyes had returned to normal and he was no longer set on bolting after Awi Bubu, so I let go of his collar.

"What was that for?" Henry asked, rubbing his neck.

"Because you were about to follow Awi Bubu right out the front door, that's why."

"Why would I do that?"

"For the same reason you told him we had the Emerald Tablet."

"I did not!" he said hotly.

"Actually, you did, Henry. But it wasn't your fault. I think he's some sort of mesmerist. Now be quiet for a minute. I need to think." I sat down and Isis came over and rubbed up against my leg, as if trying to impart some wisdom to me. I reached down and scratched between her ears. "And why did he think you were such a powerful friend? I wonder."

Isis meowed in annoyance, then batted at my ankle with her paws.

"Not," I hurried to add, "that you aren't a wonderful cat and my best friend in all the world, but I wonder at Awi Bubu's reaction, that's all. Most adults don't recognize your brilliance." Appeased by this, she started purring. Henry fidgeted in his chair, but I ignored him.

Why did the Egyptian want the tablet so bad? Why not

any of the other artifacts in our museum? Many had active curses on them; why would he not want those? Especially since this tablet seemed rather tame in comparison to the Staff of Osiris. Or did he truly believe the formula contained in it would turn base metal into gold? I'd always understood alchemy to be bunk, but perhaps I was mistaken. Many considered Egyptian magic to be nonsense, and look how wrong they were.

I sorely needed Wigmere's opinion. Perhaps he would know whether the formula was legitimate. If he didn't, he might have some other idea as to why this tablet held so much importance. He didn't want me using Will, but I refused to confide in Fagenbush. Therefore, my only choice was to pay him a visit myself. I glanced at my watch. It was nearly four o'clock. Too late to visit Somerset House today. But first thing tomorrow would find me at their doorstep.

However, I did have just enough time to create another distraction for Fagenbush to ensure he wouldn't follow me to Wigmere or interfere in any way. I leaped to my feet, eager to set up my next decoy.

"Wait!" Henry said. "Aren't you going to explain what happened?"

"Sorry. Awi Bubu is a bit of a magician and he used his trickery to get you to obey him."

"He did not!"

"Yes, he did," I said gently. It must have been unnerving to realize someone had the power to make you do something.

Henry opened his mouth to argue further.

"I'm going to set up another diversion for Fagenbush. Do you want to help or not?"

Henry's mouth snapped shut; he was torn between wanting to disagree and wanting to be in on the sleuthing. "Yes, but that old man didn't make me do anything . . ."

The truth was, although I tried my best to remove any and all curses from the artifacts, there were a few that I had not been able to get rid of. Some of them were quite vile, like the ceremonial urn with a curse that called on the waters of the Nile to swallow someone whole. Or the pectoral amulet that was cunningly inscribed with a curse that invoked Anat to pierce the wearer's heart with her mighty lance. As much as I disliked the Second Assistant Curator, I wasn't quite ready to do him such fierce bodily harm. I was looking for a way to distract and divert him, not kill him.

I rummaged through my mental inventory of cursed artifacts as I made my way through Statuary Hall. There was nothing here I could use; for one thing, the statues were all too big, and—wait a minute. I paused at a plinth nestled between a statue of Ramses II and an obelisk of the New

Kingdom. Staring back at me from behind a glass box was a jackal mask. Anubis, to be exact. It was made of wood, and its dark resin-based paint had eroded over the years, giving the mask a very sinister appearance. Once worn by priests during mummification rituals, it contained a cunning curse: anyone who wore the mask without first undergoing the rituals of purification and then making an offering to Anubis would bark like a jackal.

That would work.

But how to pique Fagenbush's interest, let alone get him to put the thing on?

"What are you looking at that ugly mask for?" Henry asked. I sighed wistfully. Awi Bubu's mesmerism tricks would come in quite handy if they allowed me to make Henry be quiet for five minutes.

"I'm thinking I can use it to distract Fagenbush." While I had told Henry quite a lot about what had been going on around here, all of it had been human-based events. I hadn't confided in him about the curses and black magic yet. For one, I wasn't sure he would believe me, and two, I wasn't sure I trusted him to not use it against me the next time we got in an argument.

"Henry. Here's what I need you to do. Go down to Fagenbush's office and sneak by his door, only sneak loudly, so he's sure to hear you."

"Why would I want that beast to hear me?"

Could he figure *nothing* out on his own? "Because, Henry," I said very slowly, "we want him to follow you up here so he'll think he's discovered something about this mask and examine it. Then, hopefully, he'll spend most of tomorrow studying it and leave us alone."

"Right. Got it." Henry saluted and tore off down the hall, which gave me about three minutes to come up with a plan. The first part was easy. All I had to do was position the glass box covering the mask so that it was askew. That would let Fagenbush know that someone—me—had recently been investigating it. But how to get him to put it on? Then it occurred to me: I didn't need him to actually put it on. He could just look closely inside it, which would mimic putting it on and thus activate the curse.

I patted the pocket of my pinafore and located a lump of old wax. I slipped behind the display box and stuck the blob of wax in the corner of one of the mask's eyes. If Fagenbush was worth his salt as a curator, he would look closely at the wax before removing it, in order to be sure removing it wouldn't cause any damage. Then I tilted the mask on its side, as if someone had knocked it over by accident. Now all that was left to do was wait for Henry.

Sure enough, I heard the clumping of his feet on the stairs. "He's coming," he whispered when he reached the top.

"Shh! Let's go." I grabbed his hand and headed down the hall. This part had to be timed just right. We hurried past the Egyptian exhibit and went to the door that led to Father's workroom. I paused there, waiting until Fagenbush appeared at the top of the stairs. He needed to see me so that he'd wonder what I'd been up to. Then hopefully his rather annoying instincts would kick in and he'd notice the Anubis mask.

There! His long, dark form appeared on the top stair. "Quick," I said to Henry, then I pushed him into the workroom, came in right behind him, and slammed the door.

Mother and Father looked up, startled, when we burst into the room. "What are you two doing up here?" Father asked.

Henry kept running, but I slowed down long enough to answer Father's question. "We just wanted to remind Mother that she promised we could decorate Easter eggs this week."

"Well, instead of storming through here like an army of invading Mongols, why don't you come have a look at this and tell me what you think?"

I had been inching toward the far door, but his words brought me to an abrupt halt. "You want to know what I think?" I asked, uncertain I'd heard correctly.

"Yes." Father turned back to his worktable. "Your mother and I are having a devil of a time with these hieroglyphs and you seem to be able to read them as if they were no more than slightly sloppy handwriting."

He'd noticed! I grew a bit lightheaded at the novelty of it all.

"We talked about asking Weems," Mother added as she put her hand on my shoulder to gently propel me toward the table. "But since the mummy incident I don't trust his discretion."

I couldn't blame her for that. "I'd be happy to help, Mum."

Behind me, Henry wandered over to wait by a large shelf against the wall.

My curiosity piqued, I cozied up to the worktable to have a look. It was a rubbing from the tomb walls of Thutmose III, and the thin parchment took up the entire table. "Here, let me get you a stool so you can see it all." Father dragged a crate closer and I climbed up. There. Now I could make out the whole thing. I frowned and began to translate.

"'Hail Thutmose, commander of all Egypt. Hail Mantu, god of war, who smiles down upon us. Hail Apep, Serpent of Chaos, whom Mantu wrestles into submission.'"

"Wait a minute . . ." I said. I felt Father watching me

closely as I reread the script. "Since when does Mantu wrestle with the Serpent of Chaos?" I asked.

"Precisely! Your mother and I were wondering the very same thing. Keep reading."

"'We call upon Mantu, O Bringer of Chaos, to aid us in setting our enemies before you, that you might visit your chaos and destruction upon them.'"

Shocked, I turned to stare at Father. "Is he saying they fight their enemies as a way of appeasing Apep? One massive sacrifice, if you will?"

"That was what we made of it, although we thought perhaps we'd translated something wrong."

Just then, there was a loud clap of thunder that had us all jumping out of our boots. Worried about Henry, who was afraid of thunderstorms, I turned to check on him. He stood stock-still, holding a set of ivory clappers in his hand. He stared at them in awe.

"Was it supposed to rain today?" Father asked as he hurried over to the window. He looked outside. "Odd, there's not a thundercloud in sight."

I ignored the window and looked over at Henry, who was carefully setting the ivory clappers back on the shelf. He shoved his hands into his pockets as if they'd been burned, and then he headed for the far door. "I'll just wait for you out here, Theo."

"Very well, Henry. I won't be long."

"So, what do you think?" Father asked, returning from the window.

"Well, it is only a rubbing," I pointed out. "So it's a bit harder to tell. If we had the actual wall in front of us, I imagine the hieroglyphs would be much clear—"

My words were cut off by a rapid yipping coming from Statuary Hall. Fagenbush had found the mask.

"Was that a dog?" Mum speared me with a probing look.

"I don't think so," I said.

Yip-yip-yap! It was closer now, as if Fagenbush were headed toward the workroom.

"Well," I said brightly. "If that's all you needed from me, I'd best catch up to Henry."

"Yes, yes, that's all for now." Father had turned back to the rubbing and was poring over the glyphs once again. "Henrietta, do have a look at this peculiar glyph."

I was dying to have a look too but decided it was more important that I be gone when Fagenbush arrived, so I scurried toward the far door that led to the side stairway. I found Henry sitting on the top step, waiting for me. "Did it work?" he asked.

"It appears so."

CHAPTER THIRTEEN

WITH A *BARK-BARK* HERE

THE NEXT MORNING, when we arrived at the museum, there was a note from Fagenbush explaining that he was ill and unable to come to work. Weems was furious and stomped around muttering about poor work habits. Perfect—not only was Fagenbush out of my way, he was in trouble too! Now I just had to steer clear of Stilton and ditch Henry, and I'd be home free. I resorted to the one thing guaranteed to send Henry running.

"Research?" he whined. "Why d'you have to do more beastly research? I thought you'd finished with that already."

"Hardly, Henry. Research is a never-ending task. And for

something as old and revered as the tablet, I've only scratched the surface."

He shoved his hands in his pockets and mumbled something about having to look for his marbles, then hightailed it down the hall. Quickly, before anyone else could waylay me, I grabbed my coat and slipped outside to hail a hansom. Thank goodness Wigmere had seen fit to give me a small expense allowance to cover cab fare. It made getting to him that much easier.

Even though I'd visited Somerset House a few times now, it never failed to impress me with its grandeur. As I climbed out of the cab, I squared my shoulders, straightened my skirt, and lifted my chin, trying to look as if I belonged there.

I nodded at the doorman, who recognized me and waved me in. I was halfway up the first set of stairs when I heard a calamitous thumping coming my way. Seconds later, Sticky Will appeared, pelting toward me. "'Ello, miss!" he said, not slowing down one whit.

"Will?"

"Can't talk now," he said and disappeared down the steps.

Another thumping, this one much heavier, came at me. I looked up to find Boythorpe, Wigmere's annoying secretary, galloping after Will, his face red with fury. He barely spared me a glance, but I saw that he had a dark black ring of what seemed to be shoe polish around his right ear. Will must be up to his practical jokes again. I sighed and briefly considered intervening, then realized this presented a perfect opportunity to get to Wigmere without having to go through Boythorpe. I hurried up the stairs and down the hallway to Wigmere's office and knocked.

"Come in," his deep voice called out.

I opened the door and stepped inside, a heavy, hushed feeling falling over me.

He looked up from the enormous pile of papers on his desk, and an alarmed expression appeared on his face. "Has something gone wrong?"

"Oh, no, sir! I didn't mean to startle you. It's just, if you aren't too busy, I have a couple of pressing questions."

He tossed a wry look at his desk. "I'm always too busy," he said. "But of course if something urgent has come up, you have my undivided attention."

All of a sudden, I felt uncertain. Were my questions about the Emerald Tablet urgent enough to interrupt him? I had no way to tell. Only Wigmere would know that.

Or perhaps Fagenbush, a guilty little voice reminded me.

Nervous now, I perched on the edge of one of the chairs facing his desk.

"What is so urgent that it brings you out of the safety of the museum?" he asked.

"Well, sir, it's about the Emerald Tablet." Was it just my imagination or had his gaze become the slightest bit frosty? "But also about a strange man who used to work for the Antiquities Service in Egypt," I rushed to add. Then I told him all I knew about Awi Bubu, his uncanny knowledge of the Heart of Egypt, and his claim that the tablet belonged to him and should be returned immediately. "Do you really think it contains a formula to turn metal into gold?" I asked at the end.

Wigmere stroked his mustache and looked thoughtful. "I doubt it, no. But what really matters is that people believe that it does. It is that belief that makes the tablet important to them."

"The inscriptions are in Chaldean cuneiform, sir. Do you have someone here who can decipher it?"

"George Peebles could, if he were here, but I'm afraid he's on assignment now, looking into a shipment of questionable artifacts from the Temple of Osiris at Abydos. He will be tied up for some time."

"Oh." My hopes fell. "What would you like me to do with it in the meantime? It *is* attracting rather a lot of interest."

He waved his hand in the air. "I've got more important things to worry about than charlatans and deranged oc-cultists. Do your parents have a safe? Could you store it there until Peebles can have a look?"

"Yes, but don't you wonder how the magician knew so much about what happened?"

"It *is* odd, I'll grant you."

I scooted even farther forward on my chair, encouraged by this. "Do you think it means there might be a leak of some sort?"

"No, I don't. Didn't you say two other people besides yourself knew of the tablet? Your brother and Limburger, was it?"

"You mean Stilton, sir."

"Right, Stilton. It's much more likely that one of them told someone about the Emerald Tablet."

"But that wouldn't explain how Awi Bubu knew that the Heart of Egypt had been returned to the Valley of the Kings. Only the Brotherhood of the Chosen Keepers and I knew that."

"And the Serpents of Chaos," he reminded me.

"Oh," I said, sitting back in my chair. "Do you think this Awi Bubu is a member of the Chaos organization?"

"No. I don't. They don't tend to show their hand the way he did. I believe he's just an opportunistic charlatan drawn to the lure of overtly magical relics—not unlike Trawley and his Order of the Black Sun."

"Sir," I began slowly. "Speaking of Chaos, there's something I need to ask of you."

He raised one of his bushy white eyebrows at me. "Yes?"

"It's regarding Admiral Sopcoate. I'd like permission to tell my grandmother about his traitorous activities—"

"No!"

I leaned forward in my chair. "But she's about to make a horrendous mistake! She's talked the admiralty into letting her hold a memorial service for Sopcoate. She would be horrified if she ever realized she'd planned such a thing for someone who committed treason against his country."

Wigmere gave an emphatic shake of his head. "If the admiralty gave her permission, they must have decided it was a worthwhile cover. I'm afraid you must honor your original promise to me and not breathe a word to anyone. Not even her."

My shoulders slumped in defeat. If Grandmother found out that I had withheld this information from her . . .

"Now," Wigmere said briskly, "have you had any luck in locating any other artifacts that Munk may have acquired when he purchased the staff?"

"No, sir, I haven't. I've been totally waylaid by the discovery of the Emerald Tablet."

Wigmere frowned. "I think Munk's cache is a much higher priority than a piece of occult memorabilia. It's an alchemical wild-goose chase, something far too many men have spent centuries looking for. It's a quest pursued by charlatans and fools."

"But Stilton seemed to think—"

Wigmere waved aside my argument with one gnarled hand. "Many scholars do not even believe there was such a thing, or at least, not anything handed down from Thoth. Emeralds weren't even mined in Egypt until the Alexandrian period, well past any time that Thoth himself would have actually lived, if indeed he did live. And what few emeralds were found in Egypt were small ones. Nothing indicates that emeralds large enough to carve a tablet upon exist anywhere in the area. No, I'd really prefer you spend your energies looking for the rest of Munk's artifacts. I don't want to risk another object of such great power slipping through undetected."

"But that's the thing, sir. It's all a horrid jumble down there. There aren't exactly tags on items announcing which lots they were bought in. And the staff wasn't cursed, exactly. It was just powerful when activated. But for the purposes of long storage or hiding, it had been deactivated. I have to assume any other artifacts of that nature will be dormant or deactivated as well."

"Which would make them devilishly hard to recognize."

"Precisely!"

"I wonder if there isn't some common thread or element that could be used to identify the Munk artifacts. Say, the artwork or the time period. If the Egyptians truly believed these belonged to the gods, then it seems likely they would need to be from the Old Kingdom. Something made in the Middle or New Kingdom couldn't possibly be old enough to have belonged to any god who might have walked the earth."

"Excellent point, sir." And one I had already thought of. "However, not all artifacts are clearly from one period. Yes, it is evident in certain artwork and pictorial depictions, but since so much of that has worn away or faded, it's not always helpful."

"Hmm. I wonder if we shouldn't have someone else down there. Someone with just a touch more experience."

I did not like the sound of this at all. Not one bit. "I'm not sure that would be a good idea, sir. How would we explain someone new to my parents?"

"I was thinking of Fagenbush."

I bolted forward, and only the firmest resolve kept me from shouting *no!*

"He's already in place and on-site," Wigmere continued. "It seems as if it would be an easy thing to get him assigned to those artifacts."

"Easy for whom, sir? As far as my father knows, I've finished that up. Weems, the First Assistant Curator, is very busy directing Fagenbush's duties with the new exhibit and would be quite put out to have him just up and switch. Honestly, it simply wouldn't work."

Wigmere studied me with his piercing blue gaze. "And this has nothing to do with the personal animosity you've shown him? Even after he saved your life?"

I fought the urge to squirm in my chair. "No, sir. While it's true we're not the best of chums, that has nothing to do with why I think this wouldn't work." Well, not much, anyway.

"Theodosia. You have taken quite a lot of responsibility on yourself, even though you are nothing but a child. I have added further to that by bringing you into my confidence and allowing you to help us when it was expedient."

Odd. I thought *I'd* been allowing *him* to help *me*.

"One of the things I don't expect you to understand yet is that one must learn to be a team player. I realize that, as a girl, one without access to other girls of your age or to sports, you haven't been exposed to teams much. But they are an important tool. One of the signs of maturity and responsibility is being able to work well with others. Even those we don't like."

A hot wave of mortification washed over me. "It's one thing not to like someone, sir, but quite another not to trust them," I blurted out. Wigmere simply looked disappointed in me.

"I've told you, Theodosia. He's been checked out thoroughly. I have no doubts as to his trustworthiness, but perhaps you are too young to understand."

A heavy silence began to grow as I struggled to think of a way to defend myself. I was relieved when the door burst open, grateful for any interruption.

Except this one. Clive Fagenbush stood in the doorway, looking furious.

Wigmere was outraged. "Fagenbush! What is the meaning of this?"

Fagenbush shut the door behind him and strode toward me in a menacing fashion. He stopped when he reached my chair, towering over me. He lifted a finger and pointed, nearly poking me in the nose.

"This—*yip-yip*—girl has put a curse on me. Twice."

I shot to my feet, swerving abruptly to avoid colliding with his finger. "I have not!"

Fagenbush opened his mouth to argue but let loose with a long yipping bark instead. He sounded extraordinarily like a jackal.

"What is going on here?" Wigmere asked as he stared in puzzlement at Fagenbush.

The Second Assistant Curator took a deep breath and tried again. "Your youngest—*yip-yap*—member of the Brotherhood—*arf!*—has seen fit to put a curse—*yip-yip-yip*—on me."

I whirled around to face Wigmere. "I have not! I haven't the faintest idea how to curse someone. All my research revolves around curse removal. Besides, it's not my fault the museum is loaded with cursed artifacts."

"She's got a point, Clive. Why do you think she's involved?"

I waited. Would he admit he'd been following me around, using me to determine which artifacts should be examined rather than doing his own research?

"Because, sir, I found her lurking near the artifacts in question."

"Maybe I just happened to identify them before you did. And maybe I was able to examine them without getting cursed. I can't help it if you're incompetent at detecting curses. All that proves is that I shouldn't have to report to you."

"Enough!" Wigmere exploded. "I will not have my agents —even my junior agents—squabbling like children."

"One of them *is* a child, sir," Fagenbush pointed out, and I have to say I admired his bravery. I would not have risked more of Wigmere's temper.

"But *you* are not. I expect the two of you to work together for the good of the organization. If you can't do that, perhaps I'll have to assign someone else to the Museum of Legends and Antiquities."

I was tempted to point out that since my parents worked there, I couldn't very well be assigned somewhere else, but I refrained.

"Now, work together or I'll find others who can. You're both dismissed."

As the first step of Fagenbush and I working cooperatively together, Wigmere insisted we share a carriage back to the museum. It was a long awkward ride, let me tell you. Fagenbush stared out his window and I stared out mine. Neither of us broke the thick tense silence, except for the low growls and small yips that emerged occasionally from Fagenbush, but as those were involuntary, they didn't really count. After a particularly long string of yaps, Fagenbush looked so distressed that I took pity on him. "It should only last for another day or two. It's not permanent, you know."

He whipped his gaze from the window and glared at me. I shrank back against the seat. "It happened to me once too," I explained. Of course, I'd been much younger then, only eight, and my parents had merely thought I was playing a game. It's much easier to get away with barking when one is a child, I'll grant you that. However, my reassurance did nothing to lessen the look of loathing in Fagenbush's eyes.

"Why do you hate me so?" I blurted out, surprising us both. I'd had no intention of asking any such thing.

"Because—*yip-yap*—you have set my career back ten years with your meddling and interference, that's why." He stopped talking for a moment, overcome with another round of barking.

"How?"

"How? Every time I manage to locate a cursed artifact, I discover that you've been at it already, either decursing it or nullifying it or removing it. I can't prove my worth if you've left nothing for me to do." He looked faintly surprised to have said so much without interruption. Perhaps the curse was already beginning to wear off.

"But how was I to know?" I said. "I thought I was the only one who could see the curses and such. I'm just trying to help."

His mouth twisted up into a mean, small knot. "You *are* the only one who can see them." His voice was laced with bitterness. "The rest of us have to utilize a series of slow, mundane tests."

And that was when it hit me. He was *jealous* of me . . . of my ability. He wanted to be able to detect the curses the way I did and save himself a load of work. And show up his peers, no doubt. "Well, being able to feel black magic isn't all tea and crumpets," I pointed out.

"Even now, when you do know I'm employed by Wigmere, you still refuse to work with me, and you set me up for these vicious pranks of yours."

I squirmed a bit on the carriage seat. "It wasn't a prank," I insisted. And it wasn't. It was a diversionary tactic to allow me to get research done without him hovering about.

He leaned forward, his long thin nose quivering. "I will not be shown up by a slip of a girl who is playing at things she doesn't understand. I will not let you keep me from my rightful duties or interfere with the important work I've been sent here to do."

"Well, I'll let you be the one to explain all that to Wigmere," I said, flopping back into the corner. Honestly. Wigmere had no idea what he was expecting me to deal with.

CHAPTER FOURTEEN

ALOYSIUS TRAWLEY COMES OUT TO PLAY

MOTHER AND FATHER DECIDED TO STAY at the museum that night, giving me an opportunity to conduct a Moonlight Test. In spite of what Wigmere had said, I wanted to conduct that one last test on the tablet before hiding it for good.

My parents had spent the whole day retranslating all the rubbings they'd taken from the annex to Thutmose III's tomb in accordance with the new translation they'd come up with. They were reluctant to quit, afraid their streak would falter if they were to leave it. Luckily, they did think to send Henry and me out for dinner late that afternoon, possibly because Henry was a pill when he was hungry.

Henry came with me to Mrs. Pilkington's pastry shop,

where she said she was very pleased to meet him and gave us each a hot cross bun, which she was making for Good Friday, the next day. They were still warm from the oven; the slightly sweet dough practically melted on my tongue. Henry positively inhaled his, which was rather embarrassing. I savored mine as Mrs. Pilkington wrapped up our meat pies. "You two have a lovely Easter now," she said as she handed me the package.

"We will, Mrs. Pilkington. You too."

We stepped out into the raw afternoon, where the biting wind had picked up; we huddled in our coats and began the long trek back to the museum. Two blocks from Mrs. Pilkington's, I noticed a tall black figure tailing us, and my stomach dropped.

Not the scorpions! Not when I was with Henry.

I glanced quickly at my brother, wondering if he had noticed, but he was busy jumping over the cracks in the sidewalk.

Half a block later, a second figure stepped out of an alleyway as we passed and fell into step behind us. Henry stopped his game and sidled closer to me. "Is that man following us?" he whispered.

"What man?" I asked, my mind whirring. So far the only exposure Henry had had to all this was as a game, an adventure to pass time in the boring old museum. But now, as I looked into his worried blue eyes, I wasn't sure he'd want to know the real truth.

"Are you blind? How can you not see that obvious fellow back there?" The scorn in his tone made me want to point out that actually there were two men, how could *he* not see that? I didn't say it, though. After all, I'd had a bit more practice at this than he had.

I pretended to glance over my shoulder, as if to look at the man he was talking about. "I'm not sure, Henry. I do remember Mother and Father talking about some intense competition from the British Museum. Perhaps that's who they work for."

"But why would they be following *us,* then?"

Bother. Seen the hole in that theory, had he? "Well, I'm only guessing. It could also just be your imagination, you know."

A furtive flutter of movement across the street caught my eye. A rather enormous thickset man was keeping pace with us. His hat was pulled low over his forehead and his coat wrapped tightly around him with the collar up. He looked vaguely familiar.

I was fairly certain he wasn't one of the Black Sunners. If I'd had any doubts, they were erased when one of the scorpions behind us crossed the street, heading toward the third man.

When the hulking brute saw him, he spun on his heel and began walking back the way he'd come. The other scorpion joined the first, and as they drew closer, he broke into a run, and then all three men disappeared down the street. I breathed a sigh of relief and turned to Henry. "See? They had nothing to do with us."

After supper, our parents returned to their workroom, and Henry and I settled down to play naughts and crosses. Henry lost two games in a row, then became bored and went to fetch the custard tart he'd been saving for dessert. "Hey! What did you do with my tart?" he came back and asked.

"Nothing at all, Henry. Maybe you left it with your marbles?"

"Ha-ha. Very funny. Now hand it over."

"But I don't have it. Really. Besides, I don't even like custard tarts. I prefer lemon."

Henry stood with his hands on his hips, scowling at me. "I'm not sure I believe you."

"Suit yourself, but think about it. I've been right next to you the whole time. Here"—I held my arms out to my sides— "search my pockets if you want."

"It's no use looking in your pockets if you'll *let* me."

Clearly, I couldn't win. "Have it your way," I said. "I'm

going to go do some more research." I didn't have time to deal with a case of the sulks. I had important things to get done.

Still put out over his losses, he merely grunted at me and picked up a book to read.

Luckily, the moon was nearly full, so there was plenty of moonlight filtering into the museum. The tricky part would be getting the tablet into the moonlight without my being seen by anyone else.

Glancing uneasily at the shadows against the ceiling, I gripped the two protective amulets around my neck and cautiously made my way to my small closet. Once there, I collected my oil lamp and slipped out of my shoes. One never knows what might be afoot, and it is better not to call attention to oneself if one can help it.

Many of the curses on the artifacts involved the dangerous dead and disgruntled spirits, the *akhu* and *mut*. If an artifact was cursed, either it called upon the power of the *akhu* or *mut* or it trapped them in the artifact itself. Once the power of the sun (Ra to the ancient Egyptians) left the sky, those disgruntled dead things came out to play. And trust me, their idea of play and my idea of play were wildly different.

As I hurried down the hallway, there was an ominous rustling up near the ceiling where the *mut* tended to gather in wait. As I passed, a large piece of shadow detached itself from the ceiling and began oozing after me. I knew better than to look at it and risk focusing my *ka,* or life energy, on it; that would act like a magnet.

I averted my gaze and broke into a run. I have also learned that if I run on my tiptoes, I make very little noise, although I can't keep it up for long.

I burst into the foyer, where moonlight spilled into the room from the large front windows. I glanced over my shoulder to see if the shadow would follow. Some of them avoided moonlight, while others were drawn to it like moths to a flame. It all depended on whether it was the manifestation of a curse or a true *mut* roaming free about the museum, not to mention which god the magician had invoked when he'd created the curse.

This one appeared to be hanging back, preferring the gaping blackness of the hallway to the silvery light of the foyer. Excellent. One obstacle out of the way, now only a dozen to go.

Next stop, the catacombs. And as much as I hated the museum at night, the catacombs were even worse.

I opened the door, wishing I'd thought to collect Isis before coming; turned up the gaslights; then made my way down the stairs. They creaked and groaned as if protesting my weight. When I reached the bottom, I shuddered violently as the sensation of a thousand bugs galloping along my spine racked through me. Not a good sign. That meant that the nearly full moon had awakened something. My eyes shot over to the statue of Anubis sitting on his shrine, the feeble light reflecting off his shiny black surface. He, at least, was still dormant.

But of course—the shrine held the Orb of Ra! It would offer me additional protection for this evening's activities.

I hurried over to the Canopic shrine, gave the statue of Anubis a friendly scratch between the ears, just in case, then bent down to open the door and retrieve the orb from its hiding place. "I'm not going to take it anywhere. I promise," I explained to the statue. "I'm just going to hold it for a bit, then bring it right back."

Feeling much more secure with the power of Ra clutched firmly in my left hand, I headed over to the wooden shield that was hiding the Emerald Tablet. The air swirled and eddied as I went, and I imagined a sense of disappointment as the *akhu* and *mut* gave way before the orb.

I had to let go of the amulets around my neck in order to pick up the tablet. Assuring myself that since I held the Orb of Ra in one hand, I'd be perfectly safe, I gripped the tablet and waited. Nothing. Good. I hurried back over to the shrine, where the light was better. After my conversation with Wigmere, I realized that if this was indeed in a dormant state, as the Staff of Osiris had been, then there should be a way to activate it.

I slipped the orb into my pinafore pocket and used both hands to examine the tablet, turning it over and over, looking for levers or keyholes or sections that might move. Nothing. It was one solid chunk of green stone.

Which tended to confirm Wigmere's theory that it wasn't terribly powerful or important, except to a few rabid occultists. All I had to do now was conduct a Moonlight Test, and then I could quit worrying about the tablet and get back to my other duties.

I hurried toward the stairs, then paused at the bottom step to whisper over my shoulder. "Honestly, I'll be right back," I assured Anubis, then I dashed up to the foyer, stopping long enough to make sure that my parents hadn't wandered down looking for me or that Flimp wasn't making his rounds. All was clear.

I made my way to a particularly bright puddle of moonlight, then angled the tablet so that it was fully illuminated. The dull green glowed brightly, and I blinked against it. Honestly, it was like a searchlight! Wait. I narrowed my eyes against the brightness and leaned in for a closer look. There! In the depths of the stone, something was moving, like minnows trapped under ice. They were symbols of some sort, but not any traditional Egyptian hieroglyphs that I recognized. And they were swimming about, but it didn't look as if they were trying to find a way out, as curses did. Nor did I have a buzzing or tingling sensation, as I did when a curse was trying to work its way out of an artifact into me. Most odd indeed. I squatted down and set the tablet on the floor, then patted my pinafore pocket and found a scrap of paper and a pencil. I wanted to copy a few of these symbols down so I could try to look them up later. I worked in silence for a few moments until I had nearly a dozen of the strange glyphs copied down. Just as I shoved the paper and pencil back into my pocket, something rubbed up against me. I grabbed the tablet and lurched to my feet, stifling the shriek that nearly erupted from my throat.

Isis.

Relief washed through me, and my racing heart began to slow. I reached down and gave her a pat. "There you are! And while I'm very happy to see you, please don't scare me so badly next time."

In answer, she butted my leg with her head, then looked up at me expectantly. I froze. The last time she'd done that was when an intruder broke into the museum. Was someone coming? I held perfectly still and strained to listen. The faint sound of whispering voices reached my ears. I glanced down at the glowing tablet I held in my hands. Where to hide it?

I looked frantically around the foyer. With all the jumbled crates and boxes, there were loads of good hiding places, but I couldn't risk someone moving the tablet before I got back to it. My eyes finally landed on the large flat basket filled with tiny, black grain-shaped rocks. It had been more than three days. The concoction should have removed the curse by now.

Using the flats of my hands, I swept all the little rocks to one side of the basket. There wasn't a smidgen of the honey-and-bread mixture left. I laid the Emerald Tablet on the bottom, then quickly swept the grain back in place until not a glimmer of green showed through. Even better, the basket was part of the exhibit itself, so no one would cart it off to the rubbish bin tomorrow.

With the tablet safely hidden, I paused to listen once more. Nothing. I began to move away, hugging the wall and flattening myself against it so I'd be as invisible as possible. Isis wound herself around my ankles and waited.

Slowly, I inched my head out of the foyer doorway so I could peer around the corner, nearly screaming as a disembodied white head with wild, beady eyes seemed to float my way. After my initial shock, sheer exasperation propelled me around the corner. "You!" I said.

CHAPTER FIFTEEN

THE SCORPION CHARMER

ALOYSIUS TRAWLEY STOPPED DEAD IN HIS TRACKS. There was an *ooph* as the many bodies following behind collided against him. He recovered himself, then sneered. "Theodosia. How lovely of you to meet us here for our midnight visit."

It seemed a bad sign he was no longer calling me O Giver of Light. "What are you doing here?" I asked, keeping my voice low so my parents—and Henry—wouldn't overhear. "It's the middle of the night!"

"Does she always state the obvious?" he asked one of the men in back of him.

"N-no, sir. N-not often."

"Stilton?"

The Third Assistant Curator peeked out from behind Trawley, blinked twice, and jerked his left shoulder. I tried to hide my deep sense of betrayal that he had let his grand master into the museum in the dead of night.

"You see what happens when you don't play fair, Theodosia? You invite us to come see for ourselves what you are withholding."

"Playing fair? How was I not playing fair?"

"By not sharing your power with us, like you'd promised."

"I promised no such thing!"

Trawley took a step closer. "You also led us to believe the power was yours. I'm beginning to suspect you merely had access to powerful artifacts, and *they* were the source of the power, not you."

I glanced at Stilton, who now had a tic in his right cheek.

"Oh no. Stilton didn't tell me, and he has been soundly punished for not doing so. He has had to choose whom he will serve, you or me, and I'm afraid he has chosen me.

"The last time you paid us a visit, I realized you were prevaricating and had no intention of ever letting us into your confidence, so I did what all men who seek power and arcane truths do when faced with such an obstacle—I took matters into my own hands and came to see for myself."

"You mean you've been here before?"

"Yes. I let myself in two nights ago and had a look around, paying close attention to the Egyptian artifacts."

Stilton poked his head out from behind his master again. "H-he was looking for the staff."

"Silence!" Trawley hissed. "I am looking for any artifacts of power. However, just because I found nothing that night did not mean I was ready to give up. As I was leaving, I noticed an otherworldly green glow coming from beneath a doorway—an unearthly light that spoke of great power. But before I discovered the source of it myself, your Egyptian watchman stopped me. But that will not happen this time, as I have brought my own reinforcements."

"What Egyptian watchman?" I asked, thoroughly confused.

Trawley glanced behind me, a look of supreme annoyance clouding his face. "*That* one," he said, pointing just past my right shoulder.

I whirled around to find Awi Bubu standing in the foyer. Honestly! We might as well put out a sign that said OPEN FOR BUSINESS with all the traffic we were getting.

"Good evening, Little Miss." The Egyptian magician bowed toward me, but his eyes never left Trawley. "I believe you know my assistant." Kimosiri's lurking frame slipped from the shadows, sending a jolt of recognition down my spine. *He'd* been the third man on the street following me earlier—the one who'd drawn the scorpions away.

"Please stand in front of Little Miss, Kimosiri, and do not remove yourself until I tell you to."

The large man nodded, then came and planted his huge self directly in front of me, effectively blocking my view of Trawley and the scorpions. I peered around his solid form.

Trawley laughed, a most disturbing sound. "You are two and we are eight. Do you really think you can stop us?"

Awi Bubu cocked his head. "Are you really eight strong? I would not be so certain, if I were you." Then he began to chant, softly at first, then louder. It took me a moment to recognize the words as the ones he'd used in his scorpion-charmer act at the Alcazar Theater.

"I do not know what you think you are doing," Trawley began, then he stopped as the scorpions at his side were tugged upright like marionettes on strings. There was another jerk as they stepped away from him. "Mefenet! Come back here. Tefen!"

Stilton's eyes were wide, his face panicked. Instead of obeying Trawley's command, he spun around and began walking away in stiff, halting movements.

One by one the other scorpions began to do the same thing. Even Basil Whiting, who seemed to be Trawley's most loyal follower, marched away against his will.

Trawley took three steps forward, then glanced uneasily as Kimosiri shifted his position and growled a warning. "What have you done to them?" Trawley looked as if he wanted to throttle the old magician.

Awi Bubu didn't speak until the last of the scorpions had disappeared. "That should do for now," he said, mostly to himself. Then he turned his attention to Trawley. "Your men are scorpions, are they not? I am a scorpion charmer, which gives me power over them. They have no choice but to obey my wishes when I call upon the scorpion goddess Selkhet."

"But they are *my* men!"

"But you have named them scorpions and so put them under the power of the scorpion goddess, and therefore they must obey scorpion charmers everywhere—although there are not many of us left."

Trawley's face grew mottled with rage. When he spoke, spittle flew from his lips. "You have not had the last word, I assure you. You will be hearing from me again, soon." He shot me a lethal glare, then followed his scorpions from the museum.

Awi Bubu nodded his head at Kimosiri. "Go and see the door is shut and locked once they have left. And do not let that watchman see you! We don't need another encounter with the police."

Without a word, the larger man followed Trawley down

the hall. Trawley picked up his pace and fairly skipped toward the door.

It was just the two of us then. Awi cocked his head to the side like a very curious, very ancient bird. "Why did you not use the Orb of Ra on them?" he asked.

My hand flew to the heavy lump in my pinafore pocket. "How do you know about that?" I asked, then frowned. "And what do you mean, *use it*?"

"I sensed an artifact of great power on your person and could determine the approximate size and shape by the power it gave off."

Now that would be a skill to possess, I thought. Come to think of it, it wasn't so different from my ability to sense curses, just more refined. "How does one use the orb without the staff?" I asked.

"Ah, there are a few things Little Miss does not yet know. We will have to save that for another time, I'm afraid. And now, since I have just done you a good turn by saving you from the eggheaded man, perhaps Little Miss will do me one and fetch me the Emerald Tablet."

Feeling a bit braver with Trawley and all the scorpions gone, not to mention the absence of the silent, hulking Kimosiri, I said, "What Emerald Tablet?"

He *tsk*ed at me. "Little Miss, I am disappointed in you. Surely there should be truth between friends?"

"Are we friends?" I asked, well and truly curious.

"I would like to think so. Allies, at the least. Why else have I shown up at such a time to help you?"

"Um, because you wanted the tablet and you were afraid Trawley and his Arcane Order of the Black Sun might get it first?"

"Such cynicism in one so young is most unbecoming."

Honestly. He sounded just like my grandmother.

Awi Bubu began wandering among the items in the half-assembled exhibit. "Have I ever given you reason to mistrust me? Have I spilled any of your secrets? Exposed your activities to your parents, perhaps? No. I have done none of these things, and yet you will not call me friend." He stopped in front of a bust of Thutmose III, then whirled around to face me. "Do you call Stilton your friend? I wonder."

"I don't see how that's any of your business," I said, stung that he'd landed on my uncertainty about the Third Assistant Curator. I had been so sure he was trustworthy, and yet he had led Trawley here.

"Ah. At least Little Miss is learning," Awi Bubu said as if I had spoken my thoughts out loud.

"Stop that," I hissed at him.

"It is in your power to stop me, Little Miss. You have only to give me the tablet and I will be on my way." Something in his voice made me study him more carefully. There was a jubilant lilt to it, as if my giving him the tablet would bring him great joy.

"I'm afraid I can't do that. It belongs to my parents' museum, and they would be very upset with me if I were to hand over something of value."

Awi Bubu barked out a laugh. "Your parents"—he practically spit out the words—"your parents are lovely people and even competent at what they do, but they have no idea as to who or what you are, or what you are up to. Do not insult me by claiming otherwise."

Who or what I was? I was suddenly hungry to know just who—and what—he thought I was. Because, frankly, I hadn't a clue.

Awi Bubu heaved a great sigh, full of regret. "I would so have preferred you to hand the tablet over to me, but if you will not, I have no qualms about taking it. My claim upon it is much greater—and older—than yours." Without even hesitating, he headed over to the basket of grain. How had he known where I'd put it? There wasn't the faintest bit of green showing.

More important, how could I stop him? Surely his absolute determination to possess it proved it had some value, even if I had been unable to detect it.

Since he wasn't much bigger than I was, I gave serious thought to simply tackling him, or I would have if I hadn't known that Kimosiri was likely to be back any moment.

"You do know you can't really turn metal into gold, don't you?" As I'd hoped, my words stopped him.

"Of course," Awi said. "But that is not the nature of this tablet's value."

"It's not?"

"No, the early translations were intentionally misleading."

As Awi reached the display case that was holding the basket, a hissing, spitting shape leaped out of the darkness, straight at his face.

Awi Bubu recoiled and his hands began to sketch a strange motion until he realized it was my cat.

"Isis!" I said.

"Isis," Awi Bubu repeated, taking a step back from her. She had planted herself in front of the tablet, back arched and fur puffed out, which made her look large and terrifying. The Egyptian magician studied her a moment, then said some words in a strange language. Arabic? Ancient Egyptian? I had no idea.

Isis calmed a bit but remained firmly in position between Awi Bubu and the tablet. Much to my shock, the magician gave me a little bow. "Very well. I will not cross your friend to possess what is mine, but be warned, Little Miss, we will meet again and I will have that tablet."

And with those words, he left the foyer and hurried down the corridor Kimosiri had disappeared down earlier.

Slowly, without even thinking, I sank to the floor, my legs unable to hold me up another second. Once she was sure he was gone, Isis left the tablet's hiding place and came over to me. She nudged my hand with her nose and began purring. "Excellent work," I told her. I went to pet her, but my hand paused in the air above her head. Why had Awi Bubu been so afraid of crossing her? Why had she guarded the tablet? These questions made me hesitate. Finally, Isis grew impatient and batted at me with her paw.

Whatever else she was, she was my dearest friend in all the world and had just saved my bacon. I picked her up with both hands and cuddled her to my chest, burying my nose in her soft fur. When I felt strong enough to stand again, I kept her in my arms and carried her back to my closet, where she spent the entire night by my side in the sarcophagus.

CHAPTER SIXTEEN
HENRY LOSES HIS MARBLES

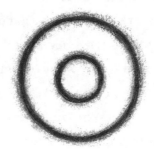

I AWOKE THE NEXT MORNING when the door to my closet burst open and banged against the wall. Isis yowled and I sat bolt upright, heart thumping painfully against my ribs. As Isis sprang out of the sarcophagus and raced for the door, I said, "Henry?"

"Why? Why'd you do it, Theo?"

I rubbed my eyes and wondered if I was having a nightmare. "What? Why'd I do what?"

"This," he said, then threw something that struck me in the chest.

"*Oof!* Henry! That was uncalled-for!"

He stepped into the room, his fists clenched. "What do

you expect when you go around ruining people's things?"

"What are you talking about?" I looked down at the projectile in my lap. It was the book he'd been reading last night. I picked it up and opened it, then gasped. The pages inside had been torn and shredded. "Henry, I didn't do this, I swear it!"

"Well, who else would have? And don't begin jabbering on about Chaos and bad guys and that rot." Two bright spots of pink colored his cheeks.

"All right," I said slowly, trying to think. "But it wasn't me. I would never ruin a book, Henry. Never."

"I don't believe you. I think you're playing tricks on me, trying to keep at this mystery game of yours."

I scrambled out of the sarcophagus. "Henry, that's not true!"

"We'll just hear what Mother and Father have to say about all this."

I froze. They would be furious, and rightly so. The only problem was, I wasn't guilty! "Henry, you've got to believe me, I didn't do it. But we'll find out who did."

He stared at me a moment longer. "Very well. If you can prove someone else did it by dinnertime tonight, I won't tell on you." And with that, he stormed away.

I sat down on the edge of the sarcophagus and flipped through the pages of the wrecked book. Who would have done this? And why? It looked like someone had tried to tear pages out with a knife. Or claws. I paused. Isis wouldn't have, would she? No. She'd been with me all night. But then who?

Anubis? With a jolt, I realized I still had the Orb of Ra in my pocket. Had he come up from the catacombs last night looking for it? I *had* promised I'd return it soon, but what exactly did a jackal consider *soon?* That seemed a bit of a stretch, as I had no idea why he would attack Henry's book if he was mad at *me,* but I had to start my investigation someplace.

I jumped up and washed my face at the basin, then took off my slept-in dress and put on my spare. I slipped back into my pinafore and hurried out to deal with what was shaping up to be a busy day.

My first stop was the catacombs to see about Henry's book. Grasping my amulets, I hurried down the stairs.

Anubis looked as if he hadn't moved a whisker since I'd last seen him. I came closer and studied his teeth and claws, looking for tiny shreds of paper or other signs that he had attacked Henry's book. I checked the floor, but it too was clean of tattered paper scraps—wait. A glint of metal caught my eye.

A niggle of dread filled me when I drew closer and saw it was an amulet. Specifically, the amulet I'd given Henry the first time he'd come down here with me.

Which meant the little beast had taken it out of his pocket when I wasn't looking and kicked it behind the shrine.

As that realization sank in, everything else snapped into place: the marbles, the tart, the book. Unprotected as he was, Henry was being haunted by something; something from the catacombs, no doubt. I lifted my eyes to the wall of mummies, not surprised to find a small pile on the floor at the feet of Tetley's mummy.

There were Henry's marbles, his crumbly old tart, and a few ripped shreds of his book. I glanced up at Tetley, awareness dawning. His *mut* was haunting Henry! The Egyptians had always believed young children were much more vulnerable than adults to spiritual influences and hauntings from the underworld. And as if that weren't enough, Henry had sounded the ivory clappers in the workroom. Normally, they needed to be clapped three times to drive away an evil spirit: once to call the spirit's attention; the second time to exert influence over the spirit, insisting it obey; and the third time to drive it away.

I hadn't given any thought to it before because I'd assumed Henry was wearing the amulet I had given him. But now here it lay, on the floor. I picked it up and slipped it over my head.

Tetley's *ba*, restless and unhappy, had now become a *mut* and was lingering on earth, moping and miserable. He was no doubt upset at the lack of a proper burial and had been busily collecting what he would need in the afterlife. They weren't exactly honey cakes and shabtis, but they were things that would sustain him and keep him entertained.

Poor Tetley! But at least I had an answer for Henry. The trick would be getting him to believe me, or at least creating enough doubt in his mind so that he wouldn't tell our parents.

Determined to make him understand, I started back up the stairs, stopping when I felt the heavy bump against my leg. I headed back over to the Canopic shrine and tucked the Orb of Ra safely away inside it. "Sorry about that," I told the statue, then hastened to get on with my morning.

Luckily, the curators hadn't shown up yet. As I crossed the empty foyer, I was so focused on my explanation for Henry that the faint rap on the window nearly made me jump out of my skin. Will! I'd forgotten we were to meet today. I went outside to join him, where he'd taken up position behind a birch tree.

"Morning, miss."

"Good morning. I'd actually forgot you were coming today."

Will snorted. "I already told you, I ain't goin' to let a couple of 'oity-toits keep me from the most interestin' job I've ever 'ad!"

"Right. Well, in this case, I don't think Wigmere would mind a great deal. So very much has happened! I'm sure he'll want to know about it as soon as possible." Then I filled Will in on all the details of the Black Sun break-in and Awi Bubu's intervention. When I finished, he whistled in appreciation. "Can't wait to 'ear what ol' Wiggy says about all that."

"Surely he will agree that it is of utmost importance. Besides"—I perked up—"you can tell him Fagenbush hasn't arrived yet so I can't very well use him. Now, did you get everything? Do you want to repeat it back to me?"

"No, I got it." He tipped his cap to me. "Be back soon, with instructions," he said.

As I pulled my eyes away from Will, I noticed a lone figure hurrying into the museum. Stilton had arrived. At the sight of him, I felt my anger at last night's betrayal return in full force. He and I needed to have a talk.

I decided to wait for Stilton in his office, ambush him, as it were. It was the least he deserved for betraying me—our entire museum!—to Trawley, leading that wretched man into our midst to steal something.

I didn't have to wait long. Stilton let himself into his office looking drawn and pale. He was clearly distracted and didn't even see me until I cleared my throat. He flinched so hard, he dropped the small white box he'd been carrying; it landed on the floor with a faint *plop*.

"Miss Theodosia!" he said. "You startled me."

"Well, I'm very sorry about that, but we need to talk."

He quickly and guiltily averted his eyes from mine and bent to retrieve his package. When he stood back up, a warm, rich smell wafted toward me. My stomach growled. Mortified, I clamped my hand over my middle and prayed he hadn't heard.

Rather tentatively, he held the box out to me. "I-I th-thought you might be hungry this morning, what with staying here last night and all."

He looked so miserable and hopeful all at once that a small portion of my ire disappeared. "Thank you," I said, taking the box. Of course, it didn't hurt that he'd brought food as a peace offering. When I opened the box, hot cross buns peeked out. "Oh, thank you!" I said again, this time with much more feeling. I plucked one from the box, savoring the warmth on my fingers.

While Stilton hung up his hat and overcoat, I perched on the edge of a chair and devoured my bun.

"Have another," he said, taking a seat at his desk.

"Aren't you going to have any?" I asked, reaching for a second one.

He shook his head. "I'm not hungry. They're all for you. And Henry, if you think he'd like some."

I took a third then closed the box, realizing I *should* save some for Henry. Besides, it might make a good peace offering over the Book Incident.

Stilton truly did look awful. He had dark shadows under his eyes, and his whole demeanor was dejected and droopy. "So," I said. "About last night . . ."

Stilton looked away and began gathering some papers. "I'm most sorry about that, Miss Theo."

I waited for him to elaborate, but he became very busy shuffling his papers and trying to get them in the right order. "Stilton," I finally said in exasperation. "What on earth possessed you to allow Trawley and the others to come into the museum after hours?"

His shoulders slumped and he tossed the pile of papers back on his desk. "I had no choice, actually."

"What do you mean, you had no choice?" Adults always had choices; it was us children who were usually boxed in.

"He would have booted me from the Order." He looked distraught at the prospect.

"Would that really have been so very bad?" I asked gently.

Stilton's appalled gaze flew to mine. "Oh, yes! It would be terrible! Th-they're my family."

"They're not much of a family," I pointed out.

He looked away and began fiddling with the pen on his blotter. "They're all I have, miss."

"But what about your real family? Don't you have any brothers or sisters?" It was rather rude, asking such personal questions, but it seemed important that I understand Stilton better. Especially if I had any hope of ever trusting him.

"Four brothers and two sisters, miss. All older than me." He glanced up and blinked rapidly. "You might say I'm the runt of the litter. In fact, my father often did," he said, making a valiant attempt at humor. He hauled himself to his feet and went over to study his bookshelf as if he were looking for something. "My brothers were all big, burly fellows, you see, and I, I wasn't. I was sickly as a child."

I could only imagine the horror of being sickly with four hale and hearty older brothers to give you grief about it. "What about at school? Surely there were others like you there."

"Not much luck there either, I'm afraid." He continued studying the bookshelf as if it were the most interesting thing in the world. "Wasn't good at sports. And, you probably wouldn't know it, but I used to stutter a bit too."

No need to spell out what that meant. I suddenly had a

vision of a scrawny, stuttering ten-year-old Stilton and all the beastliness that awaited him at school; how utterly alone he must have been.

"The Arcane Order of the Black Sun is the first place I've ever managed to fit in. They didn't care how tall I was or how strong. We shared a common interest that made everything else irrelevant." He turned from the bookshelf and straightened his shoulders a bit. "I guess you could say it's the fellowship part of it. Being united with colleagues in a common p-purpose."

An awkward silence opened up between us. "But Stilton, what *is* their purpose? Do you know? Why did Trawley break in here last night?"

Stilton ran a hand through his hair, and I saw that it was shaking. Badly. "To look for the staff that Whiting told him about. But also to test my loyalty. M-my punishment for not being able to manage you better."

Manage me?

"The loyalty test is normally used only when one becomes a full initiate of the Seventh Level, but the night before last Trawley administered it to me."

I was almost afraid to ask. Almost. "And what is this loyalty test?"

"The Trial of Nephthys." His words were clipped and short, as if it pained him to utter them.

Nephthys was the goddess of darkness and decay, the female counterpart to Seth as well as his consort. She was also thought to be the mother of Anubis, the jackal-headed god of mummification. Any ritual or trial involving her would not be pleasant.

"I was also forced to utter a negative confession."

"Like they use in the Weighing of the Heart ceremony?" That was surprising. I considered Trawley a bit of a charlatan; I hadn't realized his knowledge of Egyptian rituals ran that deep.

Stilton nodded. "'I have not betrayed my brethren,'" he repeated. "'I have not served another master, I have not uttered a falsehood. I have not acted deceitfully.' Then I was put into a man-sized box, and the lid was sealed shut." He attempted another smile. "Didn't realize I was a touch claustrophobic."

"I'm so sorry," I said, feeling as if it were all my fault.

Stilton looked up, his haunted eyes clearing a little. "It's not your fault, Theo. I had never seen that side of the supreme master before. There's something changed in him." Stilton's eyes glazed over for a moment, then he visibly pulled himself together. "Besides, there was no permanent harm done."

Which of course had me wondering what *temporary* harm had befallen him, but I decided I would bite my tongue off before asking. He had clearly suffered a great deal and the particulars were none of my business. Besides, I could look up the Trial of Nephthys later and read about the details then.

Not wishing to intrude on Stilton any longer, I thanked him for the buns, tucked the box under my arm, and got up to leave. When I reached the door, he stopped me.

"Miss Theo, if there is ever any way I can make it up to you, please let me know."

He was so miserable looking that I couldn't help but give him a reassuring smile. "I'm sure I'll think of something."

Then I went in search of Henry.

I found him playing with his tin soldiers in front of the grate in the family withdrawing room. I had time only to plop the box in front of him and say, "I've found out what happened to your book, Henry," when Grandmother Throckmorton's voice rang out from the foyer. "Theodosia! Madame Wilkie and I are here for your dress fitting!"

I closed my eyes and tried not to scream in frustration. Once I had my temper firmly under control, I opened my eyes again. "There *is* an explanation," I told Henry. "And it is *not* me. Do not tell Mum and Dad until we've had a chance to talk."

I left him attacking the hot cross buns and went to Grandmother.

CHAPTER SEVENTEEN
A DIFFICULT MOURNING

IT WAS WELL AND TRULY THE UGLIEST DRESS I had ever seen.

Madame Wilkie held it up for my inspection, and it was all I could do to keep from groaning in dismay.

It was plain and severe, the fabric so black it seemed to suck the very light out of the room.

"Well," Grandmother said with a thump of her cane. "Try it on. We don't have all day."

Madame Wilkie laid the monstrosity down on the settee and helped me out of the frock I was wearing; gray and black plaid, it seemed positively cheerful by comparison.

I shivered as she went to the settee to fetch the mourning gown.

"I've been debating whether the officiating reverend should read from Job or the Book of Common Prayer. Do you have an opinion?"

"Job is the book with all the trials heaped upon that poor man's head, right?" If I was remembering it correctly, it contained more curses and plagues than Thutmose III's war minister, Amenemhab's writings.

"Yes. It can be quite dramatic and invigorating."

"But isn't the whole point of a funeral to allow people to make peace with the one who has just passed on?"

Grandmother's face fell a little bit. "That is true."

"Ready, miss?"

At my nod, Madame Wilkie slipped the monstrosity over my head and tugged the thing into place.

Grandmother took one look at me and cheered up considerably. "Perfect. You look properly subdued and respectful."

What I looked was a fright. Not only was it the ugliest fabric ever, but it itched. I discreetly reached up to adjust my sleeve, using the opportunity to scratch at my wrist.

"Don't fidget," Grandmother ordered.

"If miss will just hold still," Madame Wilkie said, "I shall pin the hem in place and be done."

"I've had a brass plaque engraved for Sopcoate's casket," Grandmother continued. "It reads, 'Here Lies Admiral Sopcoate, an Unsung Hero.'"

Before I could even process the terrible mistake she was making, an idea exploded inside me, just like one of Henry's whirligigs.

Since there was no body to place in it, Sopcoate's coffin would be empty. How hard would it be to slip Tetley's body in there unnoticed and give that poor man a proper burial? Excitement fizzed in my veins at the thought of being able to lay him to rest. Plus, it would have the added benefit of keeping Tetley's *mut* from pestering poor Henry.

I could hardly hold still, I was so excited. In fact, I was so absorbed in trying to figure out the details of my new plan that I didn't even feel it when Madame Wilkie stuck my ankle with one of her beastly pins, and I barely even noticed when Grandmother scolded me for daydreaming.

As soon as they left, I hurried to the reading room, intent on finding everything I could about Egyptian burial rituals and ceremonies. I spent the afternoon engrossed in Erasmus Bramwell's *Funerary Magic, Mummies, and Curses* and Mordecai Black's *A Dark Journey Through the Egyptian Underworld.* Of course, I also had to consult *The Rites of the Dead* by Sir Roger Mortis.

I was so engrossed in my research that it took a few minutes to realize that Fagenbush had been standing in the doorway. "How long have you been there?" I asked.

"Long enough," he said. "I have a message for you."

I tried to pull my mind away from the Opening of the Mouth ceremony and focus on him, but it was hard.

"From Wigmere."

That got my full attention.

"He wants me to tell you that Will has been suspended, and if you continue to refuse to communicate through me, you will be too."

I leaped to my feet. "*What* did you say?"

Fagenbush took great joy in repeating his news. "Will's been suspended. And you will be too if you don't start following orders."

I stared at Fagenbush, loathing him beyond words. "You put Wigmere up to this. You can't stand it that I trust Will more than I trust you."

He took a step toward me. "Will is an ex-pickpocket. A dirty little street urchin with no sense of honor or loyalty. I have worked for the Brotherhood for eight years and lost a loved one to its mission, so of course I think I am better fit to work with Wigmere. Especially since no organization is stronger than its weakest link. In our case, that happens to be an eleven-year-old spoiled brat who has no idea what she's playing at. You're a child. Will's a child. This is no business for children."

I was so angry I was shaking. "I may well be the child here, but who is it that went tattling to Wigmere when he didn't get his way? Certainly that is more childish than anything I've done." I stormed out of the room.

My mind churning, I strode down the hallway, not sure where I was going. I could hardly believe that Wigmere would suspend Will. My stomach was in knots. What would Will do for money? Would he return to pickpocketing? I sincerely hoped not.

Not to mention that I'd been counting on Wigmere to shed some light on the meaning of the events of last night. Now I didn't even know if he had received my report before he'd suspended Will.

And so I was on my own. I had to figure out why Awi Bubu thought the tablet was so very important—and whether or not that meant it was important to us. All without Wigmere's aid.

Very well. I'd exhausted all the materials in our reading room. There was nothing left to be found on our shelves regarding the Emerald Tablet. And Wigmere's vast knowledge was unavailable to me, at least for the moment. So now what?

Really, there was only one other place that might have more information. A place so off-limits and forbidden that it would have my parents gnashing their teeth if they knew: the British Museum. Its reading room, to be exact. There was a good chance it might have something that ours didn't.

CHAPTER EIGHTEEN

THE LESS SHE SPOKE, THE MORE SHE HEARD

IT WAS SEVERAL BLOCKS TO THE BRITISH MUSEUM, but since I
was spitting mad, I arrived at Great Russell Street in no time
at all. Once there, I paused at the steps leading up to the entrance. I'd been lucky once, sneaking into the museum without calling attention to myself; I wasn't sure I'd be that
fortunate again.

Hoping for an idea, I studied the small clusters of people
on the front steps. A group of schoolgirls had just arrived,
led by a tall thin woman who looked as spare and strict as a
whipping rod. Most of the girls risked curious stares in my
direction, no doubt wondering why I wasn't in school as they
were. One of the younger ones stuck her tongue out at me.

They made their way up the stairs, and I fell into step behind them, as if I were the straggler in the group. It worked beautifully and I was able to walk in right under the porter's nose without so much as a "What are you doing here, miss?"

Once inside, I hung back in the enormous foyer while the school group headed for a flight of stairs. Though I felt a bit guilty, I was struck by how majestic the place was.

There were many corridors and stairways leading off the main hall. I took a moment to study the small signs that gave some clues as to where these hallways led: AMPHIBIAN COLLECTION, FOSSIL FISH GALLERY, READING ROOM.

I headed down the long corridor, my footsteps echoing against the stone walls and marble floors. As I drew near a large double door at the end, I began to encounter more and more gentlemen and clerks, many of whom gave me questioning looks, if not outright shocked stares. Clearly, not very many schoolgirls made their way down here. Pity.

I opened one of the heavy doors, stepped inside the reading room, and nearly gasped in awe. Books and papers rose from the floor all the way to the windows, which were nearly twelve feet up and ran the entire circumference of the room. There had to have been at least a million books in there!

There was a large round desk in the middle, and rows of reading stalls and study desks came off of it, like spokes on a carriage wheel. Truly a researcher's paradise. Indeed, most of the desks were filled with scholars. It was, I had to admit with a small sense of defeat, much grander than the reading room at the Museum of Legends and Antiquities.

I approached the center circle, where it looked like attendants were assisting visitors. One young clerk caught me hovering. His eyes widened and his mouth narrowed as he hurried over. "What are you doing here, young lady?" he asked in a library whisper.

"I'm looking for some research materials."

He recoiled slightly, as if he'd been expecting me to ask directions to the lavatory. "I'm afraid our reading room is for serious scholars only."

"What makes you think I'm not a serious scholar? I have a very important report I must write for my . . . teacher."

The man leaned forward, and his face grew red. "This is not a mere library, you know, but the research archives for the greatest museum in the world. Have you a reader's ticket?"

"Er, no." I asked myself what Grandmother Throckmorton would do if faced with this same situation. I leaned forward too. "These publications aren't meant to be seen and read by British subjects then?" I asked.

He paused a moment, trying to think up an answer to that one. "Yes, but only serious, scholarly British subjects, not the riffraff."

Riffraff!

"If you wish to look at our materials, you must apply for permission and be issued a reader's ticket." He seemed very attached to that protocol, no doubt because it kept riffraff such as myself out.

"Now," he continued, "if you don't leave immediately, I shall have to call a porter to escort you out. You don't want that sort of scene, do you?"

"Of course not, but please, if you would let me look for just a moment."

He folded his arms across his chest and shook his head.

I sighed in defeat. "Very well." I made my way back to the entrance, being sure to look as dejected as possible, which wasn't very difficult, frankly.

However, I had not truly given up. I had noticed that just outside the main doors to the reading room there were a number of other doors. Clerks hurried in and out of them, their arms full of books and papers. I was guessing the doors might lead to additional archives. My hand on the exit, I looked over my shoulder to find the obnoxious clerk watching me. I tossed him a wave, then opened the door and slipped down the hallway. Once there, I took the door immediately to my left.

The room was an absolute maze of groaning shelves and tiny cubicles and offices that closely resembled a rabbit warren. I tried to make sense of the layout, but the only sort of identification were signs with numbers on them.

I didn't know what I'd been expecting. Something more helpful, perhaps. Like signs saying BOOKS ON THE EMERALD TABLET, THIS WAY!

Many of the small offices were occupied, although a few were empty. As I sneaked down the hallway, trying to remain as inconspicuous as possible, one of the nameplates caught my eye: THELONIUS MUNK.

Munk. Could that be any relation to Augustus Munk, founder of the Museum of Legends and Antiquities? The very gentleman who'd bought an abandoned warehouse full of very intriguing artifacts that had ended up in our museum's basement? It was too great a coincidence not to explore a little further.

I poked my head into the office, disappointed when I saw it was empty. Wondering what I should do next, I stepped back out into the hallway and nearly plowed into an old man tottering my way carrying a stack of scrolls and books.

"Oh, I'm so sorry," I said awkwardly as I reached out to keep him from toppling over. He was bent with age, and his skin was the color of old parchment. His frock coat was at least fifty years out of date, and he had a few tufts of hair sprouting from his ears.

He blinked twice. "Did you fall down a rabbit hole? Or come through a looking glass? I wonder."

I smiled at him. "Neither. Are you late for a very important appointment?"

The old man barked out a papery laugh. "Hardly. I think everyone's forgotten I even exist down here. Except you, so why don't you quit hovering at my door and come in so I can put these books down."

Unwilling to turn away an opportunity when it landed in my lap, I followed Thelonius Munk into the tiny, crammed office. It was full of papers and books and dust. Quite a lot of dust, actually. I sneezed.

"Bless you," the old man said, then creaked his way over to his desk and lowered himself into his chair. "Did you tell Mother I'd be late for tea?"

"I beg your pardon?"

He blinked again. "I'm sorry." He took his glasses off and cleaned them with a corner of his vest, then replaced them on the end of his nose. "What can I do for you, Alice?"

"No, no!" I almost laughed before I realized he was serious. "I'm Theodosia . . ." I'd been about to say *Throckmorton,* then realized it was probably best if I kept my last name out of this.

"You want information on the Emperor Theodosius?" He perked up, as if this pleased him greatly.

"No, no. My *name* is Theodosia."

He held up a hand to stop me, then opened a desk drawer and rooted around. When he drew his hand back out, he was holding a large, crooked brass trumpet. He lifted one end to his ear and thrust the wide end toward me. "Speak up now," he instructed.

"I said, My. Name. Is. Theodosia."

"Oh." His face fell. "So you don't want any information on the Emperor Theodosius?"

"I'm afraid not."

He looked quite disappointed. "No one pays enough attention to him. Very important figure in history, you know."

"I'm sure he is," I said, not wanting to hurt his feelings. "What I was actually looking for was any ancient texts that connect the Emerald Tablet with the Egyptian god Thoth."

His unfocused gaze sharpened on me.

"It's for a, er, school report I'm doing."

He nodded his head in approval. "Good. I've never held with the notion that girls shouldn't be as well educated as boys." He pursed his lips and stared into space for a moment. I had no idea if he was mentally reviewing the collections to see if they had what I needed or if he was taking a short nap. Just when I was sure he'd forgotten I was there, he spoke. "Is there anything else, while I'm back there?"

I swallowed. In for a penny, in for a pound. "Well, yes,

actually. I am also looking for any information on something I came across handwritten in the margins of a research book. I wanted to see if there was a more official accounting of it."

"Well, what is it, Alice?" he asked, a bit testily. "I can't look it up if you don't tell me."

"The *wedjadeen*." When I said that, the air in the room seemed to ripple slightly, as if the word itself had disturbed something. Not good. I dearly hoped he'd heard it the first time and didn't need me to repeat it.

His eyes became glazed as he stared at the wall some more and stroked his knobby chin. *"Wedja, wedja . . ."* I held my breath, terrified he'd repeat it. Instead, he blurted out, "The Eyes of Horus. That does sound familiar."

"Is that what it means?" I asked. "Many *wedjat* eyes?"

"No," he said, "not exactly. The use of the suffix -*een* indicates a group of men. And I have heard that before, but where?" He creaked to a standing position and shuffled out from behind his desk. "I'll be back in a jiffy," he said.

I could only wonder how long he thought a jiffy was since it took him two whole minutes to get from his desk to his office door. Still, he did think he had information for me. I sat down and vowed to wait patiently no matter how long it took.

I think I may have even napped a bit, for I found myself startled as if from sleep when I heard, "Here you go, Alice."

I began to correct him, then changed my mind. It was probably best to remain as anonymous as possible.

He held a scroll in one hand and an old journal bound with leather straps in the other. It was all I could do to keep from snatching them away as he shuffled over to his desk.

He set the book down, then began to unroll the parchment, his gnarled, liver-spotted hands trembling slightly.

I scooted forward in my chair.

His eyes scanned the parchment until he finally said, "Aha!"

"Did you find it?" I asked, unable to keep silent a moment longer.

He planted his finger on the parchment so hard I was afraid he'd poke a hole in it. Then he began to read. "'The Emerald Tablet, fashioned by Thoth, whom the Greeks call Hermes Trismegistus . . .'" He continued to read from the scroll, but there was nothing to add to what I'd learned in my own research. My shoulders slumped in disappointment.

When he'd finished reading, he looked over at me expectantly. "Thank you," I said brightly, not wanting to hurt his feelings.

Without much hope, I watched him struggle to unbuckle the straps on the book. "Now, this is a diary written by one of Napoleon's men during his occupation of Egypt,"

Thelonius said. He began turning the pages so slowly I wanted to scream.

"Here!" He cackled in glee. "Knew I could find it. This man came upon one of his fellow soldiers who'd gone missing for a fortnight. He was wandering alone in the desert, half dead from exposure and babbling something about the *wedjadeen*."

The light flickered. Clearly, that was a word of some power and importance and was not to be uttered lightly.

"I have read about them someplace else," Thelonius said, "but the text isn't on the shelf where it should be. It must have been misplaced. I'll look for it, if you'd like."

"Thank you, you've been an enormous help."

Once safely back at our museum, I made straight for the family sitting room. I'd had nothing to eat since that morning, and I was starving. Hopefully there was at least a crust of bread left and a bit of jam, something to hold me over till supper.

I burst into the room and startled Henry, who dropped the spoon he'd held in his hand. He was hunched over the table, the jar of jam in front of him, and he'd been spooning out the very last drop.

My heart sank all the way down to the bottom of my hollow stomach. "Henry!" Disappointment made my voice quite sharp, I'm afraid.

He picked up the spoon and shifted his gaze to me. "What?"

"That's disgusting, eating the jam straight out of the jar." Never mind that I would have done the same myself at this point, I was *that* hungry.

Henry shrugged. "There was nothing else to eat and I was starving." He returned his attention to the nearly empty jam jar and began scraping out the last little bit at the bottom. He was hunched over his work, as if it were the most important task in the world, and his movements were a bit furtive.

Just as I readied myself to explain about the book, I noticed a faint shadow of some kind hovering close to his shoulder. He finished the last lick of jam, then pushed away from the table. He stood and carried the empty jar over to the dustbin, and the faint shadow of darkness at his shoulder followed him.

My entire body went cold. "Henry, is that a smudge of dirt there on your shoulder?"

Henry looked down at his shoulder and brushed at it. "No. I don't see anything."

When he'd brushed, the dark spot hadn't budged. Which

meant it *was* a shadow. Which meant Tetley's *mut* had gotten to Henry before *I* had gotten to *it.*

I had to lay that poor mummified man to rest. As soon as possible. There was no time to lose in putting my burial plan for Tetley into action. My hunger forgotten, I went to make the necessary preparations. First stop, Stilton's office.

I found him just packing up to leave for the day. I rapped lightly at his open door. He glanced up at me briefly, then returned to neatly stacking the last of his papers. "Hello, Miss Theo." Was he reluctant to meet my eye? Or merely feeling a bit awkward, as I was, from our last conversation?

"Hullo, Stilton. Do you have a moment?"

He stopped what he was doing and focused his full attention on me. "Is everything all right, Miss Theo?"

"Yes. I just need to ask a favor, actually."

"Have a seat," he said, nodding at one of the chairs.

"Thank you." I sat down and took a moment to smooth my skirts and try to decide how best to present my request. "I have a bit of a problem I need help with."

"Of course, Miss Theo. I told you I'd do anything I could to make it up to you." His eyebrows were drawn together in an earnest frown.

"So you did. Well, this is going to sound strange, but I need you to kidnap a coffin."

His jaw dropped open and one eyebrow began twitching so fiercely I thought it would launch itself clean off his face.

"But only for a little while," I rushed to add. "You can take it right back in a matter of hours."

"Am I to know why you need this coffin, miss?"

"Probably the less you know, the better, don't you think?"

"I suppose that depends. When did you need me to, um, procure this coffin for you? And was there a specific coffin you had in mind, or would any old coffin do?"

"Oh, no. It's a very specific coffin. And I need it by tomorrow night. Here's where you can find it . . ." And I proceeded to explain.

From my earlier research, I had made a small list of items I would need for the ceremony. Luckily, we had most of them here in the museum, although part of me felt I really had to quit treating the Egyptian exhibit as if it were a shop and I was on a shopping expedition. But another part of me simply didn't care. *Someone* had to tend to all the dark magic roaming around.

With the museum closed for the upcoming exhibition and everyone else busy in the foyer, I had the Egyptian room to myself. I was able to collect four small brass chafing dishes for incense burners, then I located two of the four vessels I would need for the purification ceremony. I found the other two down in the catacombs. I would also need a small bag of rock chips, red carnelian, to be exact. Hmm. Those would be tough, as I'd used up all my red stones a few weeks ago making Blood of Isis amulets for all the mummies in our museum during the Staff of Osiris crisis.

The only place I could think of to find carnelian chips was the repair table out in Receiving. We usually had a good supply of semiprecious stones and other odds and ends that the curators used to repair things that came in broken or damaged.

I paused at the door to Receiving, remembering my earlier encounter with the *mut* that lurked here. It could have been the one that had now attached itself to Henry, or it could have been a completely different one. Best to be on my guard.

I stepped inside the room, and my eyes searched all the corners of the ceiling. There was nothing there, which meant the shadow was most likely upstairs, attached to Henry like a limpet.

I hurried to the worktable and located a dozen small pieces of carnelian. It would just have to be enough. Shoving those into my pocket, I headed for the reading room.

There were two more vital ingredients to the ceremony. I

needed seven sacred oils, which I would have to scrounge up from our pantry at home. I also needed an *Egyptian Book of the Dead*—a collection of spells and incantations that guided Egyptian souls through the trials and tribulations of the netherworld. Without them, the *ba* might be waylaid or defeated on its journey and never reach the Egyptian underworld, or what they called Duat.

I wanted to bury Tetley, but my conscience wouldn't allow me to bury the museum's only copy of the *Book of the Dead* with him, so I'd have to write out some of the more important spells on a piece of paper. That would take at least half the night, I was certain, which meant I'd have to take the papyrus home with me.

Bother. I hated homework.

CHAPTER NINETEEN

A Tisket, a Tasket,
a Please-Forgive-Me Basket

I HAD SO MUCH TO DO ON SATURDAY THAT, for the first time ever, I was hoping Mum would forget her promise to help me and Henry dye Easter eggs. It had sounded like a lot of fun a week ago, but now, with the Emerald Tablet and *mut* hauntings, I was simply too busy for something as frivolous as Easter eggs.

Not to mention I'd been up half the night writing down spells from *The Egyptian Book of the Dead*.

Henry continued acting strangely when he came down for breakfast. His cheeks were flushed and his eyes unnaturally bright as he surveyed the sideboard. He helped himself to a bowl of porridge, a plateful of scrambled eggs, a second plate piled high with bacon and kippers, and a dozen slices of toast drenched in butter and jam.

He stolidly plowed through his meal, uttering nary a word of greeting or a whisper of conversation. My parents and I finished our meager-by-comparison breakfasts and then simply sat back to watch. When he had finally finished and licked the last remnant of jam from his fingers, Father looked at Mother in vague alarm. "Is he ill, or growing, do you think?"

"Growing," Mother said firmly, although the look she cast at Henry was a bit doubtful, and when she got up from the table, she rather casually felt his forehead.

When Father left for work, Mother promised to join him shortly then shooed Cook out of the kitchen, donned an apron, and rolled up her sleeves. "Let's get started, shall we? I'll put the water to boil. Theo, you get out the dye stuffs, if you please. Henry, go into the pantry and fetch the basket of hard-boiled eggs Cook left for us."

Mother set four pans with water on the stove while I rummaged around for the dye ingredients. When we had finished setting everything up, I went to join Henry at the kitchen table—where he was steadily eating his way through all the hard-boiled eggs.

"Henry!"

He flinched and dropped the egg he'd been cracking. "What?"

"We're not supposed to eat them! We're decorating them."

Mother left the stove to come peer at Henry in a worried fashion. "Didn't you get enough to eat for breakfast, dear?"

He shrugged. "I dunno."

Honestly! He was like a squirrel storing up nuts for the winter.

Or the afterlife.

Suddenly he pushed himself away from the table, stood, and unbuttoned the top button on his trousers. "I don't feel so well," he said with a groan. Then he waddled from the room.

With Henry gone, Mother and I attacked the remaining eggs with efficient precision. We both had more important things to do, after all. When all the eggs had been put to soak in their pans, Mum left me to watch them while she went to get ready for work.

That's the hardest part about egg dyeing: waiting for the eggs to absorb enough color. If you take them out too soon, they are too pale. Luckily, I had lots to think about and plan for as I watched them bobbing around in the colored water like little buoys.

I needed to contact Will. He hadn't shown up at the museum yesterday afternoon, and I was desperate to hear his side of the suspension story.

Which meant I would have to pay him a visit. I'd been very

lucky in the past about being in the general vicinity of where I thought him to be, then having him find me. Perhaps that luck would hold. If not, well, Ratsy had announced their address to the entire Alcazar Theater.

Besides, we had more eggs than we could ever eat. Either that or Henry would make himself violently ill eating them all. I bet they would make Will an excellent peace offering.

An hour later, when Mum had left for the museum and Henry had retired to his room with a cup of peppermint tea for his stomach, I sneaked into the pantry and prepared for my visit.

I pulled down one of Cook's old shopping baskets from its hook and filled it with a dozen of the colored eggs we had just dyed. It looked quite cheerful, if a bit empty.

I went back into the pantry and climbed up on a stool, reaching for the place on the top shelf that Henry had shown me, where Cook and Mum hid the sweets. I found a bag of lemon drops, some peppermint sticks, and some leftover ribbon candy from Christmas. There was also another stash of colored eggs, but these were much heavier than the ones I had made with Mum. These were most likely the ones Cook had filled with chocolate. My hand hovered over the bowl. These were Henry's and my most cherished Easter treat, and there were only a dozen of them. However, Henry was clearly going to eat himself into a stupor, given the chance, and I—well, there would be more next year. With a small sigh of regret, I removed seven of the chocolate-filled eggs and put them into the basket.

Now it looked positively bursting with Easter cheer. I slipped into my coat and let myself out the back door. It would be a long walk, but it seemed like a fitting penance, since I had helped get Will into trouble in the first place.

Even beautiful weather and penance did not alter Will's neighborhood. Once I entered the Seven Dials I became distinctly uneasy. The streets and alleys were narrow and filthy, and though there were people about, they weren't doing normal-people things, like shopping or visiting with one another. They just loitered in doorways wrapped in thin coats—or none at all—and looked out at the world with bleak, hopeless eyes. Even the air here seemed heavier, dirtier. Many of the pinched, drawn faces stared hungrily at my basket. I gripped the handle tighter, looked straight ahead, and picked up my pace.

I had never been to Will's house, but I remembered Ratsy calling out their address during Awi Bubu's magic show. I knew that Will's territory when he'd been a pickpocket was nearby, and I assumed that it would be close to where he lived. As I wandered deeper and deeper into this part of town, I realized that might have been a mistaken assumption.

I drew close to Nottingham Court, and my steps faltered when I saw the buildings—hovels, really. They were jumbled together and had no street numbers on them. How on earth was I to find Will now? As my heart sank in disappointment, I felt someone grab my elbow. I squealed and clutched the Easter basket with both hands then whirled around to see who was trying to steal it.

I came face to face with an enormous bowler hat perched on a pair of large pink ears. I let out a sigh of relief. "Snuffles!"

"'Ello, miss. Wotcha doin' 'ere?" As he spoke, his eyes fixed on the colorful contents of the basket and never wavered.

"I've come to visit you and your family and bring you an Easter treat. Is Will home?"

At this happy announcement, Snuffles grew quite enthusiastic. "Sure is, miss. Come on." He grabbed my elbow so I—and the basket—wouldn't get lost and led me to one of the large buildings. With long-practiced efficiency, he stepped between the small groups of people standing listlessly by the front door. Their sharp eyes zeroed in on us in a way that made me most uncomfortable. I quickly followed Snuffles into the building.

It was dank and damp and smelled of mildew and other much less pleasant things. People were camped out in the hallways. "This way, miss." Snuffles motioned for me to hurry along, which I did, following him up two flights of stairs. He led me past a series of small crooked doors until he came to the last one. He thumped once on the door, called out, "Company!" then opened it and went inside. I stood in the doorway, unsure.

I heard Will's voice. "'Oo's 'ere, Snuff?"

"Miss is. You know, the one you work wif."

Will left whatever he'd been doing and hurried to the door, looking fair flummoxed to see me. "Miss?"

Something—embarrassment?—flashed in his eyes. He gently but firmly herded me back into the hallway and closed the door behind us. He folded his arms and glowered at me, two faint spots of pink blooming on his cheeks. "Wot are you doin' 'ere?"

I cleared my throat. "Is it true that you got suspended?"

"Aye." His face relaxed a bit. "Because o' that fig-in-a-bush bloke."

"I-I'm sorry. I was certain once Wigmere heard what we had to tell him, he'd understand."

"'Tweren't your fault, miss. I didn't even get the chance to say a word. That nose Boythorpe walked me down the hallway and when I got to Wiggy's office, that figgenbush fellow was already there. Wiggy asked me if I 'ad a message from you for 'im. I told 'im, yes, and it was an important one. Then the greasy chap said, 'See what I mean, sir?'

"I turned to 'im and said, 'She couldn't very well give you the message, now could she, since you was 'ere instead of at the museum where you's supposed to be.'

"Then Wiggy said, 'Enough.' And suspended me. I asked if 'e didn't want to 'ear the important information first, and 'e said no. 'E'd wait until you reported it through the proper channels."

It sounded almost as if Fagenbush had set a trap and we'd walked right into it. "Oh dear. I'm so sorry. Here," I said, thrusting the apology basket at him.

He eyed it suspiciously. "We don't need no charity, miss."

"It's not charity, you dolt. It's an apology gift. People give them to each other all the time." And if they didn't, they should.

"Well, in that case, for the sake of yer conscience . . ."

"Absolutely. And I'm sure your brothers would enjoy it."

"Aye. That they would." He took the basket, his eyes growing wide as he saw all the goodies inside. Suddenly, I wished I'd packed real food instead of Easter treats. A roast chicken, and potatoes, a loaf of bread, and some butter and jam. Real food was what he and his brothers needed.

"I'll set things right, Will. I promise. I'll go see Wigmere as soon as I can and explain what happened. Once he sees the seriousness of all that's going on, he'll have no choice but to forgive us both."

"I 'ope so, miss, because me old gang's been on me like rats on rubbish to come back into the fold."

His old pickpocket gang, he meant. "Don't worry. We'll have you back working for Wigmere in no time," I said, hoping it was true.

"Course you will, miss. You'll come up wif somefink."

I was touched by his faith in me. So few others exhibited the same loyalty. "Thank you for believing in me," I said.

He looked fairly panicked, as if afraid I might get teary or something. "'Tain't nothin', miss. Besides, working with you is a lot more adventure than being a pickpocket."

That part was true, at least.

"In fact, miss, I been thinking." He looked around the hall to make sure no one else was listening, then inched closer. "I've decided, see, that I wants ter join the Brotherhood of them Chosen Kippers."

"Keepers," I corrected.

He drew back, looking affronted. "That's what I said. Anyways, I were asking Stokes about it one day when 'e was waiting ter get in ter see Wig. They make a lot more blunt than chimney sweeps and porters and even pickpockets. I figger if I can join up, then me mam won't 'ave to be a washerwoman till the day she up and drops dead. And me brothers? Mebbe some of them could even go to school."

"Aren't they supposed to go to school anyway?"

Will snorted. "Ain't no one checks up on 'em, miss. And we need what they can bring in just to keep a roof over our 'eads and our bellies full. But Stokes said most of 'em Kipper fellows had gone to school for a wicked long time. Them big fancy universities and the like."

"Oh, Will, how will you ever get to a university?" My heart was breaking. It was impossible for someone like him.

He looked surprisingly undaunted. "I can't, miss, but it don't matter."

"But then how will you join the Brotherhood?"

"I got somefink better than a university." He rocked back on his heels and beamed at me. "I got you."

"Me?"

"You! I figger you know more'n anyone about all the Egypshun stuff, and you can teach me."

I stared at him, speechless.

He must have taken it as a refusal, for he grabbed hold of my sleeve. "You gotter 'elp me, miss! If you can teach me about all the Egypshuns, then I can prove to Ol' Wiggy that I'm more'n just an errand boy."

As I stared into his big blue eyes, so eager and hopeful, I vowed that if he wanted a chance to prove himself to Wigmere, I would do everything in my power to help him. "Very well," I said. "I'll tutor you."

"You will, miss?" he squeaked.

"Absolutely. In fact, if you'd like, we can begin tonight."

His whole face lit up and he looked as if he might burst out of his skin. "Why? Wot are you cookin' up in that 'ead of yours, miss?"

"We-ll, it's a bit dangerous, and might be too frightening for you."

Will scoffed. "Nah, miss. Nothing scares me. Not after seeing those mummies of yours walking down the street." He shuddered ever so slightly.

I pretended not to notice. I knew better than anyone that being scared didn't mean you couldn't get the job done. "I'm so glad to hear you say that," I said, "because here's what we need to do. You remember Mr. Tetley?"

"The bad guy mummified as punishment?"

"That's the one. Well, his spirit, or *mut,* as the Egyptians called it, is haunting the museum. Haunting Henry, to be exact."

Will whistled. "Why 'im, d'you think?"

I gave Will a steely gaze. "Because he refused to wear the protective amulet I gave him, like the one I gave you."

Will swallowed. "I love me am'let, miss. Wouldn't dream of takin' it off." He fished around under his grimy shirt collar and produced the amulet I had given him.

"Excellent!" I said, surprised but pleased.

He leaned in closer. "Ratsy and Snuffles still have theirs too, miss. I warned 'em not to take 'em off. Not wif all the magic running around town these days."

At last someone who was taking the whole situation seriously! "See? You're already proving how good you'll be at this. Now, the only way to lay Tetley's spirit to rest is to give him a proper burial."

"'Ow you gonna do that, miss?"

"Well, as luck would have it, my grandmother is planning a memorial service for Admiral Sopcoate."

Will recoiled. "That traitor?"

"She doesn't know he's a traitor," I rushed to explain. "Hardly anyone does. But she's ordered a coffin for him, even though there's no body."

Will's face brightened. "And why let an empty coffin go to waste, right, miss?"

"Exactly."

"So alls we got to do is slip that Tetley fellow into the empty coffin before the service."

"Well, that's not quite all we have to do. There's a complication, you see."

"What kind of complication, miss?"

"It's hard to explain, because I barely understand it myself. I'm not sure if Tetley needs a Christian burial to be laid to rest or, since he was mummified in the way of the ancient Egyptians, if he needs ancient Egyptian funeral rites performed. He'll get the Christian rites at the memorial service, the blessing and all that, but I'm afraid we'll have to perform the Egyptian Rites of the Dead ourselves."

"We, miss?" he squeaked.

"Yes. We. And we'll need more than us to do it. You said Snuffles and Ratsy still have their protection?"

"Yes, miss."

"Do you think they could be talked into helping out? They'll be perfectly safe."

Will snorted. "Safe! You think livin' 'ere is safe?"

Good point, I thought. "Also, one of the most critical parts of every Egyptian funeral rite is the farewell feast for the deceased."

"Feast?"

"Yes, we'll have a picnic afterward, with lots of food."

Will's eyes brightened at that. "I'm sure they'll want to 'elp."

"Excellent. Now here's what I need you to do . . ."

CHAPTER TWENTY

A-Sneaking We Will Go

THAT EVENING, MY PARENTS tucked me and Henry into our beds at eight-thirty, then left for an engagement. I gave it fifteen minutes to be sure they hadn't forgotten something, like Father's gloves or Mum's beaded reticule. When I was sure they wouldn't be coming back, I slipped out of bed and headed over to the pitcher and washbasin on my dresser. Before doing any magic or ritual of this importance, it was necessary to purify oneself so that—well, I'm not sure why, to be honest. But all the ancient Egyptian priests did it, so I assumed it was important. I wasn't about to attempt the rites unpurified and then just see what happened. It did not pay to cut corners with Egyptian magic.

I washed my face and neck and behind my ears, then washed my hands twice. Next, I slipped into a fresh set of drawers, a clean petticoat, and a heavy cotton dress. I couldn't let anything made of wool or leather, anything that was part of an animal, touch my skin. I rinsed my mouth out with salt (since there was no natron at hand), and at last I was ready. My first stop was Mother's boudoir to collect one of the seven sacred oils I would need.

I tiptoed into her room and studied the small assortment of bottles, jars, and brushes on her dressing table. When I was younger, she used to let me play dress-up and put her combs in my hair and fluff her powder on my cheeks. A wave of longing for those simpler days swept through me, leaving me nearly breathless. I missed that innocence, that special alone time with Mother. Instead, here I was pinching her perfume so I could prevent a fake mummy's very real ghost from haunting my younger brother. With a sigh of frustration, I snatched the small crystal bottle of rose geranium oil from her dresser and shoved it into my pocket.

Next, I made my way to Father's dressing room and filched the Macassar oil he used on his hair. Two down, five to go.

I headed downstairs to the pantry where I knew Cook and Mrs. Murdley, our housekeeper, stored the household oils. Hopefully, I could find what I needed there.

I was in luck. Betsy, the housemaid, was prone to coughs and chest ailments, so we had a good store of camphor oil and eucalyptus oil. There was also a thick green bottle of cedar oil and a small bottle of lavender oil. I still needed one more. Then I remembered—the wretched cod-liver oil! A year ago, Cook had gotten it into her head that Henry and I needed daily doses of the foul stuff. After exactly three days of that, we'd had enough. In one of our moments of perfect accord, we had taken the hateful brown bottle and hidden it.

I hurried to the old Huntley and Palmers biscuit tin where we'd stashed it. The ugly brown bottle was still there! Dusty as you please, but more than three-quarters full. Excellent.

I carefully placed all the bottles of oil in a large, flat-bottomed basket, covered them with a tea towel, and set it by the back door. I returned to the pantry and got an even bigger basket and began collecting things for Tetley's funeral feast. I was sorely tempted to take the Easter ham, but I was certain Cook would notice that. Instead, I took a leftover meat pie, a cold chicken, a tin of biscuits, and part of a lemon cake that we'd had for tea. If anyone noticed them missing, I would simply blame it on Henry's newfound enormous appetite.

Which brought me to my last problem: Henry. More specifically, how to get him to come with us to the museum.

I was sure he wouldn't want to go and equally sure that he, or more important, the *mut* who'd attached itself to him needed to be there in order for the ceremony to work.

I pondered this problem as I lugged the heavy second basket over to the door. The floor behind me creaked, and I froze.

"Theo? Is that you?"

I dropped the basket with a *thunk,* glad it wasn't the one with all the oils in it, then turned around. "Henry? What are you doing up?"

"I heard noises and came to see what was going on." He glanced at the basket I'd just dropped and at the second one by the door and perked up. "I say, are you running away?"

"No," I said carefully. This part would be tricky. If I asked Henry outright if he wanted to come with me, he'd say no. He'd made it quite clear what he thought of all these activities of mine. I had to find a way to make him want to come without his knowing it was what I'd wanted all along.

Henry crossed the kitchen and squatted down to look at what was in the baskets. "Well, if you're not running away, what are you doing?" He reached for the lemon cake and I swatted his hand away.

Nursing his hand, he narrowed his eyes at me. "You're play-acting at your mysterious game again, aren't you?"

"Something like that," I admitted. "But I know you don't care for it, so I didn't invite you."

His eyes dipped back down to the basket. "So why d'you need all that food then?"

"It's for a picnic. After the game."

"Where's this picnic going to be?"

"At the museum."

"And you're going to eat all that?"

"No. Some friends are coming with me." Then, as if on cue, there was a light scratch at the back door.

Henry jumped. "What's that?" he hissed.

"My friends," I said, and opened the door. Will, Ratsy, Sparky, and Snuffles stood there, nearly hopping on their toes with excitement.

"Let's get a move on, miss. Makes me nervous to stand in one place so long."

"Hullo," Henry said.

"'Ey, mate!" Sparky said. "Will didn't tell us you was comin' too."

"He doesn't want to come," I said.

Henry shoved me aside with his elbow. "I never said that. Let me just get my coat."

He ran over and grabbed an old jacket from a hook near the pantry and slipped it on, and I fought down the urge to cheer. It had worked! He was coming with us. And I hadn't had to cosh him over the head and drag him the whole way.

The fog had moved in, casting a chilling, thick pall over our neighborhood. The street lamps glowed eerily through the gently undulating wisps. Henry scooted a bit closer to Sparky.

"Oy, watch out, mate. You're standing on me toes!"

"Oh, sorry," Henry said, then sidled closer to me.

Will and his brothers, on the other hand, seemed quite comfortable marching along the dark streets of London, as if they did it often. I, however, was greatly relieved to see the tall spires of the museum come into sight. Will's steps faltered slightly. "Looks a bit different at night, don't it?"

"Yes, it does." It was an unusual building to begin with, very Gothic looking, with tall towers and odd spires here and there that seemed very sinister when observed on a foggy night with no adults around.

"'Ow're we going to avoid that watchman of yours, miss?"

Flimp! I'd nearly forgotten about him. "The back entrance, I think. It's more of a storage and unloading area, so he probably doesn't check there that often. Besides, it's farthest from his post."

Will gave a nod, then motioned for his brothers to follow.

We scuttled across the deserted square and around the side of the building to the loading dock.

When we reached the back door, Will and his brothers stepped aside to make room for me to open it. I looked at Will. "Er, I don't have a key. I was hoping you could, you know . . ." I waved my hand vaguely.

"You want me to pick it, miss?"

"If you wouldn't mind."

"I say, you can do that?" Henry stepped forward. "Can I watch?"

"Course, mate." Will set the basket down and drew something very small and thin from his pocket. He gently inserted the pick into the lock and poked around. Henry bent over so he could get a closer look, his nose practically resting on the doorknob. We all waited, holding our breath, until there was a faint click. "Got it," Will said. Then he opened the door and we all went inside.

CHAPTER TWENTY-ONE

An Unexpected Sacrifice

WHY IS IT THAT THINGS ALWAYS LOOK so very different in the dark? While the receiving area was a large room, it felt positively cavernous at night. I fumbled my way over to the switch to turn up the gaslights. The boys behind me gasped. Annoyed, I turned to *shh* them, then saw that they were all staring wide-eyed at the coffin that was laid across two benches. Good. That meant Stilton had been true to his word. I quickly checked the brass plate Grandmother had ordered to be sure this was Sopcoate's coffin. It was.

Henry broke the silence. He came over next to me and patted the casket. "It's just an empty coffin, nothing to worry about."

"We're not afraid of no coffin," Sparky said, puffing out his chest a very little bit.

Snuffles and Ratsy agreed.

"'Ush, you jabberers," Will said, then turned to me. "What now, miss?"

"First, we have to purify the place," I explained. Henry rolled his eyes, but I ignored him. Being a responsible older sister was a great burden sometimes.

"Here," I said, thrusting one of the oil-containing jars at Henry. "Make yourself useful and sprinkle this on that side of the room." Then I handed a lotus-shaped goblet to Snuffles and gave him similar directions. Ratsy and Will took the other oils and went to the other sections of the room. Not wanting to appear a complete idiot, I muttered the prayer invoking purification very quietly, under my breath.

When that was done, I handed out the four small braziers. "Put these in each corner of the room," I instructed them.

Will took the small dish. "What's this for?"

"Incense, to purify the air."

"You mean like they use in church?"

"Er, not exactly like that. Incense is very difficult to find, so I thought we'd just light lucifer matches and let the smell of the burning matches purify the air."

"Matches, miss?" Sparky perked up. "Can I do the honors?"

"Yes, if you promise not to burn anything else."

"Promise, miss." I gave him the matches and he busily got to it. I must say, he lit each match on the first strike, something I was rarely able to do.

It was time to collect the mummy. I had no idea how heavy it would be, so I had Will, Ratsy, and Sparky come with me. Henry and Snuffles were left to keep watch on the receiving area.

As the boys followed me down the corridor to the basement door, Will looked around nervously. "This place seems right different after dark, it does."

"I bet you 'ave some might 'ealthy rats around 'ere, miss," Ratsy added.

Perish the thought! It was all I could do to deal with Egyptian curses, restless *mut,* and a troop of urchins—I simply couldn't bear the thought of rats on top of all that.

When we reached the door to the catacombs, I opened it as slowly as I could in order to minimize any squeaking. I turned on the gaslights, then led my band of merry men down the stairs. While I was grateful for so much stalwart company, I was also a little concerned as to what effect so much *ka* would have on the artifacts.

Specifically, on the jackal statue.

We reached the bottom, and Will and Sparky looked slightly subdued as they stared at the row of mummies. Ratsy must have been far more used to dark and gloomy places due to his profession, for he merely whistled in appreciation. Then he pointed at the statue of Anubis that sat atop the Canopic shrine. "Hey, I've seen that dog before!"

Not wanting to discuss *that* particular trick, I diverted everyone's attention by asking, "Do you all have your protection on?"

"Right 'ere, miss." Will clutched his amulet and held it out for me to see. Ratsy and Sparky did the same.

"Excellent," I said. It was so nice having boys who listened to me, as opposed to Henry, who fought me at every turn. "You two take the mummy's feet," I told Ratsy and Sparky. "Will and I'll get the shoulders."

"Too bad you don't still 'ave that staff, eh, miss? Then you could just wag that thing at 'im and off 'e'd go."

"True," I muttered. But it was rare that Egyptian magic ever worked to one's advantage that way.

"On three," Will said. "One, two, *three.*" With a series of grunts, we lifted the mummy, which weighed much less than one would think. Best not to dwell on why.

We began the precarious journey up the stairs, which required a lot of juggling and instructions. I glanced nervously at Anubis, trying to gauge how all this life force was affecting him. It was hard to be one hundred percent certain in this gloomy light, but he appeared to be unchanged. I wondered briefly what he would think of our ritual tonight, his being the god of mummification and all, then I put that thought aside as Sparky bumped his elbow against the banister and nearly bobbled the mummy.

When we reached the top of the stairs, I made everyone stop so I could make sure Flimp hadn't picked that precise moment to make his rounds.

"Don't take too long, miss," Will muttered. "This thing is right clumsy to 'old on to."

Once I was certain the coast was clear, we made our slow, bumbling way down the hall to the receiving dock. When we arrived, Henry leaped to his feet. "What took you so long? You've been gone for ages."

"It was only five minutes, Henry. Besides, I thought you weren't afraid of the museum."

"I'm not," he said. "I was just worried maybe Flimp had caught you."

"Well, he hasn't. Put him down gently," I instructed when we reached the coffin.

Once we had Tetley safely settled in the casket, I stepped back and studied him. Such a spiritual conundrum. Did a Christian man who'd been mummified according to ancient Egyptian custom require a Christian burial or an Egyptian funeral rite? If it hadn't been for Tetley's *mut* clinging to Henry like a macabre shawl, I would never have attempted what I was about to do. However, if Tetley was buried without his *ba,* then it might stick with Henry permanently. I couldn't risk that. I could only hope that by covering all the bases, Tetley would find peace at last.

"All right," I said, my voice suddenly solemn as the weight of what we were about to do settled on my shoulders. "This is serious business. Poor Tetley's eternal soul may be at risk." Not to mention Henry's. "So listen carefully to my instructions and do precisely as I tell you. First, the anointing with the sacred oils."

I turned to the tray where I'd set out all the oils I'd collected from home. In some ancient ceremonies, the priests had used their finger, while in other time periods, they used a piece of wood carved to look like a finger. I didn't have one of those, and I was highly reluctant to use my own finger, so instead I was using Cook's pastry brush. With the boys standing around in a semicircle looking appropriately serious, I began.

"I anoint thee, Osiris—"

"I thought his name was Tetley," Henry said.

"It is," I hissed at him. "But the ancient Egyptians always identified the deceased with Osiris so as to invoke his powers. Now be quiet." I cleared my throat. "I anoint thee, Osiris, with these sacred oils given to us by Ra in order that you may be purified and sweet smelling when you reach the Hall of Judgment." With that, I placed a smudge of lavender on his head. Next, I dipped the pastry brush into the cedar oil and touched the area over his heart. "That your heart may be pure and strong." I anointed his elbows and hands with the rose geranium oil. "That your limbs can fight off the demon hordes of the underworld who block your way." I dabbed Macassar oil on his ears. "So that your ears may be open to sound." Cod-liver oil went on his feet (as far away from his nose as possible!), so that they would carry him the entire length of his journey. And so on, until, at last, I once again smeared the top of his head, this time with the eucalyptus oil.

"Hey," Snuffles said with a loud sniff. "I can breathe!"

Will nudged him. "Shh."

"Osiris has now received the sacred oils, which shall bless him and make him whole again on his journey to join Ra." I set the brush down and took a deep breath.

"Now what?" Ratsy asked.

"Actually," I whispered, "next there was usually a sacrifice of some sort of animal, but I've decided to skip that part."

"I should think so," Henry said.

At that precise moment, there was a small thud off to my right. We all startled and looked toward the sound. There stood my cat, Isis, holding a dead mouse in her mouth. As we watched, she walked toward us as calmly as you please and laid the poor rodent at the head of the coffin.

Dumbfounded, I could only stare at her.

"'Ow'd you train her to do that, miss?" Will's voice was tinged with awe.

"I didn't!"

"Is it time for the feast yet?" Snuffles asked hopefully.

"Almost," I said. But before I could resume, there was a sound of clattering, like . . . like claws on a marble floor.

I looked up at the door just as the jackal came bounding in. He trotted past our small circle, and the boys drew back with a collective *"Oh!"*

Panic shot through me; I looked to see where Isis was, wondering what the jackal would do when he saw her.

But oddly enough, he never even glanced in her direction. He *click-clacked* his way over to the head of Tetley's coffin, sat on his haunches, then looked at me as if to say, *You may continue.*

Well, he *was* the god of mummification and an important funerary deity.

With one last nervous glance in his direction, I resumed the ceremony by picking up a small iron adze and gently touching Tetley's eyes and mouth four times. "Osiris, I restore to you your sight and your speech so that you may defeat the demons in the underworld as you travel to be with Ra." Next I picked up the small bag of carnelian chips and repeated the gesture and the spell. I wasn't one hundred percent certain what the carnelian was supposed to do, but since it had been included in most of the accounts of the ceremony, I thought it must be important. "May the power of Ra shine down upon you; may the restorative powers of Osiris be at your fingertips and speed you on your journey. May your *ka* and *ba* be united again." As I said those last words, I touched the bag of carnelian to Tetley's chest, just over his heart. The air shimmered, and my spine tingled.

"What's that?" Will asked.

"You felt it too?"

He nodded as his gaze darted nervously around the room.

Just then, there was a faint sighing sound from Tetley. I swallowed the scream that rose in my throat and took a step back. His mouth was open and his chest was expanding, as if he were drawing in a huge breath. Faint tendrils of something—mist? life force? *mut?*—began to rise up from my poor brother like steam from a boiling kettle. He squeaked and went still, his arms frozen at his sides, his eyes wide.

"Is it supposed to do this?" Ratsy asked.

"I'm not sure," I confessed, my heart beating so wildly I could scarce get the words out.

The mist that had been hanging over Henry now undulated in Tetley's direction. Slowly the spirit began to ooze

241

down into the coffin. Just as I started to breathe a sigh of relief, it paused, hovered for a long moment as if reconsidering, then began to ooze back up and move in Henry's direction again.

Had it changed its mind? Did it not want to go to the afterlife any longer?

Even as my poor mind scrambled for some solution to this problem, the jackal made his move. With a low growl in his throat, he bared his sharp teeth and raised his hackles. We all took a step back.

As the jackal advanced, the *mut* mist maneuvered itself so that it was behind my brother, using him as a shield! The jackal ignored that and lunged to Henry's right side, snapping at the mist behind him. The mist scooted out and quickly began seeping back into the coffin, the jackal snapping and growling at it the whole way. The mist gathered just above Tetley in one large mass, then rushed into the mummified body until the last wisp of it was gone.

Tetley gave one last sigh, then fell still.

The jackal went over to the coffin and sniffed. Apparently satisfied, he gave one sharp bark and wag of his tail, then took off back the way he had come.

Trying to hide how shaken I was, I looked around at the others. Their faces were all pale and wide-eyed.

"Blimey, mate! Look at that." Sparky pointed at Henry.

My brother was rigid with shock, and his hair had turned white. Not all of it, but his cowlick was now white. Blimey indeed.

"Henry," I said rather sharply, since I was nearly out of my mind with fear. Jerkily, his head swung around to look at me. "Are you all right?" I asked, more gently this time.

"I-I think so," he said, but his voice sounded a bit hollow and far away.

"Can we eat now?" Snuffles asked.

"Er, no. Just one more thing: May the food we are about to eat bless your body and give it strength in the afterlife. Amen."

"Now?" Snuffles said.

"Now," I said.

As Will and his brothers fell upon the picnic basket, I hurried over to Henry's side. I felt his forehead, which seemed the right temperature. He slapped my hand away, which was a good sign, but the faraway look in his eyes wasn't. I leaned in closer and whispered, "Henry? Are you sure you're okay?"

He turned his head in the direction of my voice and nodded.

"Do you want to come have something to eat?" I asked.

He shook his head no, and I took advantage of his stunned state to administer a firm warning. "I told you you needed to be careful about the magic around here. I'd actually hoped you'd never have occasion to believe me, that you'd stay blissfully ignorant. I'm sorry this had to happen."

"'S okay," he said, then frowned. "What exactly *did* happen?"

I looked into his eyes and saw the fear and unease lurking there. "Nothing much. The smell of the oils just made you lightheaded, that's all."

He stared at me a moment, then nodded and went to sit with the other boys.

I felt sick about this, even worse than I'd felt when Isis had been struck by a curse. I could only hope it would have no lasting effects.

Just as we were packing up the last of the funereal feast, Stilton came looking for me. "Miss Theo?" he asked, looking surprised to see so many of us.

"Oh, hullo, Stilton," I said. "Thank you so much for your help. We're done, so you can take the, er, coffin back now."

That's when he saw the mummy formerly known as Tetley in the coffin. Slowly he advanced on it, a strange look on his face. He glanced from Tetley, to me, then back to Tetley. "You're seeing that he gets a Christian burial, aren't you, miss?"

"Yes, Stilton. It's the least we can do for him."

A resolved look appeared on Stilton's face as he quietly

closed the coffin. "That's right decent of you, miss. I'll take him back now."

Before I'd even ventured down to breakfast the next morning, I heard Mother shriek, "Henry! Your hair!"

I yanked my frock over my head and ran downstairs to the dining room. Henry stood behind his chair as Mother stared at him in concern. Father was talking, and he didn't sound too happy. "What on earth have you done, young man?"

Being called young *anything* always boded ill.

"I-I," Henry stammered and then threw me a pleading look. That, at least, was a good sign. It meant he wasn't going to hang me out to dry.

"He got lemon juice in it," I said as I stepped into the room. "After you left the kitchen yesterday, Mum, we began playing at being . . . alchemists. And, as alchemists, we pretended we were creating a formula that would turn lead into gold."

"And what was in this alchemical formula of yours?" Father asked.

"Lemon juice. And vinegar. And a bunch of other things I can't remember," I said. "Maybe oils. I think we used some of the oils from the pantry." It seemed smart to add that last bit, just in case anyone ever noticed that all the various oils in the house had been moved. The truth was, by the time we got home last night, it was so late and I was so tired, I couldn't remember where I'd gotten which sacred oil.

Father's mustache twitched, and I couldn't tell if it was in frustration or in amusement. "I guess we should just be grateful *your* hair didn't turn white. Or fall out." He turned a stern eye on Henry. "I hope you've learned your lesson about meddling in unsupervised scientific experiments."

Henry hung his head. "Yes, sir."

"Very good. Now, let's enjoy this wonderful Easter breakfast Cook has prepared for us."

Other than that incident, Easter Sunday was lovely. We all got dressed up in our best finery, Mum and I wore our Easter bonnets, and we went to church. Being inside a church feels a lot like being inside a museum; the air feels heavier, more important somehow, as if the weight of all that spiritual worship were somehow physical. Henry fidgeted a bit until I gave him a piece of wax I found in one of my dress pockets. He played with that until the service was over.

After church we had a special luncheon. Mum had even invited Uncle Andrew, which was a wonderful balance to Grandmother Throckmorton, who showed up in her black mourning clothes, a beady-eyed crow to the rest of us cheerful spring bluebirds. I did my best to ignore her and reminded myself that she had no idea the man she was mourning was neither dead nor a hero.

After we ate, we collected the baskets we had decorated and hunted for the eggs Mum had hidden. It would have been an absolutely perfect day if not for the small lump of dread and nerves sitting in my stomach. Although I was thrilled to have Henry back to normal—if a bit peaked and subdued—I was terrified that it might all go to pieces at the funeral if our ruse was discovered. Polite society had been most put out when they'd found a fake mummy at one of their receptions; I could only imagine how they'd react if they came across one at a solemn occasion like a memorial service.

CHAPTER TWENTY-TWO
SOPCOATE'S MEMORIAL SERVICE

THE CHURCH GRANDMOTHER HAD FOUND was very grand, even if it wasn't Westminster Abbey. It had enormously high ceilings with stained glass windows that cast pools of green, red, and gold light down on everyone. Rows of columns lined the aisles of the church, and organ music filled the empty spaces high above.

To my great relief, the casket was already in place up near the altar. Henry and I exchanged a glance, his lock of white hair a comforting reminder of why I'd had to do what I'd done.

For Grandmother's sake, I was pleased to see that the church was nearly full. There were many men in naval uniforms, including a number of rough-looking sailors in the very back. The crowd fell silent as a long, sorrowful note came from the organ, and the service began.

The reverend talked about ashes to ashes, dust to dust (which doesn't make much sense when you're speaking of someone who'd been lost at sea), and the bombazine of my mourning dress itched horribly. The black gloves I'd been handed by the page were far too big and made my hands look large and misshapen. I tried to tug them tighter. Next to me, Henry fidgeted, but I said nothing as I was half certain that tugging at one's gloves and sleeves also qualified as fidgeting. Then I caught Father looking at me out of the corner of his eye and did my best to hold absolutely still.

Just as the reverend got to the part about leaving all our worldly desires behind, I had the distinct sensation that I was being watched. Moving slowly so as not to attract Father's attention, I turned to look behind me. The sea of faces were all staring intently at the minister.

"Quit fidgeting," Father hissed.

I pulled my gaze from the back of the church and stared dutifully forward, vowing to at least look as if I were paying attention, if not for Sopcoate's sake, then for Grandmother's. I occupied myself by coming up with a plan just in case anyone opened the casket or noticed how heavy it was.

Just when I'd decided that a fainting spell would be the

only way to halt a disaster, the fine hairs at the nape of my neck stirred again. I reached up and rubbed them, hoping it was just the stiff, wretched fabric of my collar. But no. The sensation increased until my shoulders positively itched with it. Someone was definitely watching me. I could feel their *ka* focused on me, and I did not like it one bit.

However, I dared not risk turning around again. First, it would call too much attention to myself and alert whoever it was that I was onto him. Second, Father was watching me again.

When at last the service was nearly over, Grandmother stood up and held out her hand to Father. He took her arm and escorted her up to the coffin. She paused with her hand lingering over the casket, and my heart leaped into my throat. Would she open it?

Her fingers touched the casket, and then she picked up a spray of lilies and laid it over the top. She bent her head as the minister said a final prayer.

My knees went weak. We'd done it! The funeral was over and no one had discovered our secret. I closed my eyes, said one last quick prayer for Mr. Tetley's soul, and wished him peace. When I opened my eyes again, I found Henry smiling at me. I smiled back, nearly giddy with relief.

The congregation rose from their seats and began making

their way outside. As I walked the length of the cathedral to the open doors, I paid close attention to the crowd, trying to identify whoever had been staring at me so fiercely.

Once outside, people milled about on the steps, chatting with one another and murmuring kind thoughts about Admiral Sopcoate, who didn't deserve a single one of them. As they all mingled, I continued to search the faces as unobtrusively as possible.

Mother and Father were deep in conversation with Grandmother and someone from the admiralty. Henry had planted himself at the far side of the church steps, taken a tin soldier out of his pocket, and was quietly playing with it. He still looked pale, I thought, as if he were just getting over a long illness.

I'd had no luck identifying the person who'd been staring at me, and I was considering joining Henry on the cathedral steps when I caught a furtive movement out of the corner of my eye.

An old sailor with white hair and beard looked away quickly, as if he didn't want me to know he'd been watching me. Why would he be watching me?

He glanced in my direction again and our eyes met briefly. He had a patch over one eye and there was something almost familiar about him. Although, truthfully, it was very difficult to tell sailors apart. In their uniforms and spit and polish, they all looked confusingly alike unless you knew them. Had he served on the *Dreadnought*, by chance? Had I met him there?

He turned and began limping away as if hurrying somewhere important.

I decided to follow the sailor to the corner, just to be sure he wasn't up to no good.

I'd taken no more than two steps when a wave of sensation, like a hundred beetles marching along my spine, swept over me. The sensation was so strong that if I'd been at the museum, I'd have immediately conducted a Second Level Test. Could the sailor have a cursed artifact on him?

I glanced at all the unprotected people gathered near the church then quickly hurried to the street corner. I turned onto the side street, but there was no one in sight. No old sailor, no cursed artifact. Just as I began to leave, a bulky shape stepped out of a recess in a wall and said, "Gotcha!"

I started and then stared in puzzlement at the old sailor, who was tucking an amulet back into a box. As soon as he shut the lid, the beetle sensation along my back stopped. He smiled at me through his salty white beard. "I knew that would get your attention."

At my blank look, he added, "Curiosity *did* kill the cat, you know."

May I just say that it is not a good sign when someone begins a conversation that way?

"What's the matter, don't you recognize me, Theo?"

How did he know my name? His voice was familiar, but I couldn't quite place it. I shook my head. "No, I'm afraid I don't. Have we met—oh!"

The sailor lifted the eye patch and I found myself staring into the face of Admiral Sopcoate. "You!" I breathed, shocked to the very core of my being.

"Me, Theo. In the flesh. Lovely of your grandmother to organize such a fancy memorial service for me. I couldn't have planned a better one myself. A ripping good time, hearing what everyone had to say about me."

I thought of all the naval men just around the corner who'd have raised no end of questions at the admiral's reappearance. I could hardly credit the man's daring. "Is that why you're here? Curiosity?"

"No, not curiosity. That was just an added benefit. I'm afraid I'm here to pay you a little visit."

Oh dear. It was never good news when a Serpent of Chaos wished to pay one a visit. It was then that it occurred to me that he might have the others with him. I glanced behind me.

"I'm quite alone," he said. "Well, me and Mr. Webley here." He patted his pocket.

"Who?" I hadn't met a Serpent of Chaos named Webley.

"Webley," he repeated, then reached into his pocket and pulled out a pistol. Slowly he raised it so it was pointing at my chest.

My insides felt like runny custard. "What do you want?" I asked, trying to sound as if having a gun pointed at me were no big thing.

"You mean, other than revenge?"

I tried to swallow but found my mouth was too dry.

"Luckily for you, there is something we want more than revenge, Theo. Something we want very badly. Something you can give to us and thus assure you'll live to be twelve."

"What's that?" I croaked.

He leaned forward. "The Emerald Tablet."

I blinked in surprise. Honestly! Had someone taken out an advertisement in the *Times*? How did everyone know we had the wretched thing? I opened my mouth to protest that I didn't have it, but he waved the gun at me. "I'm fairly sure one of your lovely governesses must have warned against lying." He laughed, an ugly sound. How had I ever thought he was jolly?

"W-why do you want it? It just talks about alchemy. Surely the Serpents of Chaos don't believe they can turn lead into gold," I scoffed.

"Or maybe you're not as smart as you think you are.

Maybe it has powers and properties that the great, meddle-some Theodosia doesn't know about."

"What does it do then?"

"Oh, I'm afraid that is on a need-to-know basis, my dear. And quite frankly, you have no need to know." He took a step closer. "What you do need to know is that we will do anything—anything—to get our hands on it. Do you understand?"

I nodded.

"Very well. Bring the tablet to Cleopatra's Needle on Friday afternoon. Let's say around five o'clock, shall we? During your parents' exhibit opening? I think that should provide a nice diversion and allow you to slip away unnoticed, don't you?" He brought the pistol up higher, so that it was pointed directly at my face. "Be there. If you fail to deliver it, my dear, not only will *your* life be in danger, but that of your grandmother as well. How do you think she will take to the fact that she invited half the admiralty to the funeral of a traitor?" He laughed again, and my skin fairly curdled off my bones.

"Theo? Theo, where've you gotten to?" Mother's voice came from just around the corner. She must have come looking for me. And as much as I wanted her to find me, I did *not* want her to find Admiral Sopcoate's pistol.

Sopcoate took a step back and waved the gun in Mother's

direction. "Say nothing to anyone. Be there, or you and your grandmother will be food for the fishes at the bottom of the Thames."

And with that he turned and ran down the street. Fighting back a sob of relief, I hurried toward the sound of Mum's voice.

"There you are, dear. Come along. It's time to go to the funeral repast at your Grandmother's—are you feeling all right? You look rather pale." She put out a hand and felt my forehead, which I knew to be clammy and damp with fear.

I took the opportunity to lean up against her for a moment, to absorb some of her strength and chase away the horrid chill that had come over me. "I'm not sure I like funerals," I said, Sopcoate's warning still ringing in my ears.

CHAPTER TWENTY-THREE

THE *WEDJADEEN*

THE ONLY GOOD THING to come of my run-in with Sopcoate was that my parents decided I wasn't feeling well. That made a perfect excuse for all of us to avoid going to the funeral luncheon at Grandmother's house. I supported this whole-heartedly by leaning my head back against the cab cushion and making as pitiful a face as I could.

It wasn't hard. My nerves were still twanging like plucked strings. When I glanced down at my hands, I saw they trembled slightly. I clutched them together and folded them in my lap.

"Are you sure you're not feverish?" Mum asked, putting her hand to my forehead again. "You still look a bit flushed."

"I think I am just overset from the funeral. That's all."

Henry stared at me with big, worried eyes. I tried to give him a reassuring smile, but I'm afraid it wobbled a bit. I closed my eyes and tried to calm my nerves.

"How a girl who spends as much time as you do in a museum full of dead things can get overset at a funeral is one of life's mysteries I'll never understand," Father said as he rapped on the carriage roof, signaling the driver to be off.

I opened one eye and looked at him.

"Not that I'm not grateful." He winked.

I shut my eye quickly. Did that mean he thought I was faking? Wouldn't that just cork it? The one time I was most certainly *not* faking, Father thought I was. Sometimes I worried that he saw far more of what went on than he admitted. That was a disturbing idea.

"I for one will be glad to get back to the museum," Father said heartily. Clearly, he didn't like funerals any more than I did. Probably for different reasons, however.

"I suppose I should take Theo home," Mother said reluctantly.

I rolled my head to look at Mother. "I am feeling a bit better, now that we're away from that church and all that incense. I would be happy to lie down quietly in the family withdrawing room if you and Father would like to get back to work."

Mother gave me a brilliant smile. "How understanding of you, darling. Thank you."

Henry let his head drop back against the seat in resignation.

That settled, Father called out new directions to the cabby and we headed toward the museum.

When we arrived, the curators seemed a bit surprised to see us back so soon. Stilton startled so badly when he saw us that he bumped into the row of shabtis he was just setting up and sent them tumbling into one another until they were all lying flat.

"Be careful, you dolt!" Weems growled, then pasted a smile on his face and came to greet us.

Mother began removing her gloves, pulling off one finger at a time. When Weems was close enough, she said, "I really don't think it's necessary to call our employees names, do you, Mr. Weems? Name-calling seems to me the province of bullies who have no other skills with which to motivate their employees. But that's not the case with you, is it?" She looked up suddenly and met his gaze head-on. "I would hate to think we'd made a mistake about you."

The foyer was filled with dead silence as we all watched Weems's face turn bright red. Nearly everyone looked ready to cheer. Finally, Father cleared his throat. "I believe the weapons up in the workroom are ready to be crated and moved down here, if you would see to that, Weems. Fagenbush, that scarab collection is also ready to be moved."

Weems blinked rapidly, his Adam's apple bobbing in distress. "Yes, sir," he said through his pinched lips. He turned and minced angrily from the room. Fagenbush followed.

Mother smiled brightly at the others. "It's beginning to look like an exhibit around here," she said, then she went to find a work smock.

Of course, the truth was that, in spite of what I'd told my parents, I had no intention of lying down. There were far too many things I needed to attend to. For one, how had Sopcoate known about the Emerald Tablet? Only a handful of people knew it was here at the museum: Stilton, Wigmere, Fagenbush, Will, Henry, and Awi Bubu. I was quite certain that Will, Henry, and Wigmere hadn't told him. Nor had Fagenbush, if Wigmere's judgment was correct. And while I could quite easily see Stilton letting slip the existence of the Emerald Tablet to Trawley, I was sure he wouldn't want it to fall into Chaos's hands. The same went for Trawley. If Stilton *had* told him about it, he'd want to keep it for himself and not give it to Chaos.

Which left Awi Bubu.

Was he a Serpent of Chaos? It would explain so much:

how he knew about the Staff of Osiris and the Heart of Egypt, his enhanced powers. And it made sense that Chaos would recruit people from the Antiquities Service in Egypt.

It also fit in with Awi Bubu's claim that he was an exile from his homeland.

But if he was a Serpent of Chaos, wouldn't he have just taken the tablet that night he was here? He'd had plenty of opportunity. And he'd never once threatened me, which was something the other Serpents did quite frequently.

But if he wasn't a Serpent of Chaos, he clearly hadn't told me everything he knew about the Emerald Tablet either. For Chaos to want it, it had to be very powerful indeed, most likely destructive. That Egyptian and I needed to have a chat. I wanted to know the truth about the wretched tablet. *Now.*

The next step would be to get to Wigmere and tell him what I had learned. I was so desperate to get his take on all this that I briefly considered telling Fagenbush so he could enlist Wigmere's aid. However, if the leak about the tablet hadn't come from Awi Bubu or Stilton, then Fagenbush was my next best suspect. Perhaps he worked for the Serpents of Chaos but had been assigned to infiltrate the Brotherhood of the Chosen Keepers as a means of keeping tabs on them? If that was the case, I didn't want to tip my hand to him. Or give him any more information than was absolutely necessary.

Which meant I had to get him out of the way so I would be free to come and go as I needed without risking his following me. What sort of distraction could I arrange in the next half-hour? Father had assigned Fagenbush to assemble the scarab collection this afternoon. Scarabs . . . oh!

I hurried to the Egyptian exhibit. There was one scarab there that had defied all my attempts at removing the curse that infected it. Luckily, it wasn't a serious curse, merely an unpleasant one.

Glad for the hideous funeral gloves I still wore, I slipped the lapis lazuli scarab from its case and hid it in my pocket. Now I just had to sneak this cursed scarab in with the others without Fagenbush noticing. A fine trick indeed, when he paid attention to my every little move.

I went to the foyer and waited for an opportunity to present itself.

A short time later, when he returned lugging a crate, I made my move. I pushed away from the wall, threw a guilty look over my shoulder, then hurried down the east corridor and out of sight.

"Dash it all." His voice echoed down the hall where I waited. "I forgot the display board upstairs," he told Stilton. "I'll be right back."

But of course, he didn't go upstairs at all—he began following me. I turned and continued down the hallway, then made a wide sweep through Receiving and came up the west hallway, effectively circling back so I could reach the foyer before he caught up to me.

As I sailed into the foyer, Stilton jerked in surprise, dropping the shabti he was holding and causing all the others to tumble over again.

"Sorry about that," I murmured as I headed for the crate of scarabs.

Stilton sighed. "It's not your fault, Miss Theo."

Furtively, I set the cursed scarab on top of the ones Mother had found in Thutmose III's tomb, then I bent over the crate and peered in as if I were looking for something. When Fagenbush appeared in the breezeway, I glanced up at him, then quickly skulked away.

"What was she doing?" he barked at Stilton.

"Who? Theodosia?"

"What other *she* did you happen to see in here? Yes, Theodosia."

"I-I don't know. She was just looking at the scarabs. Did you find the display board?"

Fagenbush ignored Stilton's question, strode over to the crate, and began digging through the scarabs.

I waited quietly in the hall until I heard Stilton say, "Dear heavens, what is that stench?"

Which meant Fagenbush had touched the cursed scarab.

Of course, I knew what that stench was: dung. Ox dung, to be exact. Scarabs were actually small stone statues of dung beetles, which the ancient Egyptians considered sacred. This particular scarab held a curse that caused one to smell of ox dung for a few days. When I heard Sweeny chime in with "Smells like a barnyard in here, it does," I knew the scarab had done its work. I used the ensuing confusion to slip out unobserved.

With luck, Fagenbush would be distracted by that disaster for a while. If he wasn't, well, at least I would be able to smell him coming.

I was halfway to Oxford Street before I heard someone calling after me.

"Wait up, miss!"

I turned to find Sticky Will hurrying after me and was surprised at how glad I was to see him. "What are you doing here?"

"Tryin' to follow you, miss," he said, finally catching up to me.

"Is something wrong?"

"No. I jest wanted to begin me training as soon as we could. I figgered followin' you around would be a good start."

I hated to disappoint him, but I simply didn't have time . . . wait a moment. Maybe I did. Maybe he should come with me to confront Awi Bubu, as backup. If something went wrong, he could go for help. Plus I could bring him up to speed on the way. "Excellent, let's begin, shall we?" The thing was, if I was going to take Will's desire to become a Chosen Keeper seriously, I had to keep him informed of everything, and that meant any magical goings-on, any Serpents of Chaos activity. If his education was to be complete, then he had to know about anything and everything. Not to mention, he was always an excellent audience and oohed and aahed appreciatively. With that in mind, I filled him in on the morning's developments, and by the time we reached the Alcazar Theater, he was up to date.

"I knew this would be better than stuffy ol' school," he said, his eyes wide. "D'you want me to comes in with you?"

"No, I think it better if you stay out here. If I'm not out in half an hour, you can go for help."

His face fell a bit. "Aw, miss. That's no fun, runnin' fer 'elp."

"I know, but if Awi Bubu really does belong to Chaos, you'll need help, believe me."

Reluctantly Will agreed, and, feeling much safer with someone watching my back, I went to find the magician.

Luckily, Will had directed me to the back door that he and his brothers used to sneak in without paying for their tickets, so I didn't have to come up with any hastily cobbled-together explanations to get into the theater.

Once backstage, I quickly found my way to Awi Bubu's dressing room. My anger had been reduced to a slow boil on the way over, but even so, I thumped loudly on the door. I would have flung it open were it not for the fact I was afraid he'd actually be dressing.

The door opened and I found myself staring up into the broad dark face of Awi Bubu's assistant.

"Who is it, Kimosiri?" Awi Bubu asked.

"It's me," I said.

Kimosiri grunted and stood aside to let me pass. Inside the dressing room, Awi Bubu was sitting at a small table with a map of the stars spread out in front of him. I could recognize some of the constellations, but there were scores of lines and numbers and other notations littering its surface.

A strange smile touched Awi Bubu's lips. "Ah, Little Miss. I was just thinking of you." He looked down at his chart. "Does Little Miss know where she was born, perchance?"

His odd question caused the tirade I'd been planning to stutter to a stop. "I beg your pardon?"

"I asked if you know the place and time of your birth."

"I was born on November twenty-eighth in our house on Queen Anne Street. Not that it's any of your business."

"Ah, but it is, you see. For Little Miss is incorrect. She was not born at her house on Queen Anne Street. She was not even born in Britain, I believe."

"What are you talking about?"

"I went to the registry office to see the time and date of Little Miss's birth so I could consult the astrological charts—"

"You did what? Without my permission?"

Awi Bubu merely shrugged. "I do not need your permission. However, imagine my surprise to find that there is no record of a Theodosia Throckmorton being born on British soil."

I felt like he'd just punched me in the stomach. "Wh-what do you mean?"

"I mean that wherever you were born, it was not in Britain."

"O-of course I was! You're daft! Perhaps the people at the registry office just didn't want to give you the information?"

Unperturbed, Awi Bubu shrugged again. "Or perhaps Little Miss does not truly know the circumstances of her birth. Have you spoken with your parents about this?"

"Enough!" I said. "That is not why I'm here." Unwilling to waste any more time on his preposterous nonsense, I remembered the whole reason I'd come. "Do you work for the Serpents of Chaos?" I blurted out, rather artlessly.

Awi Bubu turned to his assistant. "You may leave us, Kimosiri."

The giant, silent man nodded his head once, then slipped

out the door, closing it softly behind him. When we were alone, Awi Bubu leaned back in his chair and folded his arms. "No, Little Miss. I do not work for any manifestation of chaos, serpents or otherwise."

"Have you told anyone else about the Emerald Tablet?"

"Indeed not."

From his shocked look, I had to admit he appeared to be telling the truth. Which meant the leak to Chaos came from elsewhere. Even so, he still owed me a great deal of information on the tablet.

"Very well then. Tell me about this Emerald Tablet. The truth this time." I folded my arms and glared at him. "What does the tablet *do?*"

"I thought Little Miss understood. The tablet's value lies in the information it contains, not in any innate power it possesses."

"Rubbish. The Serp—some very evil men are after it, and they would not be after it if it did not have some immense power of destruction."

Awi Bubu grew very still. "Who are these men?" he asked.

"Why should I tell you if you haven't seen fit to tell me the truth?"

"Because perhaps I could help you."

"Help me! Ha! The way you can help me is by telling me the truth."

His gaze sharpened and I felt his will nudge up against mine, urging me to tell him.

"Stop that!" I yelled.

The sensation disappeared. Awi Bubu turned away from me and began rolling up the chart in front of him. "Very well. It is as I said. The Emerald Tablet has very little power itself. Its true value is that it is a map, a series of directions that lead to a cache of Egyptian artifacts of untold value. Artifacts few even dream exist."

"What sort of artifacts?" I asked, but I had a sinking feeling I knew what was coming.

"Artifacts that have been wielded by the gods and goddesses of Egypt themselves. Artifacts that still hold the power of those gods, destructive power that man was never meant to control, power over life and death," he said.

My knees suddenly felt weak and I backed up to the lone chair against the wall and sat down. "How many of these artifacts of the gods are there?" I asked.

"We do not know. Some have been lost through the ages, but there are still many that exist."

"Reginald Mayhew," I muttered, thinking of the British undercover agent Wigmere had mentioned a few weeks ago.

Awi Bubu sprang forward, looking as if he wanted to shake me. "What do you know of Mayhew?"

Shocked, I reared back. "What do *you* know of Mayhew?"

"I know that he laid claim to some things that did not belong to him and that he had no right to touch."

"I heard he got them from a Frenchman," I said without thinking, and then the penny dropped.

Thelonius Munk had mentioned a Frenchman wandering in the desert, babbling about the *wedjadeen*. And when we'd been researching the staff, Wigmere had discussed a small group of dedicated men who'd smuggled the artifacts out of the Alexandria Library. Could it be? I glanced at Awi Bubu sharply. "Are you one of the *wedjadeen?*"

Before I finished uttering the word, Awi Bubu sprang across the room, clamped one hand over my mouth, and made a snatching gesture with the other, as if he were plucking the word from the air itself. The sound of running footsteps sounded in the hall outside, and Kimosiri burst in, panting heavily and looking very afraid.

CHAPTER TWENTY-FOUR
BOYTHORPE'S REVENGE

AWI BUBU PRESSED HIS WIZENED FACE so close to mine our noses were almost touching. I could see small beads of perspiration on his upper lip. "Never, *never* utter that word out loud. Do you understand me?"

Stunned, I blinked rapidly and said through his fingers, "Yes," which came out rather like a croak.

"Come all the way in and close the door," Awi Bubu instructed Kimosiri as he stepped away from me. "Have you never wondered why my faithful assistant does not speak, Little Miss?"

Before I had a chance to admit the question had crossed

my mind, Awi Bubu continued. "He too uttered that word once. And they cut out his tongue."

Kimosiri opened his mouth and shoved it in my direction. I bit back a scream as I stared into his tongueless mouth.

"Now you must go," Awi Bubu said, herding me toward the door. "Others may be here for you soon."

"For me?"

"For the person who has dared to utter that word. I cannot keep you safe just yet, so you must go."

"But who are *they?*" I asked, thoroughly confused and more than a little alarmed.

"Quickly! There is no time. I will explain the rest tomorrow when I pay your mother a visit. Kimosiri, follow her until she reaches the museum, then return at once."

The larger man hesitated.

"I will be fine," Awi Bubu assured him. "I can make the necessary explanations to the others should they show up. Besides, they will not harm me. I do not think."

Before I had time to ask any more questions, Kimosiri escorted me out of Awi Bubu's dressing room, down the hall, and out the rear door. He was a bit taken aback to find Will waiting for me.

"Miss!" Will's eyes lit up with relief when he spotted me, then he frowned as he saw Kimosiri looming behind. "Everything okay?"

"Yes, it's fine," I reassured him. Then I turned to Awi Bubu's hulking assistant. "As you can see, I already have an escort. You can go back to Awi Bubu."

He didn't budge, just stood there and eyed me suspiciously.

"Go. Back. To. Your. Master," I intoned, trying Awi Bubu's mesmerism trick on him.

The hulking brute merely raised a mocking eyebrow at me. Bother. That meant there was more to it than just the vocal inflection. I tried a different tack this time. "Truthfully," I said, "Will can see me safely home. If those others come, it's best if you're here to help your master."

Kimosiri shifted uneasily on his feet, then looked over his shoulder toward the theater.

"Go on," I encouraged him. "You know that's where your primary duty lies. Go."

Something that looked very much like relief spread across his face. He folded his hands in front of his body, gave a short bow, then went inside the theater.

Once we were alone on the sidewalk, Will turned to me. "Where to now, miss?"

"Somerset House," I said. "There is no longer any doubt. I simply must get in to see Wigmere."

Will's eyebrows disappeared up into his scalp. "Somerset 'ouse, miss? Are ye sure about that? 'Cause I'm not sure that's the best place for me, if'n you know what I mean."

I glanced at him distractedly. "You're right. It's probably best you wait outside, out of sight of the windows."

Will's shoulders slumped ever so slightly with relief.

We were quiet on the walk to Somerset House. There were so many things Wigmere needed to know! He had to be made aware that Chaos was after the tablet, and this new information that Awi Bubu had provided, that the tablet was in fact a map to a cache of artifacts containing untold destructive force—well, wasn't that the exact sort of thing the Brotherhood kept an eye on?

Not to mention the Brotherhood would likely want to know about something called the *wedjadeen,* whatever it turned out to be.

When we reached Somerset House, Will took up position on the side of the building, and I crossed the enormous empty courtyard on my own. The doorman waved me in, and I proceeded up the stairs. I tried to put my thoughts in some order so I wouldn't burst in on Wigmere and sound frantic and hysterical. It seemed especially important to be on my very best behavior with him right now.

I paused at the landing of the third floor. I'd really hoped to avoid Boythorpe; I simply didn't have the reserves necessary to spar with him. I squared my shoulders and darted past Boythorpe's door, praying he wouldn't see me.

No such luck.

He was up and out of his office in two seconds flat. "Excuse me!" he said in a smug, officious voice. "You can't go down there."

"Oh, it's all right," I said, ducking around him. "Wigmere's expecting me." Or he would have been if he'd had half an idea of how much I had to tell him.

Boythorpe flung himself in front of me, both arms opened wide to block my way. "He is most certainly not expecting you. I have, in fact, been given very specific instructions regarding you and your visits."

My stomach sank. "You have?"

"Yes. I have been ordered to tell you to leave at once and report anything you have to say to Wigmere through Mr. Fagenbush, your proper contact. You will be made to use the correct channels, or else."

"Whose orders are these?" I asked, the full impact of what he'd said crashing over me. I was not to have access to Wigmere any longer?

Boythorpe drew himself up importantly. "They come from someone much higher than you. Now, please leave or I will have to call someone to escort you out."

Escort me out! Like a common thief or vagrant? "There's

no need," I told him, trying to keep my voice steady and cheerful. "I'm leaving."

Will was more put out by my reception than he had been by his own suspension. "What is that 'ay-brained prig thinking of, cutting you off from Wigmere?" he demanded. "'Oo does 'e think 'e is?" He paused a moment. "I know! I'll go in and create a diversion, then you can sneak past 'im, miss. It'll be just like old times."

I just shook my head, too distraught even to speak. I tried to tell myself I was upset at having to manage all this without Wigmere, but the truth was, Boythorpe's orders to refuse me entrance cut deep.

The walk back to the museum seemed to take forever, the heavy, leaden sky perfectly mirroring my mood. Once there, I found I simply didn't have the energy to tackle any research or curses, or even to see Henry. I most certainly wasn't up to seeing my parents; I was afraid I would blurt out questions about my birth. What had they been keeping from me all these years?

Where was I born, if not in Britain? Or, worse, had I been born in Britain but under a different name? Was I an orphan, perhaps, whom Mother and Father had taken pity on? What if I wasn't really from this family? That would explain so much! Why Grandmother disapproved of me; why I had these unusual talents that no one else seemed to possess.

As much as I'd longed for answers to those questions, I'd never imagined *these* answers.

Isis, sensing my mood, appeared at my ankles and followed me to my closet, where she curled up in my lap and kept me company until it was time to go home.

At dinner that night, I found my eyes going back to Mother time and again, studying her face, trying to see any similarities between her features and mine. Finally Father got so exasperated he said, "Good heavens, Theodosia, stop scrutinizing your mother as if she were a particularly troublesome translation."

"Sorry, Father," I muttered, turning my attention to the mutton on my plate. To make matters even worse, we were having boiled mutton for dinner, my absolutely least favorite.

"Alistair," Mum said reproachfully. Then to me she said, "Is there anything wrong, darling? Something we need to talk about?"

Here was an opening I could use. "Actually, yes, Mother. I was wondering if you could tell me about the day I was born?"

There was a clank as Father dropped his fork and Mother gasped, her cheeks growing pink. After a surprised minute, she frowned. "Theodosia, that is most inappropriate to bring up at the dinner table. Surely a girl of your age knows that."

My face turned bright red in embarrassment. Indeed, I *hadn't* known that. In fact, Mother never made a fuss about propriety or being vulgar or any of those sorts of things. That was one of the reasons she annoyed Grandmother so.

And even through my extreme embarrassment, I could tell that her overreaction meant she was hiding something. A something so terrible it couldn't be discussed at the dinner table.

CHAPTER TWENTY-FIVE

FROWN NOT ON HUMBLE BIRTH

THE NEXT MORNING, I thought seriously about staying home. In fact, the only thing that got me out of bed was the driving need to find another opportunity to talk to Mother about where I was born.

As I washed my face, I searched for signs of Mother in my features. I would even settle for Father's plainer looks. But while Mother had lovely rich chestnut hair that curled gracefully into a topknot with charming little tendrils escaping, my hair was straighter than a poker and the most nondescript color ever invented. Once in a while, when the sun shone brightly, I thought I could detect a straw-colored glimmer or two, but since the sun never shines in London, what good did that do me? And it wouldn't curl, no matter how long we left the curling iron on it. My hair burned before it curled!

My eyes weren't the least bit Mum-like either. Instead of being rich chocolate brown like hers, my eyes had some of every color in them, which sounded good but actually was a lot like greenish mud. Henry and Father had blue eyes, so I'd always thought Mother's brown and Father's blue had simply gotten mixed up in me. But with Awi Bubu's revelations still ringing in my ears, I realized that might not be the case at all.

There wasn't an opportunity to get Mother alone all morning. Once we got to the museum, it was even worse. Weems wanted to ask her a question about the placement of the Sekhmet statue, no doubt sucking up to her after his set-down yesterday. Father also remained in the foyer, checking up on how Fagenbush was coming with the assembly of Thutmose III's war chariot. The only one missing from all of this was Stilton, which was just as well since I needed to catch him alone. I still owed him a thank-you for his help Saturday night and I wanted to let him know that the funeral had gone off without a hitch. I had meant to tell him yesterday but was so distracted by Sopcoate's unexpected appearance and demands that I'd forgotten.

I made my way down the hall to Stilton's office, surprised to find the door closed. I raised my fist to knock but was stopped by the sound of voices. Who could Stilton be talking to? Everyone else was in the foyer.

"You aren't supposed to be here." I couldn't tell if that was panic or outrage I heard in Stilton's voice.

"You've been ignoring the grand master's summons for days, ever since you missed the meeting Saturday night."

I knew that voice. It belonged to Basil Whiting, Aloysius Trawley's second in command. And why hadn't Stilton warned me that he would be skipping a Black Sun meeting? I had no desire to draw even more of Trawley's ire.

"I haven't been ignoring anybody," Stilton said. "We've been up to our ears in work around here, trying to get ready for the new exhibit. I can't get away without raising suspicion."

"Have you forgotten that you swore an oath of loyalty?"

"N-no. Of c-course not!"

"Loyalty to the grand master comes before even your job," Whiting said.

"Then how does he expect me to eat or put a roof over my head?" Definitely outraged, this time.

"Such mundane matters are not his concern," Whiting said.

Stilton started to speak, but Trawley's second in command talked over him. "No more excuses. The grand master says you need to choose."

"Choose?"

"Yes, choose whom you will serve—him or the girl. And be sure you choose right, or you'll think the Trial of Nephthys was a walk in the park. Master says this is your last warning."

With a start, I realized the conversation was over. The floor creaked as Whiting headed for the door. In an instant, I leaped back to the wall and slipped behind the suit of armor there.

Whiting came out of Stilton's office, checked the corridor, then hurried toward the back entrance. This was a most disturbing development. Clearly, any pretense of cooperation was being cast aside, and it was now open war. The only question now was, Whom would Stilton choose?

My heart was still pounding as I slipped out from behind the armor. I needed to talk to Stilton and—

"There you are!"

I whirled around to find Fagenbush glaring at me. "Come into my office," he ordered.

I glanced around to be sure no one would see us, then reluctantly followed him inside. I'd never been invited into his office before, and I wasn't sure I cared much for it. I was surprised to find it much neater than Father's or Stilton's, but it most definitely felt like enemy territory. I held myself stiffly and waited.

After he closed the door, the smell of ox dung became overwhelming. "How do I remove it?" he growled at me.

"Try scraping your boots on the grass—"

"Do not pretend this isn't your doing."

"I have no idea what you're talking about."

He ground his teeth and clenched his hands, but changed the subject. "You went to visit Wigmere yesterday."

As it wasn't a question, I didn't bother to answer.

He stepped toward me and I resisted the urge to pinch my nose with my fingers. Whoever would have thought that I would *miss* the smell of boiled cabbage and pickled onions?

"What message did you have for Wigmere? He's instructed you to give it to me."

I forced myself to turn casually and say, "I was just paying him a social visit. To see if he was planning on attending the exhibit opening. That is all."

"You liar!" Fagenbush snarled at me. "You are jeopardizing my career with your stubbornness."

I whirled on him. "My stubbornness! *My* stubbornness? Have you shown me one iota of trust or kindness or anything that indicates my trusting you wouldn't be a huge mistake?" Even as I railed at him, my mind raced like a motorcar engine. Who had told him I'd been to Somerset House? Boythorpe? Or Wigmere himself?

He took a step closer, nearly backing me against the wall. "And where else did you disappear to yesterday afternoon? You were gone much longer than a quick visit to Somerset House warranted. Who else are you associating with? I wonder how Wigmere will feel upon hearing it."

Something in me snapped. I was sick of being watched and observed like some specimen in a jar. I was tired of all these wretched adults thinking I was just playing a game. I raised my finger, pointed it at Fagenbush's chest, and took a step toward him, forcing him to back up a bit. "You want to know what happened yesterday? Fine, I'll tell you. Admiral Sopcoate"—Fagenbush's eyes widened—"yes, *that* Admiral Sopcoate, showed up at the memorial service, that's what. Furthermore, he demanded I hand over the artifact that everyone keeps telling me is nothing but worthless occult drivel." I cocked my finger back then poked Fagenbush in the chest—hard. "So you take that information to Wigmere and see what he has to say, why don't you."

Then, while he was still sputtering, I strode out of his office and headed for the upstairs workroom. Since I'd gathered a good head of steam, it seemed like a fine time to get Mum alone and ask her about where I was born. Until I did that, I would be able to concentrate on little else.

I found her alone in the workroom, poring over the remaining steles from the dig.

The question I'd been burning to ask her dissolved on my tongue. I glanced at the stele on the table in front of her. "Anything interesting?"

"Oh, yes. Lots."

I waited a moment longer, gathering up my courage, until Mother finally said, "Was there something you needed, dear?"

I tried again. "Mother," I began, my mouth growing dry. The question I was about to ask terrified me. Or maybe it was the possible answer that was so disturbing. I cleared my throat and tried to lighten my tone, as if this were simply a casual conversation and my entire identity didn't hang in the balance. "Was I born at home, like Henry, or was I born in a hospital?"

Mother's whole body went still, just for a second, and

my insides turned to jelly. She clearly did not like this question.

"Why do you ask, dear?" Not much of an answer, that. In fact, I recognized it as a major avoidance tactic, one I used quite often myself. My unease grew. "No reason, really. Just curious."

"Do you remember when Henry was born?" Mum said brightly. "How funny he looked? Just like a little old gnome. And old Dr. Topham was there?"

"Yes, Mum. But I want to know about when *I* was born." My voice came out a little more stern than I had intended. Mum blinked at me, and I stared into her dark brown eyes—. eyes that were nothing like my own. A cold feeling of dread filled me. Why wouldn't she answer the question?

"Well." Mum gave a nervous little laugh. "It's an unusual story, really. You weren't born at home or in a hospital. You were born in Egypt."

Whatever I'd been expecting, it wasn't this. "Egypt?" I repeated stupidly.

Mother gave that nervous laugh again, her cheeks flushing faintly pink. "Yes, I'm afraid so. Your father and I had been working on an excavation of an ancient temple site when I discovered I was in the family way. However, the rainy season came early that year, and there was major flooding, which made travel impossible. Especially in my condition. When the rains finally stopped, it was too late for me to travel, so I stayed and continued my work."

In Egypt. I was born in Egypt. Before I could wrap my mind around that, she continued.

"As I said, I had decided to keep working. I felt perfectly fine, strong and healthy, and I saw no reason to be confined to my hotel room. I would have gone quite mad, I'm sure. However, eager child that you were, you came three weeks earlier than expected and caught us off-guard." She cleared her throat. "You were born in the temple I was working in at the time."

A temple! "Whose temple was it?" I asked, nearly afraid of the answer.

"It was a temple dedicated to Isis."

Well, at least it wasn't a Seth Temple. "Why did you never tell me this before?" I wanted to know. Was she ashamed?

"Well, it was a bit of a scandal, all the way around. I was the first archaeologist to give birth on a dig," she said, her voice drier than dust from the Sahara. "Not to mention the sheer impropriety of it all. In fact, your grandmother still hasn't forgiven me. Such a vulgar thing to do, you know. Have a baby in a far-off foreign land on heathen soil."

"Is that why she dislikes me so?"

"Oh, Theo, darling. I don't think she dislikes you so much as she is worried for you. She is convinced that your being born and spending your first months of life in a strange land has ruined your chances of being a proper British miss. Pure rubbish, but that's your grandmother for you. Your father, however, was quite taken with the whole situation. Called you our most precious artifact."

"He did?" Her words stunned me. *I* was my father's most precious artifact? How could that be? My eyes began to prickle and burn.

However, before I could embarrass myself with a full display of waterworks, there was a shout from below: "fire!"

CHAPTER TWENTY-SIX
A MOMENTARY TRUCE

MOTHER AND I RACED TOWARD THE SHOUTING. When we arrived in the foyer, we found Father flapping his morning coat, putting out a burning statue. Underneath the smell of smoke, ash, and dung, I caught the rotten-egg stench of sulfur. That did not bode well.

"What happened?" Mother asked, hurrying forward.

With the fire now safely out, Father let his coat hang limply at his side and ran his hand through his hair. "I'm not sure. The blasted thing just burst into flames. Weems?" He turned to the First Assistant Curator. "What did you do to it?"

"N-nothing, sir." Weems squirmed uncomfortably.

"Well, it didn't just spontaneously combust," Father said.

"I-I'm afraid it did," the unfortunate Weems continued. "There is no other explanation."

"Tell us exactly what you were doing before it burst into flames," Mother suggested.

Weems scrubbed his hands over his face, as if trying to wash away the memory. "Well, I had just unwrapped the statue from the roll of felt she came down in—"

"Where's the felt?" Father asked.

Weems pointed to the dark green fabric that had fallen to the floor. Father bent down and picked it up, then rubbed it between his fingers and sniffed it. "Go on."

". . . and set her on the display column."

"How, exactly?" Father asked.

"Like this." Weems took the statue from Father and set it carefully down on the column. Faint bits of dust and ash swirled in the glinting rays of the morning sun, casting the black basalt statue in bright light. There was a faint *swoosh*, then a crackle as the statue caught fire again.

Father gave a shout of surprise and whipped his coat up and began beating at the flames once more. "Quit doing that!" he shouted.

Poor Weems looked sick with bewilderment. He obviously had no idea how he kept managing to set the statue on fire.

I, however, did. And as much as I disliked Weems, I knew

it had nothing to do with him. Clearly the statue of Sekhmet was cursed.

It was a very cunning curse, actually, and one I'd seen only a few times before. Ancient magicians would curse a funereal object so that when it was brought out into the sun, it would burst into flames. In this way, they hoped to discourage tomb robbers from plundering the pharaohs' tombs.

When at last the flames were out again, Father looked haggard. "Maybe it's the plinth," he said, bending down to look at it. But of course it wasn't. I saw Clive Fagenbush watching Weems with a knowing glint in his eye; then our gazes met and a look of understanding passed between us. Fagenbush also knew what had caused that fire, and it was no plinth.

"Here, Father," I said, stepping forward at the same moment that Fagenbush did. "I'll just take that back up to the workroom for you."

Fagenbush glared at me, furious I'd offered first.

"Oh, thank you, Theodosia. That would be best, I think." He turned to Weems. "And you, I think it best if you go work on the guest list for Friday's reception. I can't risk you incinerating anything else."

"Very well, sir," Weems said, trying to look as if he weren't the least bit demoralized by all this.

I took the statue from Father, careful to touch only the

very top of its head and its feet. Sekhmet was the lioness-headed goddess who represented the destructive force of the sun, and she and her ancient priestesses were a tad vengeful. They often coated such statues with various poisons, so that if the flames didn't get you, the poison would. With luck, some of the ash would cling to the surface and would act like a rubbing, allowing me to read the cursed hieroglyphs that had been used. I was surprised at how cool it was to the touch, but that simply confirmed it was magic, not the principle of combustion, that was at work here.

When I reached the workroom, I carried the statue of Sekhmet over close to the window, careful not to let the feeble sunlight touch it. Unfortunately, even with a faint film of ash on the statue, I couldn't make out the hieroglyphs that formed the curse, and until I knew those, I couldn't remove it.

Very carefully, I moved the statue toward the faint rays of sun coming in through the thick glass. I held Sekhmet so she wasn't quite touching the light itself, only brushing against some of the dust motes dancing in the sun.

It worked. The statue didn't catch fire, but it began to heat up, and as it did, the faint hieroglyphs became visible. Because I wasn't in the direct sunlight, the inscribed hieroglyphs on the statue didn't move and swarm so much as pulsate, so even though they were faint, they were stationary and therefore easier to read.

Working quickly, before the statue actually caught fire again, I peered closely at the symbols. Destruction. Chaos. Power of the sun. Avenger of wrongs. Our lady of slaughter. Honestly! We were lucky the statue had only burst into flames!

From what I could make of the inscribed spell, the curse on this statue called down the fires of the desert on anyone who moved it from the darkness of the Temple of Thutmose III into the sunlight.

Once I'd clearly seen all the hieroglyphs, I moved the statue over to the workbench, being careful not to touch it against anything. The curse confirmed what I'd thought: it had been devised so tomb raiders wouldn't steal it. However, that presupposed that all tomb raiders could read the hieroglyphs, which most definitely wasn't the case.

Wait a moment. I looked down at the surface of the statue, but the symbols were already fading. Bother. I picked it back up and went over to the window, paying careful attention to one specific hieroglyph.

Behind me, the workroom door opened. "Perfect timing," I said. "I need your opinion." Then I turned around. It wasn't Father, as I'd expected, but Fagenbush. And he had a most strange look on his face—as if his normal sneer had been tainted with a glimmer of hope.

"You need *my* opinion?" he repeated, clearly unsure he had heard correctly. It was an odd moment, and it felt as if something I couldn't even identify hung in the balance. Uncomfortable, I turned back to the statue and said, "I need *a* second opinion; now hurry, before this thing catches fire again."

There was a long pause, then I heard his footsteps behind me. As he drew closer, I noticed that the scent of ox dung was growing fainter. The curse must be wearing off.

"What have you found so far?" he asked.

"The usual for Sekhmet: Chaos. Power of the sun. Avenger of wrongs. Our lady of slaughter. But see this glyph here? That's the one I need a second opinion on. What do you think it translates to?"

Fagenbush leaned in closer and angled his head. "'Tomb.' No, 'temple.'"

"Yes!" I beamed at him, and he blinked in surprise. "I made that exact same mistake. But it is 'temple,' isn't it."

He nodded.

"Which makes the whole thing quite odd, because the inscription claims that this statue was to remain in the *Temple* of Thutmose III for all eternity, not in his tomb, as I'd first thought. The only problem is—"

"There isn't any Temple of Thutmose III." Fagenbush looked at me, and I could practically see the gears whirring in his head.

"Exactly. At least, none that's been discovered yet."

A very long, very charged silence filled the room, making me a bit uncomfortable.

"Keep an eye on this for a moment, would you? I need to go get something to remove the curse with." Then, before he could say no, I rushed to the door and nearly flew down to my closet, where I had left my curse-removal kit. I snatched it and hurried back up the stairs. Inside the workroom, Fagenbush was poring over some of the steles that littered the worktable. As I approached, his eyes zeroed in on my satchel, but he said nothing.

I lugged it over to the table and began rifling through it until I found a small yellow tin, which I set on the worktable next to the statue.

"What is that?" Fagenbush asked.

"Beeswax," I told him as I opened the tin. "It won't remove the curse entirely, but if I rub it over the entire statue, it will act as a barrier between it and the rays of the sun, effectively nullifying the curse until I have a chance to research it fully."

He stared at me oddly. "Beeswax," he said, his voice flat.

"Yes. Watch." I dipped a corner of a nearby rag into the

wax and began rubbing it over the statue. "It won't hurt the basalt the statue is made of," I pointed out. "And see how nicely it polishes it up?"

By the time I finished the first coat of wax, my hands began to itch. Frowning down at them, I realized I had a nearly overwhelming need to wash them. Which made no sense, since I was wearing gloves, the way I always did. Ignoring the sensation, I dipped the rag into the wax for a second coat, then stopped.

What if some element of the curse had managed to work through both the rag and my gloves? That thought had me putting down the rag and the statue rather quickly. "Do you want to put a second coat on? I need to go wash my hands. But be careful, the statue might be transferring something itchy."

He looked up sharply at me, and I was suddenly painfully aware of all the decoy artifacts that I'd put in his way. "Truly," I said, holding up my hands. "My palms are itching fiercely, so be careful."

His face relaxed, and he picked up the rag and dipped it in the wax tin. I glanced briefly at the steles scattered on the worktable, worried that he'd finish the second coat of wax and have a chance to search for references to "temple" before I returned. Then I reminded myself I was only going to be gone a minute. How long did it take to wash one's hands?

CHAPTER TWENTY-SEVEN
A TALE OF TWO BUBUS

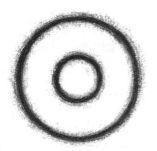

WHEN I REACHED THE LAVATORY on the first floor, I was stunned to see Awi Bubu waiting there. My hands stopped itching immediately "Awi Bubu?"

He gave a little bow. "Little Miss."

"Wh-what are you doing here?"

"Your mother and I finished our meeting a quarter of an hour ago."

Then it dawned on me. "You made my hands itch!"

He looked absurdly proud of that fact.

"How did you do that?"

"It is but one of my talents. Is there somewhere we can speak alone?"

"Very well." I tried to think where best to take him. We could be too easily overheard in the reading room. The catacombs were out of the question; who knew how he'd react if he saw any of the artifacts down there? The way things were going, he'd want them *all* back. "We'll go to my, er, room," I finally said.

I led him to my small closet, relieved when we didn't run into anybody else in the hallways. I opened the door and motioned for him to walk in first, my heart racing in anticipation. Was I finally to learn what was going on?

Awi Bubu studied the small room, his keen black eyes missing no detail, seeing everything from my frocks on their hooks to the blanket folded at the foot of the sarcophagus. He fingered the blanket and looked at the sarcophagus curiously. "Little Miss never fails to surprise me," he said. "And I have not been easily surprised in many, many years."

I shrugged, unsure what to say to that.

Without further comment, he turned to the wall behind him and wrote three hieroglyphic symbols on it with his finger, then repeated the gesture on each of the other three walls. Even though I watched closely, I could not make out which symbols he'd used. "There," he said at last. "Now Shu cannot carry our words to others."

"Why would the god of air do that?" I asked.

"Because the *wedjadeen* are sworn to protect the secrets of the gods; it is our sacred duty."

I flinched as he said the forbidden word, then realized he'd said *our*.

"If the gods hear us speaking lightly of their matters, they will report it to others, others who might not be as sympathetic as I am to Little Miss's predicament. For Little Miss has, indeed, guessed rightly. I am a *wedjadeen,* one of the Eyes of Horus, although an exiled one—that part of my tale is true."

We both froze at a scratch on the door. He stared at the door as if seeing *through* it, then nodded. "It is only your cat. Let her in."

It was indeed Isis. She stalked into the room, and I closed the door behind her.

"You may as well sit down, this is a long tale."

I settled myself on the floor with my back against the wall and held Isis in my lap. We both watched Awi Bubu, who seemed to be waging some inner war with himself.

"I have come to the decision that I must tell you all, even though it is against our rules. This half knowledge you have pieced together is too dangerous. Best that you know the full truth. Besides, I am convinced that you play some important role that I do not yet understand."

Afraid to utter a word lest he change his mind, I merely nodded.

"We are," Awi Bubu said, "a most ancient and honorable group of men. Our roots go back to the long-ago high priests of the New Kingdom during the reign of the heretic pharaoh Akhenaton, who tried to advance his one god, Aton, over the gods and goddesses who had ruled Egypt since the beginning of time. We live in small villages, poor villages, that attract no tourist or archaeological attention. Our fathers and our fathers' fathers held the same positions we do. We have one precept: guard and protect the sacred artifacts of the gods until the one true pharaoh can be restored to his throne. That is our entire reason for existing.

"When the Persians invaded Egypt, they brought their gods with them and tried to inflict them on our people. Though we wore the yoke of Persian oppression, we were successful at avoiding heresy and kept to our own gods, but it was hard. After decades of diligent manipulation, we managed to restore an Egyptian to the throne once more. All was well, for a time. But Egypt had grown weak under foreign oppression, and her gods were angry with the new gods brought to her land. The Persian king Artaxerxes attacked, and Nectanebo II fled with a small party of Egyptian priests and made his way to Macedonia. And so when it came to pass that Alexander conquered Egypt, there was much secret rejoicing, for the blood of the pharaohs flowed in his veins."

"But wait!" I said, thoroughly confused. "Alexander's father was King Philip of Macedonia. How did Alexander come to have Egyptian blood then?"

"His father was not Philip but Nectanebo II, although only a handful knew of this, the *wedjadeen* among them. However, we had not counted on the influence of the Greeks holding such sway over the young Alexander. Soon, he began to combine our Egyptian gods with his Greek ones, an abomination in our eyes. The high priests reasoned and argued with him, but their protestations fell on deaf ears. They were hesitant to act, however, for he was a true son of Egypt. When Alexander died and his general Ptolemy assumed control, it became a different matter. No blood of Egypt flowed in that general's veins, and he had no right to call himself pharaoh. Even so, he continued Alexander's work, building new temples, merging his gods with our own, committing sacrilege.

"When he finally built the Serapeum in Alexandria, he sent a call out to all the temples to bring their most sacred artifacts for housing in this great monument. The high priests held a council among themselves and decided they would not do what this impostor pharaoh ordered. Instead, they brought lesser artifacts to the Serapeum. Their most sacred, true artifacts, they entrusted to a small, fiercely committed band of magician priests who called themselves the Eyes of Horus, the *wedjadeen*. We swore to guard these relics for when the true pharaoh rose again.

"And so we have. Deep in the desert, we guard the sacred gifts given to us by the gods, keeping them from the hands of the ignorant and the ambitious.

"Of course, Egypt is a large place and has many temples. We did not, unfortunately, get all of the artifacts. Some of these treasures slipped through our hands. A few made their way to the Serapeum and were looted when it was razed to the ground. Others never left their temples and were later discovered by adventurers and looters. But we know of all of them. And we will continue to search the world until we have every last one."

"And the Emerald Tablet is one of these artifacts of the gods?" I asked, my mind reeling with what I'd learned.

"No. The Emerald Tablet is the sole map to the hidden location where all the artifacts reside. With that map, a man would have access to all the powers of the ancient gods, artifacts capable of such massive destruction as to make your Staff of Osiris look like a child's toy. Since man was not meant to wield that much power, Chaos would reign forever."

"So that's why Sopcoate wanted it," I muttered.

"Unfortunately, these artifacts were not a secret. They

were the relics our temples proudly held for our people. Even though centuries have passed, rumors of their existence still abound. There are some men who keep an ear out for that sort of rumor, eager to find that which the gods have decreed should remain hidden. And that, Miss Theodosia, is why you must relinquish the Emerald Tablet to my keeping. So that I may return it to my fellow *wedjadeen* and we may rest, knowing the last record of our whereabouts has been recovered."

"But I thought you said you were an exile. How could you go back?"

"The tablet would gain me entry. The honor brought to me by returning the tablet would restore my standing, and I would be *wedjadeen* once again." His face changed as he said this, the longing and hope transforming his aged features.

I was quiet a long moment, digesting this. It's hard to explain why, but I think I believed him. For one, his account fit with the few bits and pieces I'd been able to acquire. Even so, this was a lot to absorb. And the only corroboration I had was a few scribbled words in the margins of books. It seemed as if caution might be called for. "How can I be sure you'll return the tablet to the Eyes of Horus?" I asked. "How do I know you aren't an opportunist or an adventurer, just like the men you claim to want to avoid?"

Awi Bubu broke into a smile. "A most excellent question,

Little Miss. I knew my faith in you would be well founded." Then his smile disappeared and his face grew clouded.

"I hope that by telling Little Miss all that I have told you, you will understand why it is so important that you give me the Emerald Tablet to return to safekeeping. We have guarded these secrets for millennia; I'm afraid it is only us who can keep them safely out of harm's way."

"You said you'd been exiled. What for? How do I know it wasn't because you tried to use the artifacts yourself for personal gain or tried to hand them off to someone you shouldn't have?"

His expression grew solemn at the memory. "As a young man, I let a most powerful artifact slip through my fingers. I was young and arrogant and overconfident and did not realize the danger the piece was in."

"Very well. I'll need to think about this, though. You can't expect me to decide what to do this moment."

Awi Bubu's face fell slightly, as if he'd expected that very thing. "We don't have much time . . ."

"No. We don't. But I need to be certain that if I give you the tablet, I can still keep my family safe."

Awi Bubu nodded. "Fair enough." He made his way to the door, then paused. "How will I know when you decide?"

"You mean you won't be able to tell just by the way the air feels?"

He gave me a reproachful look.

"I'll send a message," I said. "Or come round myself."

"When you have decided, you can find me at the theater. But it would be wise not to wait too long in the deciding."

And didn't I know it! He was halfway out the door before I remembered. "Wait!"

He paused, looking hopeful. "Yes?"

"You were right," I said. "I wasn't born here in Britain. I was born in Egypt. In an Isis Temple, to be exact. November twenty-eighth, 1895."

"Ah," he said, as if many things had been made clear.

I felt a soft nudge at my knee and looked down to find Isis wanting to be petted. As I bent to stroke her soft fur, I asked in a quiet voice, "Do you think that's why I'm so . . . different?" I sensed Awi Bubu's eyes on me, but I was feeling too exposed to meet his gaze.

"If by *different,* Little Miss means 'so gifted in her dealings with Egyptian magic,' then the answer is yes. The time and location of your birth set you on an unusual path. If you had an Egyptian calendar here, I could even tell you the prophecy foretold on the day of your birth."

"Really?" I stood up. "We do have one, actually. Father picked it up in Cairo two years ago."

Awi Bubu raised his eyebrows. "Yet another surprise," he murmured. "I suggest you consult it then. Much will be

made clear when you do." He folded his hands in front of
him and gave his small signature bow. "I hope to hear from
you soon regarding the other matter." Then he left.

My curiosity was a ravenous beast, driving me to the reading room and the ancient Egyptian calendar there even
though I had many other things that demanded my attention. I went into one of the small rooms where I had left off
translating the calendar ages ago, before so much Egyptian
magic run amok had intruded on our lives. I found the old
papyrus that Father had bought and began scanning for the
proper season, the season of Inundation. Once I found that,
I began trying to figure out which date corresponded to
November 28. It was the very last day of the last month of
Inundation.

*This is a day of great pleasure for all the gods. All offerings
made to the gods on this day shall be joyfully received. They will
accept the offerings into their hearts and great favor shall come
from these offerings.*

Slowly I set the papyrus on the desk, frowning in puzzlement. This didn't explain anything; all it did was talk about
offerings to the gods! Honestly! How did Awi Bubu expect
this to make anything clear—oh! I glanced back and reread
the portent. Then I sat down, hard, on the chair next to the

desk. I had been born in a temple—the Temple of Isis. Did that mean the Egyptian gods thought I was . . . *an offering?* And that they had accepted me into their hearts and granted me special favors? And what if those favors were special skills?

Once again, Awi Bubu had answered a question in such a way that I was more confused than ever.

CHAPTER TWENTY-EIGHT

THOSE SERPENTS, THERE'S NO PLEASING THEM!

THE NEXT DAY, when everyone else was downstairs putting the final tweaks and touches on the Thutmose III exhibit, I was busy in my parents' workroom rechecking Father's translations on a number of the papyruses and steles. For one thing, having work to do calmed my frayed nerves. It was also easier to think when my hands were busy, and heaven knew I had plenty to think about.

Besides, after what I'd learned from the cursed Sekhmet statue yesterday, I was positive there had to be something here that could shed more light on the subject.

I finally found what I was looking for midmorning. It was

an official decree from the head priest at the Temple of Montu.

The Temple of Montu. There wouldn't be a priest dedicated to a funerary temple in a tomb. That made no sense. My pulse quickened as I recalled the inscription from the Sekhmet statue. *Housed in the Temple of Thutmose III for all eternity.* The only temple we'd discovered in the Valley of the Kings was a very small one dedicated to Montu inside the tomb of Thutmose III. This decree referred to a different structure altogether. One that had yet to be discovered.

Unable to contain myself a moment longer, I put the papyrus down and hurried to the foyer, hoping to pull Mum aside and give her the news.

Downstairs, Father was in wild form, working in his shirt-sleeves with his hair mussed. Mum was working just as hard, if a bit more neatly, though even she had a trace of cobweb dangling from her skirt hem. I refrained from pointing that out, as I have learned that while adults thrive on giving children constructive criticism and tidying nudges, they rather hate receiving them. Besides, I had much more important things to discuss with her. However, before I could catch her eye, there was a knock on the door.

"Who in the blazes could that be?" Father asked.

Vicary Weems, who'd been forbidden to touch any of the exhibit artifacts and assigned to put the final touches on the reception, jumped up from where he'd been reviewing the RSVPs. "I'm sure I don't know, sir, but I will find out post-haste."

Weems opened the door to find a liveried footman standing there wringing his hands. I recognized him from Grandmother's house, and an unpleasant feeling settled in my stomach.

"I've been sent to fetch Master Throckmorton," the footman said.

"I'm sorry, but he's quite bus—"

"John?" Father interrupted Weems, put down the display cards he'd been setting in place, and hurried over to the door. "Is everything all right?"

"I'm afraid not, sir. Madam has sent me to fetch you. There's been an incident, you see. I'm afraid there's been a break-in. She's been burgled."

"A break-in!" Father exploded. "Was anyone hurt?"

"No, sir."

"Have the police been called?"

"Yes, sir. They're there right now, but she was feeling quite unsettled and requested you come around at once."

It was hard to imagine Grandmother being unsettled. More likely, she wanted someone to rail at.

"Very well," Father said, reluctance and urgency warring on his face. "I'd best go see how she's doing," he told Mother.

"I suppose you should," she agreed.

He combed his hair with his fingers. "Where's my coat got to? I wonder."

"It's right here," I said brightly, removing it from the display case where he'd set it.

"Oh, thank you, Theo," he said, putting it on.

"Don't forget your hat," I reminded him, picking it up. He speared me with a sharp gaze. "Your hair is a bit mussy," I explained.

His face cleared and he took the hat from me.

"Father, I think I should go with you to comfort poor Grandmother."

He looked at me rather oddly then, aware, no doubt, that *comfort* was not the usual effect I had on Grandmother. "We have grown closer of late," I pointed out to him.

"True. Well, if you think you'll be of help—"

"I do," I said firmly. Besides, the uneasy feeling in my stomach was growing stronger. There was only one day left to meet Sopcoate's demands, and with his recent threats to Grandmother's person, I did not think this incident was a coincidence.

We arrived at Grandmother's house to find the constables just leaving. Father stopped to ask them some questions while I went in search of Grandmother. I found her in the drawing room, drinking a glass of sherry. It was only one o'clock in the afternoon, but I suppose if one is burgled, one makes allowances for that sort of thing. I hesitated at the door. "Grandmother?"

"Oh, Theodosia! Is your father with you?"

"Yes, ma'am. He's speaking with the constable in the entryway."

"Oh, the horror of it all. That someone would break into my home and perpetrate such an assault on my personage!" Even though she was distraught, I noticed she still sat ramrod straight in the chair.

"Assault? Did they strike you?" I asked.

"Not me, but poor Beadles. They cracked him on the head. He's got quite a goose egg. Cook's tending to him in the kitchen."

Just then Father came into the room. He went over to Grandmother and gave her a kiss on each cheek. "Thank heavens you're all right," he said.

"All right? I'm not all right! My privacy has been violated, my home invaded!"

"Yes, but at least *you* aren't sporting a goose egg," Father gently pointed out.

Grandmother sniffed and took a deep drink of her sherry.

"The constable said they didn't get much. Only a necklace of yours?"

"Yes, that's the oddest thing! They came in through the servants' quarters, beaned poor Beadles when he came to see why Cook and Rose were screaming, then went straight to my bedroom and rifled through my jewelry. After all that effort, they only took one thing."

"And what was that?" I asked, holding my breath.

"My emerald necklace," she said. "That is all."

"Well, that doesn't make any sense," Father said.

It did if you were trying to send a message, I thought.

I left Father to comfort Grandmother and went in search of Beadles to see if he could give a description of the intruders. I found him in the kitchen holding a slab of beefsteak to his head. Cook and Rose fussed over him like two hens. Cook saw me first. "Oh, miss! Did ye hear the news? Come to comfort your gran, have you?"

"Er, yes." I came into the kitchen tentatively. "H-how are you, Beadles? I'm terribly sorry you got hurt." I was uncertain how he would react to any sympathy from me, as he and I were not on the best of terms. I had not yet realized how the sheer novelty of being attacked lowers normal social barriers.

"Why, thank you, Miss Theodosia. I suppose one needs to

be grateful it wasn't worse," he said, not sounding the least bit grateful and in fact sounding just the tiniest bit bitter.

"Do you mind if I ask how many there were?"

"There were two of them. At least," he added for good measure. "Big blokes too. Big as oxen, they were."

"Did either of them have a white beard, by chance? Or an eye patch?"

He looked startled. "Why, yes, miss. They did! How did you know?"

Bother. I'd managed that poorly. "I was just guessing. It seems like those who act like blackguards should look like blackguards."

"Quite right, miss," he said, and then returned to his tale. He'd been jumped by two, no, maybe three ox-sized men with fists as big as hams. By the time he was done with his tale, it was impossible to locate the small knot of truth at its center. I could only confirm that Sopcoate in his currently favored disguise had been one of them. With this important confirmation, I went back to the drawing room.

Once Grandmother had been properly fussed over and calmed down, Father and I returned to the museum. Nearly frantic over the lost time, he returned to his exhibit with renewed focus, allowing me to slip out unobserved.

For I had made up my mind. Clearly, Sopcoate and Chaos

would stop at nothing to get the tablet. However, I couldn't simply hand over an artifact that pointed the way to objects with as much power as the Staff of Osiris held. The world would never be safe again.

If Wigmere had been available to me, I could have asked his advice, but according to Boythorpe, I was persona non grata. Stilton was being pressured by the Black Sunners, and I had no idea where his true loyalties lay. That left me only one person to turn to.

Awi Bubu and the *wedjadeen*. Or the Eyes of Horus, as he called them. I was dreadfully unsettled about all this, but deep down it seemed like the only thing to do. Even though, if I thought about it too long, there were so many reasons not to. How did I know he was telling the truth? Not only about the *wedjadeen,* but about the tablet itself? On the other hand, if he was telling the truth, the consequences were too grim to bear thinking about.

Plus Wigmere and Trawley and scholars in general didn't seem to view the tablet as all that important on its own, so even if I had made a grave miscalculation, we'd only be out one occult artifact.

Of course, the trick was how to keep the tablet out of the hands of Chaos while also keeping my grandmother—not to mention myself—safe. I planned to dump that dilemma in

Awi Bubu's lap. If he was truly a member of one of the world's oldest and most secret organizations, then he should have plenty of ideas.

As I let myself into the back door of the Alcazar Theater, I couldn't help but wonder if Awi Bubu *lived* in his dressing room. And if so, did the theater manager know?

The dressing room door opened immediately to reveal a looming Kimosiri. He nodded his head and gestured me inside. Awi Bubu stepped toward me and bowed. "So Little Miss has made up her mind." It was not a question. He knew.

I nodded. "Only if you can devise a plan that will keep my grandmother and the rest of my family safe."

"No one is absolutely guaranteed safe," he said. "Little Miss, for example, could be struck by a motorcar on her way home. But I will do everything in my power to be sure that our actions do not bring danger to your family's doorstep."

I guessed that would have to do. "Very well," I said. "I'm hoping you have a plan?"

"I have many, as I have done nothing but plot and plan since I first learned the tablet was here in London."

"Yes, well, whichever of them you choose, it has to happen tomorrow, because that is the deadline Sopcoate has given me."

"This I know, Little Miss."

"Very well, then. What's your plan?"

"Little Miss's parents have their grand opening tomorrow, is this correct?"

"Yes," I said. "A huge event, with lots of uppity-ups and the museum board and important members of society coming to view their newest exhibits."

"So it would be very easy for Little Miss to slip out unobserved."

"Very easy," I agreed. "That's why Sopcoate chose that time to meet."

Awi Bubu nodded, then thought for a moment. "You are no doubt being followed by one of Sopcoate's men, and one of the Bald One's as well."

"Do you think I've led them here? I'm sorry, I didn't notice anyone . . ."

Awi Bubu waved his hand. "It is of no matter. Kimosiri and I will be gone by Saturday. I have made arrangements on a ship bound for Marseille. As soon as I have the tablet in my hands I will depart for that ship and return to my homeland." The longing in his voice was palpable. "Anyway, as I said, we will assume you are being followed, so tomorrow, during the height of the grand opening, you will bring the tablet to the meeting place that Sopcoate has arranged, as if you plan to hand the tablet over to him. This way, you will appear to be cooperating, and whatever else happens after that will not be your fault."

"What *will* happen afterward?"

"The Bald One will not be happy that you are giving away a treasure he wants so badly. He will make a move to block this trade off, I think. We will pit two opposing forces on one another and use the ensuing chaos"—he permitted himself a small smile at the joke—"to step forward and retrieve the tablet from under their noses. The Black Sun will be no match for the Serpents, and the chase will be on. However, your place in the exchange will be over. You will have handed it over to Sopcoate as he demanded and fulfilled your part of the bargain."

"But how will both of you get it from the Serpents of Chaos? There will be many of them, and there are only two of you."

He gave his formal little bow. "I am a magician, Little Miss. I will have many tricks up my sleeve. Although it would not hurt if you brought the Orb of Ra with you."

We were both silent for a long moment as we imagined how this plan might play out. Finally, I sighed. "I suppose it's our best shot."

"So I believe, Little Miss. Once Kimosiri and I have gone, do not say anything to anyone about the Eyes of Horus. It is a most secret organization, and I have risked my life by bringing you into my confidence."

"Then why do it?"

"Because I quickly learned that by allowing you only half-truths, you were becoming too dangerous. And because the mark of Isis is upon you."

"Oh, please, let's not start that again."

Awi Bubu grabbed my shoulders with his wiry hands. He gave me a gentle shake. "Little Miss must accept this. You were born in the Temple of Isis, at the foot of the great goddess, on a most auspicious day. She has accepted you as her gift, and you must be respectful of that. Even now, her servants tend to you—"

"What servants?" I scoffed. Maybe if I sounded scornful, the whole thing wouldn't be so terrifying.

"Your cat. The jackal. By whose power do you think they live? Whom do you think they serve?"

"Y-you're talking nonsense. Please stop."

"No, Little Miss. I am not talking nonsense. This is one of the reasons I agreed to help your parents regain their firmin in the Valley of the Kings. Little Miss must go with them. You must return to the land of your birth."

"I'd be only too happy to return to Egypt, but why is it so important to you?"

"Because I feel certain that Little Miss has a significant role to play. The goddess has marked you for a reason, and that reason will not be found here in London. And there is one more thing." He paused for a moment, the air in the room growing even more solemn. "If something goes wrong tomorrow and I do not emerge triumphant, Little Miss must promise to return the tablet to Egypt on my behalf."

"Don't be silly, nothing is going to happen to you!" My voice sounded the tiniest bit shrill. I cleared my throat and tried again. "You yourself said you're a magician, you can make this work."

"But if I don't," he repeated doggedly, "I want Little Miss to promise. Your parents' request for permission to dig will be approved. I have already arranged this. Now I just need your promise."

When I hesitated, he took a step toward me. "Kimosiri cannot do it. A hulking foreigner who cannot speak? He would be questioned at every turn. No, it is you that must go. The information in the tablet cannot fall into the wrong hands. The artifacts it leads to, they would cause untold destruction, even open the boundaries between life and death. You must promise me that you'll return it to Egypt if I cannot." His black eyes bored into me until finally I had to say, "Yes! Yes, I promise already!"

His face relaxed and he bowed. "I am most grateful. And

now you must go. I have much to prepare for tomorrow's rendezvous."

"This is goodbye, isn't it? There won't be time tomorrow, not if you're trying to snatch the tablet from Chaos."

"Yes, it is goodbye. At least until you return to my homeland. Then I will find you and we will meet again." He nodded his head at Kimosiri, who came over to escort me to the door. My mind was so full of questions and emotions that I hardly knew where to begin. I turned to look back at Awi Bubu, whose slight figure was limned by the faint light in the room, and I was suddenly struck by how very much I would miss him. Even though he and I had appeared to be at odds for the last weeks, I somehow trusted him.

CHAPTER TWENTY-NINE

THE GRAND OPENING

IT WAS ALL HANDS ON DECK beginning early Friday morning. Father had us up and out of the house at the crack of dawn with hardly a moment spared for bolting down some toast.

It was a long, painful day, which I spent feeling as if I were tiptoeing across hot coals. Not only were all the adults frantic with last-minute details, but I was utterly consumed by my upcoming appointment with Sopcoate.

Father was barking, Mum was soothing, Weems was prancing, and Fagenbush skulked silently. Stilton was a twitching, flinching, shuddering wreck. I tried to get him alone on three different occasions that morning, but he evaded me each time.

Henry was heartily sick of all of us and had retired to the family room with yet another book. Even Isis grew impatient with me when I tried to pet her and ended up squeezing just a bit too tightly. She gave a yowl of protest and left.

I finally decided to make myself useful by going to the reading room and researching the curse on the Sekhmet statue. I also wanted to see if I could find a mention of a temple dedicated to Thutmose III. I had no luck with either of those but did manage to stay out of everyone's way until it was time to get dressed for the reception.

At ten minutes to four, Father tracked me and Henry down in the family withdrawing room; we had both changed into our Sunday best. Father looked quite dashing himself in his frock coat. "Both of you stay out from underfoot now," he reminded us. "And for heaven's sake, don't create a scene." He gave me a pointed look before heading back to the foyer.

At four o'clock on the dot, the small string quartet struck up the first note, a long vibrant sound that echoed throughout the entire museum. The show had begun.

Without a word between us, Henry and I took up positions on the second-floor balcony overlooking the foyer where we could watch the entire goings-on.

Vicary Weems stood at the front door (the idiot man was even wearing his ridiculous spats!) and checked people's invitations before he allowed them inside. Honestly! He was as bad as that librarian at the British Museum.

His face had been scrubbed even shinier than normal, and his hair was pasted so smooth and flat it looked as if someone had taken shoe polish to his head. His ears, however, still stuck out rather jauntily, as if they were determined to listen in on every conversation that took place that evening.

It was hard to be a dandy with ears like that.

The board members were among the first to arrive, all looking quite posh in their frock coats and striped trousers. Grandmother arrived shortly thereafter and immediately asked for me.

Henry smirked, and I gently elbowed him in the ribs before getting to my feet. I brushed off my knees and motioned frantically for Henry to come with me as I made my way to our waiting grandmother.

I dodged a server balancing a tray of champagne flutes and nearly trod on Grandmother's silk slipper. I braced myself for a scolding, but she simply said, "There you are. Where have you been hiding yourself?"

"Henry and I are doing our best to stay out of the way, Grandmother," I explained. "I think I've had enough of parties for quite a while, thank you."

She looked at me sharply to see if I was being fresh. When she was satisfied I wasn't, she gave a brief nod. "Excellent.

It's nice to see you beginning to develop some sense, even if your parents aren't."

It took enormous effort to bite back a retort, but I managed it, then quickly retreated to our hidey-hole before I could change my mind. Henry joined me a moment later, only he'd had the good sense to pilfer a number of canapés. He further surprised me by offering to share them.

"Thank you," I said. Even though there was no room in my stomach for food—it was too full of nervous butterflies—I took two, not wanting him to think I was ungrateful. Besides, it could be a long night and it wouldn't hurt to have a bit of sustenance. Even prisoners awaiting their death sentences received a last meal. Surely I was entitled. Although I doubted very much that two canapés counted as a full meal.

I nearly choked on the second canapé, however, when I saw Wigmere's regal figure arrive. He was the head of the Antiquarian Society, so it made sense that he would be here; nonetheless, the sight of him was like a stab to my heart. I was very glad I was hidden from his view, since I was not sure I could bear seeing him face to face. I suddenly decided it would be wise to leave early.

But I had one last thing to do. I motioned Henry closer.

He widened his eyes a bit. "Now what?"

Then I told him of my plans. All of them. I did it for a number of reasons: I wanted desperately to repair the trust between us; I missed that and wanted it back. Also, in spite of my best efforts, Henry had now experienced the very worst sort of Egyptian magic, and there was no point in trying to keep it a secret from him anymore. And as Awi Bubu had said, half knowledge could be dangerous. And last: "I think it would be better if you didn't come, Henry. I'd like someone to stay behind, a person who can tell others what has happened if"—I swallowed—"if something goes awry."

Henry looked relieved, then embarrassed. He glanced down at his highly polished boots, which he was scuffing against the floor. "I'm sorry I didn't believe you," he mumbled.

"Oh, Henry! I so wish you'd never had a reason to believe me. It was my hope to keep you, along with the others, safe from all this."

"I know, which makes me feel even more wretched that I made fun of you. You're not playing a game, are you? It's all real, isn't it?" He looked at me, his eyes still hopeful that I was just playing.

"Yes, Henry. It's all real."

He was quiet for a long moment, then asked, "Do you have any more of those amulet things?"

"Of course." I took the gold *wedjat* eye that Wigmere had given me—my most powerful amulet—and slipped it around Henry's neck.

He looked down at it before tucking it into his shirt, out of sight. "Thanks," he said, staring at the balcony in front of him as if it were the most fascinating thing on earth. "I don't think I'm like you, Theo. I'm not brave about things I can't see."

My chest ached a bit, and my eyes grew damp. "You're brave in other ways, Henry. Do you mind very much staying behind tonight? To bring in a cavalry charge if I'm not back in a few hours?"

Again, a relieved look passed across his face. "I'd be glad to," he said, with an extra bit of emphasis on *glad*.

"Excellent. I'll be meeting Awi Bubu at Cleopatra's Needle at five. If I'm not back by six-thirty, I guess you'll have to go ahead and tell Mother and Father I've gone missing."

"But you'll be back long before then, won't you, Theo?" His bright blue eyes (so unlike mine) pleaded for reassurance.

"I plan to be, Henry." I reached out and ruffled his hair, just like Father had a hundred times before, and was surprised at how silky it was. "See you in a bit, then," I said, and slipped down the hallway to my closet.

I retrieved the tablet and the orb from their hiding place, put them in my satchel, and made my way to the west entrance.

The grand opening had been planned for late afternoon in order to take advantage of the daylight to show the exhibit at its best. Unfortunately, there wasn't much daylight. The fog had come in thick and dirty and foul—even so, I felt utterly exposed leaving the museum, as if even the wind had eyes that were watching me.

Of course, according to Awi Bubu, the wind *did* have ears and reported to others, so it wasn't as if I were being all that fanciful. I gripped the satchel even tighter and clutched the Blood of Isis amulet so firmly that one of the edges poked clear through my glove.

It was taking my life in my hands, trying to cross New Oxford Street at this hour and in this weather. No one could see a thing, and half the drivers had gotten out of their carriages and were leading their horses along so as not to risk driving them straight into another carriage or, worse, an omnibus or motorcar. Fog does strange things to sound, so that wasn't a reliable guide either.

Once across Oxford Street, I kept my steps brisk and purposeful. The fog was even thicker over there, which did quite a lot to hide the dilapidated buildings and their distressed occupants, but it was quite spooky knowing they were there, just hidden in the fog. I think I'd rather have been able to see them.

When I turned down Garrick Street, I heard a sound that chilled my blood: footsteps echoing behind me. Would Sopcoate make his move for the tablet before I reached the meeting place? I clutched the satchel handle even more firmly, pausing only long enough to tell if the footsteps would pause as well. If they did, it was a clear sign I was being followed.

I waited, and the muffled footsteps slowed to a standstill. The sharp tang of fear tingled on the back of my tongue. I resumed walking at an even faster clip. I had to reach the meeting place before Chaos caught up to me.

Or was it Trawley and his scorpions? Stilton had been very busy at the reception, and I had told him nothing of my plans. I tried to comfort myself by remembering that Awi Bubu was counting on the scorpions following me. That was part of our plan.

I just wished the plan weren't so nerve-racking. I longed to break into a run and hurry to the Embankment, but it was so foggy, I was afraid I'd lose my way.

My nerves were strung tighter than a harp. I did my best to ignore the steps behind me and tried to peer through the pea soup to locate the next street. Coming up from behind me, a shape loomed out of the fog on my left. I started to run, but it grabbed my arm.

CHAPTER THIRTY

THE STILTON STANDS ALONE

"'ANG ON, MISS! Don't jump out of yer skin now."

All that adrenaline turned to warm runny treacle and left me weak in the knees. "Will!"

He rocked back on his heels, peering at me with a worried look on his face. "You thought I was one o' them Chaos blokes, didn't you?"

"Or one of the scorpions. Either way, I'm glad it's you." The truth was, I could have happily kissed his cold red cheek.

"Well, that's why I'm 'ere, miss. To wotch yer back."

My heart soared at his words, at the sheer relief at not being alone in all this. And then I remembered what was at stake for him. "Oh, Will, you can't! It's too dangerous—"

He puffed a bit. "'Ow's that? It's too dangerous for me but not for you? Not ruddy likely. Besides, this is me neighborhood. I know it inside and out."

"That's not the kind of danger I'm talking about. Wigmere will be furious with us, and I'm afraid it will completely ruin any chance you might have for a future in the Brotherhood of the Chosen Keepers."

Will set his mouth in a stubborn line. "I'll have to take me chances, miss. It's wot people do, we watch each other's back. I'm not lettin' you go in there alone."

At his firm declaration of support, my eyes began to sting. I blinked rapidly. "But Wigmere won't take kindly to your going rogue like this."

Will was quiet for a long moment. A wide range of emotions played across his face: frustration, disgust, resignation, and resolve. "Doesn't make no difference, miss. I got to do wot's right. Letting you go in there alone ain't right."

Unable to help myself, I threw my arms around him, nearly beaning him with the heavy satchel. "Oh, Will."

"Geroffme!" he said, sounding a bit panicked as he pushed me away. Once I was safely at arm's length, he straightened his jacket and cleared his throat. "Now, we can't stand here jawing all night. Let's move out."

As we headed down the street, I heard someone else behind us. I started to mention it to Will, but he said, "Don't worry 'bout 'im, miss. It's just Ratsy. We work better in pairs."

"Oh," I said, understanding. "He watches your back like you're watching mine."

"Exactly, miss." Will beamed as if I were an exceptionally bright pupil.

On the way to the Embankment, I explained to him the plan Awi Bubu and I had worked out. Will decided that he and Ratsy would get in position and hide until they thought things couldn't possibly get any worse, and then they'd make their move.

The rest of the journey passed in solemn silence, our footsteps muffled by the fog. I could barely make out Will next to me, and I couldn't hear his brother at all, which seemed unusual in and of itself.

The hardest part was when we reached Wellington Street and had to march past Somerset House with its hundreds of windows. I couldn't help but think of Wigmere, glad that he was attending the exhibition opening and not sitting in his office. That would have made it worse somehow, having to actually sneak by him.

Then we were on the Embankment, clinging to the garden side of the walk. The fog reeked of the Thames, and the well-spaced lampposts cast a peculiar greeny-yellow light down on the concrete. It was cold and damp enough that there was little other traffic. It was impossible to see more than a few yards ahead, and I was half afraid we'd walk right by Cleopatra's Needle. Not to mention that Sopcoate and his band of Chaos agents could step out of the fog and ambush us at a second's notice. I readjusted my grip on the satchel.

At last the monument came into view. Actually, it wasn't the needle itself I saw first but the hindquarters of one of the sphinx guardians. I stopped walking and put my hand on Will's arm. "We're here." I whispered just in case Sopcoate had decided to come early.

Will nodded. "You go on, miss. Whistle if the coast is clear, then we'll come get in place."

"Whistle?" I asked. "Don't you think that's a bit obvious?"

Will rolled his eyes. "What signal would you rather use?"

"How about if I just clear my throat?"

Will looked at me askance.

"Loudly," I added.

"Oy, all right, now get moving before them others get 'ere!"

Feeling horribly exposed, I crossed the Embankment, darting out from the shelter of the trees in the park to the concrete steps that led up to Cleopatra's Needle. There was no sign of anyone else. I climbed the short flight of stairs to

the base of the obelisk, careful to watch my footing on the slick wet pavement. I peeked around to the other side to see if anyone was lurking there. There wasn't.

That left the stairs down to the dock on the Thames. I stepped around to the back of the needle and peered down, but all I could see was thick billows of fog undulating gently in the breeze coming off the river.

I cleared my throat, then waited.

Very faintly, almost as if they were merely heavy raindrops, the pitter-patter of footsteps could be heard, one set off to my left, the other on my right. I dearly hoped I hadn't made a horrid mistake by allowing Will and Ratsy to accompany me. Not that I could have stopped them, but still . . . After Henry's recent disaster, I could hardly bear the thought of being responsible for anyone else's safety.

I sat on the bottom step, tucked my satchel under my knees, and settled in to wait. Sopcoate had said to meet at five o'clock. It was a quarter to now. I assumed that Awi Bubu was in position somewhere, but that was only a guess.

Before long the sound of more footsteps reached me. They were coming from the left, opposite the direction we had come. I couldn't see anyone yet because of the fog, but I strained to listen, and there seemed to be dozens of them. Surely that couldn't be right? How many men did Chaos need to hand off one simple package?

The first figure emerged from the mist, and I recognized the short, barrel shape of Sopcoate immediately. He had traded his sailor disguise for a top hat and an enormous overcoat against the weather. My heart sank at the sight of the tall German on Sopcoate's left, von Braggenschnott. He had a personal vendetta against me and was a bit of a loose cannon.

I got to my feet as the rest of the Chaos agents appeared out of the mist. There were nearly a dozen of them. Sopcoate stopped when he was alongside the sphinx. "You've come," he said. "You must have gotten my warning."

At the reference to my grandmother, my temper flared. "Yes, that was quite brave of you, burgling a defenseless old woman." My anger still fizzing through me, I lifted my gaze from his and surveyed his followers. "Just how many men do you need to take possession of one measly tablet anyway?" Perhaps not the wisest thing to say, but there was something about having my back to the wall that made me throw caution to the wind.

Von Braggenschnott's single hand twitched and he took a step forward. Sopcoate reached out and stopped him. "We have learned to underestimate you at our own peril. Furthermore, we thought we'd need the others to subdue you."

A small alarm bell went off in my head. Subdue me? That did not sound good.

"You see, we have no intention of leaving you behind this time. You're coming with us. You are arguably too valuable to eliminate, but you are far too much of a liability to leave behind. Not only can you identify me and the others, but your instinct and talent for meddling is uncanny. Besides, when we find the cache of the gods, your unique skills might come in handy."

They meant to kidnap me! Why had I ever thought they'd keep their word?

He took three steps closer. "You have interfered with our plans for the last time. We will take you with us and make you an agent of Chaos, whether you wish to be or not."

A squeal of fear rose sharp and hot in my throat, but I swallowed it back. This was far worse than I had ever imagined. It had never occurred to me that they'd take me with them.

"Before we proceed, I want to see the tablet. I'll have none of your tricks now, so open the bag slowly."

I leaned over and set the satchel on the damp concrete step, then opened it and drew out the dull green tablet. Sopcoate's eyes fastened on the artifact, and his face lit up. "It is ours, then. We will finally have access to all the power of the gods. Hand it over."

There was a faint rustle behind me. "I'm afraid there has been a change in your plans." Awi Bubu's voice floated down from his hiding place up by the needle, filling me with relief. His tone possessed an underlying menace that I'd never heard before.

Sopcoate took a surprised step back. "Who are you?"

"Merely an Egyptian who has a more valid claim to this artifact than you do."

Sopcoate barked out a laugh. "The only valid claim is that of the one who can take it by force. As you can see, you are greatly outnumbered."

There was the scuff of a heavy shoe on the concrete up by Awi Bubu. "As you can see, I do not come alone," he said.

Sopcoate laughed again. "One man—even such a large one as that—does not put the odds in your favor."

"Perhaps not, but then, I have never been one for putting my faith in odds. I put my faith in higher things. Ah, look. We have even more company."

Sopcoate whirled around to see where Awi Bubu had been looking at the gardens that abutted the Embankment. Eight men wearing long flowing cloaks stepped out from behind the trees. The lamplight reflected off the bald white head of the middle one: Aloysius Trawley. Almost against my will, my eyes searched the scorpions; I felt a sharp stab of disappointment when I spotted Edgar Stilton among them.

He wouldn't meet my gaze.

Awi had been right. Stilton had led Trawley right to us. Even though we'd counted on that for our plan to work, it still hurt.

Trawley's wild eyes zoomed around our small gathering. After pausing briefly on Sopcoate, he finally looked at me. "You have lied to us," he accused. Before I could answer, he took a step forward. "Repeatedly. And after we trusted you and took you into our family. I even had my men watching out for you."

"Watching out for me? Kidnapping me at every turn is more like it."

Trawley flung his hand theatrically in Sopcoate's direction. "Is that why you give what is rightfully ours to these men?"

"Ha!" I didn't mean to laugh, but honestly. As if I were willingly giving anything to anyone. "I *give* nothing to them. They have threatened my family if I don't hand it over."

"Then perhaps *we* shall have to threaten your family as well."

There was another flicker of movement in the trees behind the scorpions. More reinforcements? I wondered. But the tall figure remained tucked behind the trees and didn't come forward. A moment later I caught a faint whiff of ox dung. Fagenbush. Had Wigmere sent him to help?

As if hearing my question, Fagenbush shifted slightly so

that our eyes met. Then he very deliberately turned his back on me and disappeared into the trees. My heart sank like a stone. I tried to tell myself that he was only one man, that he couldn't have made that much difference against these odds, but I still felt wretched, as if the last, final connection had been broken.

"Enough of this!" Sopcoate said, the authority in his voice from years of ordering men about cutting through the group. "It is we who have come for the tablet, and it is we who will leave with the tablet. And the girl."

Beside him, von Braggenschnott smiled.

Trawley smiled back. "Not so fast. We are evenly matched, I think, and I will have the tablet. You may have the girl. She is far too much trouble."

"Don't I know it," Sopcoate muttered. Then, louder, he said, "Actually, I think you will find that we are not evenly matched."

Trawley frowned, then looked to his row of men, as if counting them. As he reached the men to his right, Basil Whiting and two others took two giant steps toward the men from Chaos. Trawley looked annoyed. "Make no move until I order you," he barked.

"But Supreme Master," Whiting said, "we no longer take your orders, I'm afraid. We have found a new master, one who is much less of a joke."

Trawley looked as if he'd been slapped when the full meaning of Whiting's words penetrated.

"Shall I count for you?" Sopcoate offered, his voice almost pleasant. "Eight plus three equals eleven. Eleven to five are odds I like very much."

Trawley looked from Sopcoate to Whiting, then back to Sopcoate, his despair and impotent fury mounting.

There was a soft, awkward sound as someone cleared his throat. I looked over to find Stilton stepping away from the remaining scorpions and coming forward to stand on my right. "Um, four," Stilton said to Trawley, sounding most apologetic. "I'm afraid there are only four of you."

For a moment, in spite of the grimness of our situation, my heart soared. Stilton *hadn't* betrayed me. Or not fully, anyway. If my face hadn't been so frozen with fear, I would have smiled at him.

Before Trawley could finish processing the full devastation of his ranks, Sopcoate spoke. "I'm tired of these games. Give me the tablet. Now!"

Behind me, Awi Bubu raised his voice in a familiar chant. I moved to the side a bit so I could better see what he was doing.

He was staring at the scorpions with his arms raised like an orchestra conductor's, chanting away.

But nothing happened. Well, Stilton lurched forward and

made as if to attack the Serpents of Chaos single-handedly, but none of the other scorpions moved. I reached out to snag Stilton before he got himself in trouble.

Trawley looked smug. "Your parlor trick will not work this time," he said. "My men have put wax in their ears to drown out your attempts to command them."

Uh-oh. We had not anticipated that.

"Enough of this chatter!" Admiral Sopcoate yelled. "Seize the tablet. I'll get the girl!"

However, as Sopcoate reached for me, Awi Bubu leaped down the few steps that separated us and grabbed the Emerald Tablet from my hands. Before Sopcoate could so much as bellow, Awi Bubu was moving around to the back of the obelisk, toward the ramp that led to the river.

CHAPTER THIRTY-ONE

WILL BE NIMBLE, WILL BE QUICK

MANY THINGS HAPPENED AT ONCE. Von Braggenschnott shouted something in German as he and four others scrambled after Awi Bubu. Sopcoate bellowed in rage, leaped forward, grabbed me, and held me in an iron grip. There was a shrill cry of attack as the remaining Serpents of Chaos, including Trawley's former colleagues, threw themselves on Aloysius Trawley and his three remaining men.

Ignoring Sopcoate's viselike grip biting painfully into my shoulder, I craned my neck around in time to see Kimosiri step forward to block von Braggenschnott and the others from reaching his master. But there were too many. As Kimosiri fought single-handedly with three of them, von

Braggenschnott and another Serpent pelted down the ramp after Awi Bubu and the tablet.

I held my breath, praying that the magician had managed to get away. My hopes were quickly dashed when I saw four Serpents of Chaos escorting him back up the ramp.

Sopcoate's gloating voice tickled my ear. "We had all the exits covered."

Kimosiri, who'd just knocked out the third man he'd been fighting, turned to see his master held captive. With a bellow of fury, he launched himself from the obelisk step onto the group of seven Serpents surrounding Awi Bubu.

There were now so many bodies around the little Egyptian that I couldn't catch a glimpse of him.

Stilton stood rather helplessly nearby, looking from Sopcoate to me, unsure what to do. "Go help them!" I told him.

"But what about you?" he asked.

"I'll be fine, go!"

He stiffened his jaw, clenched his hands, and then ran up the steps to where the others were and threw himself into the melee. I closed my eyes briefly and realized that if we survived all this, he and I would have to have a serious discussion about strategizing.

From somewhere in the midst of all those men, I heard Awi's voice call out faintly, "The orb, Little Miss, the orb!"

Kimosiri detached himself from the flailing arms and legs and staggered to my side. He was holding his left arm awkwardly, and blood streamed from his nose. He reached for my satchel to retrieve the orb for Awi.

My hand snaked into my pocket where the orb lay, a cold hard presence against my leg. "Kimosiri!" I yelled. "Here!" He looked up from the satchel, and before Sopcoate could guess at my movement, I yanked my hand from my pocket and lobbed the orb at Kimosiri.

Except it is hard to throw something when one is being held in a viselike grip, so my toss fell rather short. Kimosiri dove to the ground, caught the orb, then was back on his feet again in one flowing movement. He waded into the fight once more, wielding his elbows and feet like billy clubs.

A second later, golden light burst from the huddle of men. Some fell back, clamping their eyes shut against the fierce glow. Through the thinned crowd, I was able to see Awi Bubu on his knees tapping out a quick pattern on the orb's symbols. There was a faint humming sound, then the evening exploded in a deafening roar and a flash of blinding light.

Sopcoate kept a tight hold on me as we were knocked to the ground.

I blinked my eyes repeatedly, and when I could see again, Kimosiri was helping Awi Bubu to his feet; Awi still had the tablet in his hand. The rest of the Chaos agents lay scattered on the ground, some of them quiet, some groaning.

Catching my eye, Awi Bubu tried to bow, then grimaced painfully and clutched his side. He turned to leave, and Sopcoate called out, "Wait!" as he struggled to his feet, dragging me along with him.

Awi stopped, and I saw now that one of his eyes was swollen shut, and his left arm hung at an odd angle. He was bleeding from a cut on his lip, and there was a long gash along his forehead. He held his body gingerly, as if something were broken.

Sopcoate reached into his pocket, then I felt the press of something cold against my temple. "The girl," he said quietly. "If you don't hand over the tablet—and that orb—I'll kill the girl."

Everything inside me went still, and every clever or useful idea I'd ever had flew from my head.

Awi Bubu seemed rather stunned too. He looked at me, then at Sopcoate, then at the tablet itself, the lone map to a cache of artifacts so powerful they made the orb seem like a child's toy. What horrid mayhem could Chaos create with power such as that? Even so, I couldn't quite nod my head to give him permission to leave. I'm not *that* brave.

Awi Bubu's shoulders slumped. "Very well," he said.

Still keeping the pistol firmly against my head, Sopcoate said, "Put them on the bottom step."

His eyes glued on Sopcoate, Awi Bubu did as instructed.

Sopcoate lifted the gun from my temple and waved it at Awi. "Now back away slowly."

As Awi slowly backed up the steps, I heard a rustle of movement from behind the sphinx. Had Sopcoate heard? I slanted my gaze toward his face, but he was totally focused on Awi Bubu's progress up the stairs.

Which is why he never saw the rock that came flying through the night air and thwapped him sharply in the forehead. He bellowed, then let go of me as he staggered with pain. That was the only chance I needed. I ducked down out of his reach. He bellowed again and tried to come after me but was assaulted with another rock, this one striking his hand and causing him to drop his gun.

Without pausing to think, I leaped after the gun and kicked it with all my might, sending it swirling into the darkness.

With the gun safely gone, Will raced out of the shadows and headed straight for the tablet and orb sitting on the bottom step. "Run, miss!" he shouted. Without breaking his stride, he snatched the artifacts from the ground, jumped over two of the bodies lying in his way, and disappeared into the trees lining the far side of the Embankment.

"After him!" Sopcoate bellowed.

The few remaining Serpents of Chaos left their positions standing over the fallen Black Sunners and took off in hot pursuit.

Awi collapsed to his knees. Kimosiri knelt beside him, but Awi waved him away. "No, go after the boy. See that he is safe."

Kimosiri paused, clearly not wanting to leave. "Go, my faithful friend," Awi said with command in his voice. "And may the gods be with you."

As Kimosiri got to his feet, he sent Sopcoate a look of such utter loathing that I was surprised it didn't strike him dead on the spot. Then Kimosiri loped into the trees after the others with long powerful strides.

I tried to stand, but my legs weren't working properly, so I began to crawl over to Awi Bubu, who had collapsed completely once Kimosiri was out of sight. Before I could reach him, something snaked out and grabbed my clothes to pull me back.

"Oh, no, you don't." Blast! Sopcoate held on to me like a bulldog.

I strained against his grip, hoping my beastly dress would tear and let me escape, but no such luck. Using my skirt as a sort of fishing line, he began reeling me in. I strained even harder, using everything I had to get away from him.

A figure emerged from the thick fog behind him. I blinked, unable to believe my eyes. Then a sturdy cane arced through the air and descended on Sopcoate's head with a resounding *thwack*. He dropped me like a hot potato and whirled around to find—

"Grandmother?" I said in disbelief.

CHAPTER THIRTY-TWO
A TALE OF TWO GRANDMOTHERS

My grandmother paid me no heed and raised her cane again. "Get. Your. Hands. Off. My *granddaughter!*" she said, emphasizing each word with another blow from her cane. Sopcoate ducked and managed to avoid some of the blows. "How *dare* you!" *Thwack!* "And what are you doing alive?" *Thwack!*

Before Sopcoate could answer that question, Grandmother connected solidly with his skull and he crumpled to the ground.

"Grandmother?" I could barely believe my eyes. But before I could say anything else, a racking cough drew my attention. "Excuse me a minute, ma'am," I said, then rushed over to Awi Bubu's side, afraid of what I'd find.

He was still alive, but his breathing was rapid and shallow.

Grandmother joined me and lowered herself a bit creakily onto the stair. With her eyes firmly fixed on the Egyptian, she asked me, "Are you all right, then?"

"Yes, Grandmother. Thank you for the assistance back there. How did you know where I was?"

"Henry," she said shortly, then stopped talking when Awi Bubu struggled to speak.

When no words came out, she moved closer to Awi Bubu and removed her gloves. I stared open-mouthed at her as she shoved them at me and then began rolling up her sleeves.

"Close your mouth, Theodosia," Grandmother ordered. "You don't want to take in any more of the night's evil miasma if you can help it. It's not healthy."

My mouth snapped shut.

"Do we know the extent of his injuries?" Grandmother asked, gently examining the gash on his forehead.

"N-no," I stammered. "I haven't had a chance to determine those yet."

Awi Bubu's voice came so faintly we had to lean in close to hear it. "I believe my left leg is broken, as are a number of my ribs." Then he coughed, which made him wince in pain, and collapsed back into silence.

Grandmother became all business. "If he took that hard a blow to his midsection, then we'll have to keep an eye out for internal injuries or a punctured lung." She leaned in so close to Awi Bubu that their noses were practically touching. "Is that blood on his mouth from a cut, do you think?"

I could only stare at this woman who had clearly done something with my real grandmother.

Once she was convinced the blood was from the cut on his lip, she began palpating his sides, looking for broken ribs. With her eyes fixed on her patient, she asked offhandedly, "How long have you known Sopcoate was alive?"

A sick, metallic taste filled the back of my throat. I thought about fibbing. I could tell her I had only found out that night. Instead, I blurted out the truth, the weight of all those secrets simply rushing out of me. "Since he disappeared," I said.

Grandmother laid her coat on top of Awi Bubu. "We need to keep him warm," she said. "Hand me your coat."

As she folded my coat up into a pillow and placed it gently under Awi Bubu's head, she sniffed. "Why did you not tell me?"

"I was told I couldn't. That it was a matter of grave national security. That no one, not even my family, could know."

Our eyes locked for another long moment, then she turned back to the man on the ground. Her next words shocked me more than all the other shocking things that had happened that night. "Good girl. I'm pleased to know you have the sense to keep a secret of that nature if you have to."

I began to wonder if I was stuck in one of those nightmares where reality was so intertwined with bizarre distortions that it felt frighteningly real, and when you finally wake up, you're weak with relief. Surely that was the reason I found enough courage to blurt out the next question. "How do you know so much about taking care of injured men?"

She dabbed at Awi Bubu's face with her fine Belgian lace handkerchief. "When I was a girl I longed to follow in Florence Nightingale's footsteps. More than anything, I wanted to attend her school and march off to the Crimea to help tend to our country's brave and injured.

"Unfortunately, my father would have none of it. Nursing was for the poorer classes, and he was appalled to think of a child of his dirtying her hands, and reputation, with nursing work."

Grandmother? A nurse? I simply stared at her as my mind struggled to absorb it all.

Awi Bubu began to cough horribly, as if he were trying to dislodge a lung. His face was drawn with pain when he was done.

"We need some bandages to stabilize his ribs," Grandmother said. "I'll be right back." She slowly rose to a standing position and then disappeared behind the nearest sphinx.

As soon as she was out of sight, Awi's hand reached out and clutched at my sleeve.

"I'm right here," I assured him. "I haven't gone anywhere."

He opened his mouth and tried to speak, so I leaned closer.

"Our plan. It did not go so well. Did it?"

Afraid discouragement would worsen his condition, I said, "It went well enough. We have the tablet, I think. Will is quick and resourceful and knows this neighborhood. We'll get you patched up, then you can return it to the *wedja*—er, return it, just as we planned, and resume your place among them."

"No, Little Miss. Now it is I who must play the skeptic. That will not happen." He was interrupted by another coughing fit, and this time, blood came up. I looked around frantically for Grandmother, but she was still ripping bandages from her petticoats. Awi tugged at me again, this time more urgently. "You must honor your promise," he said, then went limp.

Pure panic jolted through me. "Oh, do hang on, Awi.

Hang on!" I ordered. Then I remembered my amulets. I lifted the two from my neck and placed them on his chest.

After a long moment, his eyes fluttered open. "The information in the tablet cannot fall into the wrong hands." He grabbed my arm and tried to lift himself up. "Promise! Promise me you will do this thing."

Terrified he'd cause himself grave injury, I said, "I promise. Now lie back down before you kill yourself."

He eased down and his grip loosened. "Leave an offering on the altar in the Temple of Horus at Luxor. The Eyes will know of it and come for you." Then he coughed once more and fell horribly, wretchedly silent.

"Grandmother!" I cried.

Grandmother hurried over, her hands full of bandages. "What's happened?"

"He's collapsed," I said.

"It may be just as well." She leaned over and felt for his pulse. "He is still alive, although his pulse is erratic. Here, rip off his shirt so we can bandage those ribs and keep them from poking about into something vital."

Some small part of my mind registered the irony of Grandmother Throckmorton telling me to rip off a man's shirt. I reached down and yanked gently; the thin torn cotton came away easily. Then I gasped.

There on the base of Awi Bubu's throat was a tattooed Eye of Horus. The very same design that Stokes had worn, that all of the Brotherhood of the Chosen Keepers wore.

Beside me, Grandmother sniffed. "That's a rather heathen-looking mark," she observed as she bent down and began bandaging his ribs.

There was the sound of a footstep on the pavement behind us, and I was terrified that the Serpents who'd been chasing Will had returned.

But it was Clive Fagenbush who stood on the Embankment behind me. His black eyes were glittering and unreadable in the dark. He stared at me a long moment, then glanced down at Awi Bubu. His next words would have shocked me to the core if there had been any part of me left to shock.

"I've brought help," he said.

And indeed he had. No sooner had he uttered those words than a group of men emerged from the fog and headed in our direction. One of the men—a doctor—broke away from the group and hurried forward, a large satchel in his hand. "Let me through," he said. He knelt at the wounded man's side, and Grandmother began briskly rattling off Awi's condition. The doctor looked at her once in surprise, then rolled up his sleeves and got to work.

Bodies continued to swarm out of the fog. Scores of them

carried stretchers, and they quickly moved along the Embankment, collecting the fallen, including, I was glad to see, Sopcoate. He would not get away this time. I recognized another of the fallen and rushed to his side before they could cart him away.

Stilton sat leaning back against Cleopatra's Needle, his face drawn and pale. He clutched his left arm, which seemed to pain him greatly. "It came true, you know."

"What came true?" I asked, sitting down next to him.

"Your prophecy for Trawley. 'The Black Sun shall rise up in a red sky before falling to earth, where a great serpent will swallow it.'"

"How so?"

"Well, half the Black Sun was lured into joining the Serpents of Chaos, effectively swallowing up Trawley's organization. And look." He pointed to the horizon, where the setting sun had turned the dark gray clouds a fiery red.

We were both quiet for a long moment, then he spoke again. "I-I'm sorry, miss. I've been a fool."

"Shh," I told him. "They'll have you patched up in no time."

Stilton shook his head. "No, miss. I've put you in danger. That's inexcusable. I just never realized how unhinged Trawley was. I know you can never forgive me. I'll hand in my resignation to your father tomorrow, first thing."

"Don't be daft," I told him.

Poor Stilton blinked. "B-beg p-pardon?"

"Stilton, you joined the Black Sun in good faith. You had no idea who or what Trawley was, or what he was capable of doing, or that he would kidnap people off the streets, did you?"

"No, miss. None at all."

"And as soon as you discovered that, you left him. Then to top it off, you put yourself in grave personal danger to make amends. I don't know about you, but in my book, that's good work."

Stilton's mouth opened and closed, but no words came out. Which was just as well, since two men arrived to put him on a stretcher. "Take good care of him, he's on our side," I told them.

"Very well, miss." They laid the stretcher on the ground and very gently helped him onto it. When he was secure, each man grabbed an end and lifted.

"Theodosia." Wigmere's deep, familiar voice reverberated like a bell.

Slowly I turned to face him. "Sir," I said cautiously.

Using his cane, he limped toward me as fast as he could, then put his hand on my shoulder. "Are you all right? Are you hurt?"

For some reason, his question made my eyes sting a bit.

"I'm fine, sir. But Awi Bubu is in rather bad shape." Afraid I would begin bawling like a baby, I hurried over to the doctor and asked, "Will he be all right, do you think?"

"He has a good chance," the doctor said. "This woman here may have helped save his life." Surprised at this praise, Grandmother got flustered and stood up to smooth out her skirts. "Well . . . ," she began.

"Lavinia?" Wigmere said, looking at Grandmother strangely. "Is that you?"

Grandmother's head jerked up at the sound of Wigmere's voice. "Charles?" The two of them stared at each other awkwardly for a long moment, a moment where entire paragraphs of unspoken things passed between them.

"Sir!" the doctor interrupted. "You should come see this."

Alarmed at the urgency in his voice, I followed Wigmere over to the old Egyptian's side.

"Look." The doctor pointed to the wedjat eye tattooed at the base of Awi's throat.

Wigmere's eyes widened as he took in the ancient symbol, and then he looked sharply at me. "Who is this man?"

"It's rather a long story, sir," I said.

"Yes, of course. And you are cold and exhausted. As no doubt you are, madam," he said to Grandmother.

"I am fine," she said, rather stiffly. "Would you care to explain how you know my granddaughter?"

"I am afraid that, too, is a long story," Wigmere said, rubbing his temple.

Clutching my hands together tightly, I took a step toward Grandmother. "Remember what I said about national security?" I tilted my head in Wigmere's direction.

"Oh," Grandmother said, her eyes widening as she looked from Wigmere to me and then back to Wigmere, her expression a little less frosty. "I see."

Wigmere appeared relieved, which proved he knew my grandmother rather well indeed.

"I do need to speak with her for a moment before I have our carriage take you back to the museum," said Wigmere. "We could, of course, take you each directly home if you'd prefer, but it would raise fewer questions if you both returned to the exhibit opening."

"Of course we'll return to the museum," Grandmother said. "But we'll use my carriage, thank you."

"Lavinia . . . ," Wigmere said, and then the two of them moved away to speak more privately. I was burning with curiosity but wasn't brave enough to follow them. I'd pushed my luck quite enough for one day.

Feeling somewhat exhausted, I sat down on the bottom of the concrete steps and waited for someone to tell me what to do next. Within moments, a large shadow loomed over me.

It was Fagenbush. I was so tired that all I could manage was "Thank you for bringing help. That got rather out of hand."

His long nose twitched and I could have sworn I saw a faint glimmer of humor touch his lips. "One could say that." Then he did the most extraordinary thing. He lowered himself to the step and sat down next to me. Oddly enough, I was too tired to even try to scoot farther away.

He propped his elbows on his knees and watched with great interest as the men from Somerset House finished tidying up. All the fallen had been put on stretchers by now and were being carted away.

"They clean up rather like ants after a crumb, don't they?" he said.

I smiled. "Exactly like ants after a crumb," I agreed.

Fagenbush reached down and picked up a stray leaf from the pavement. "That was excellent work you did on the Sekhmet statue," he said. "I've confirmed your translation, and you're right, it does appear to be referring to an important temple."

I swung my gaze back around to him to see if he was pulling my leg. "Really? You've confirmed it?"

He nodded.

Then I couldn't help it. "Why?" I blurted out. "Why are you being nice to me all of a sudden?"

He shrugged awkwardly. "Why did you ask for my help on the statue?"

Because he was close at hand, I almost said, then realized it was more than that. I was tired of loathing him. It took a surprising lot of energy, and there were just too many truly important things I needed to spend that energy on. I shrugged too.

"Exactly," he said, his voice as dry as a bone.

I thought for a moment. "Does this mean we're friends then?"

A small, bitter smile crossed his lips. "Don't know that I'd go that far. We'll start with not enemies."

"Wigmere will be so pleased," I murmured.

"Excuse me." A stern-looking woman wearing a nurse's uniform and a no-nonsense expression stood over me. "I'm here to check on the child."

"Of course," Fagenbush said, getting up. "I'll leave you to it."

When he left, I told her, "I'm fine."

"We'll let me be the judge of that." Her attitude brooked no disagreement. Honestly! She was as bad as a governess.

Against my protests, she led me over to one of the waiting unmarked carriages and shooed me inside, where she proceeded to give me a quite thorough (and embarrassing) examination.

"Well, there doesn't appear to be any sign of damage of any sort." She sounded so disappointed I had to resist the urge to apologize.

"Let's get you cleaned up then." She whipped a damp cloth out of her bag and thoroughly washed my face, hands, and wrists. Next she brushed the tangles from my hair and set it right. She even produced a needle and thread and repaired my ripped dress with terrifying efficiency. When she was finished, she said, "You're to wait here for Lord Wigmere."

"Yes, ma'am," I said, and then she left me to stew in my own thoughts and wonder what Wigmere would have to say.

A few minutes later, the carriage door opened and I braced myself to face Wigmere; I was overjoyed to see instead Will's dear familiar head peeking in. "Oy," he said, getting in and closing the door.

I hopped to my feet, nearly cracking my skull on the carriage roof. "You made it! Do you have the tablet with you?"

"Nah, I 'id it in a real secure location, miss. No one'll ever find it."

The carriage door opened again and Will stopped talking. Wigmere appeared in the doorway. "Excellent," he said. "I need to speak with both of you, and here you are."

He climbed into the carriage, then rapped on the ceiling and called out instructions to take us to the museum. "Your grandmother decided I could drive you back myself since we still have a few things we need to discuss."

"Sir." I rushed to begin. "I'm so sorry but I tried—"

He held up his hand to stop me. "You carry no blame in this incident, Theodosia."

That stopped me cold. "I don't?"

"No. Nor you," he said to Will, whose jaw dropped at this announcement.

"I'm afraid it's us who have let you down. Me, to be precise." He fell quiet for a moment and looked out the window at the passing buildings. "I tried to treat you like a junior agent, Theo. A smaller version of the many agents I have working for me." He turned his craggy gaze to me. "But you're not. You're . . . something else entirely and I shouldn't force you into a mold you don't belong in." Something very tight and painful in my chest began to loosen. I couldn't say anything for fear that if I opened my mouth, my voice would wobble horribly.

"And you." Wigmere turned his fierce attention to Will. "You have reminded me how true loyalty and trust can mean more than the most expert knowledge and experience."

Will flushed bright red all the way to the roots of his hair. He tried, unsuccessfully, to squelch his goofy smile. "Does that mean I can 'ave me job back?"

"Yes, you are reinstated as of ten minutes ago."

Will bobbed his head in thanks, then hesitated a moment before rushing to ask, "Does that mean I can maybe be one of them Chosen Keepers? Someday?"

I held my breath, afraid Wigmere wouldn't be willing to go that far.

Will scooted to the edge of his seat. "I 'ave a plan for learning all that Egypshun stuff I need to know."

Intrigued, Wigmere said, "You do?"

"Aye." He jerked his head in my direction. "Miss 'ere's agreed to teach me all she knows."

Wigmere looked startled for a moment, then began to laugh, a great warm, rolling sound that filled the carriage. When he was done, he murmured, "If she can't turn a pig's ear into a silk purse, no one can." Louder, he said, "Unorthodox, admittedly, but if you can learn what you need to over the next few years, I will certainly consider it. As I said, loyalty and sheer doggedness are just as important as knowledge. Now, I believe we are here."

The carriage rolled to a stop. Will motioned for me to go first, but Wigmere held me back. "I need to speak with her a moment," he said.

Will nodded, then hopped out to wait. I turned to Wigmere expectantly.

"I will be in touch tomorrow," he told me. "We still have much we need to clear up. And if your parents notice you were gone, you are to tell them you and your grandmother went for a ride. That was her idea," he added.

I was dying to ask how he knew her, but almost as if he were reading my mind, he said, "Best hurry back in. It would be a shame to have them miss you this late in the game." And with that, he rapped on the ceiling, forcing me to jump out or go back to Somerset House with him.

Coward.

CHAPTER THIRTY-THREE
ALL MUMSY WAS THE BROTHERHOOD
(OR, OF CABBAGES AND HORUS)

THE EXHIBIT RECEPTION WAS A HUGE SUCCESS, and the museum doors opened Saturday morning to throngs of people waiting to see Thutmose III, the Napoleon of Egypt. Mother and Father and all the curators were out in full force, answering people's questions and directing them to the most interesting bits.

As happy as I was for them, I couldn't get into the proper frame of mind. Sitting high up on the main staircase, tucked out of sight, I was too worried about Awi Bubu and his injuries. To make matters worse, Henry was at home with our housekeeper, Mrs. Murdley, packing. He would be heading back to school late that afternoon. I was feeling quite alone.

Just as I let out another sigh, a small figure appeared at the foot of the stairs. I sat up straighter. "Will?"

"'Ello, miss. Wotcha lookin' so sad about?"

"Oh, lots of things," I said, getting to my feet and brushing off my skirts.

"Well, this might cheer you up. Wiggy's sent me around wif the carriage. Says you're to come see 'im and the Egypshun. If you can get away, that is."

My spirits soared. "Of course. No one will even notice I'm gone in this crush."

"Well, come on then, shake a leg."

Once we were in the Brotherhood's unmarked carriage and under way, I noticed that Will was fairly beaming. "You look like the cat that's got at the cream," I said, curious as to why he was in such good spirits.

Will's smile deepened. "I promised 'im I'd keep mum, miss."

I tried to be irritated that he was keeping secrets from me, but his happiness was so infectious that I couldn't hold on to it. I peppered him with questions the rest of the way: Had he seen Awi Bubu? How was the old Egyptian doing? What about Kimosiri? But Will said nothing, merely grinned like the Cheshire cat and shook his head.

At last we arrived at Somerset House. Will and I hopped out, and the doorman waved us in. We hurried up to the third floor, where I paused. "How are we going to get past Boythorpe?" I asked quietly.

"No need to, miss. 'E's been suspended."

"Suspended? Boythorpe?"

"Aye, miss. Fer not lettin' you in to see Wigmere the other day."

I stopped dead in my tracks. "You mean Wigmere hadn't given that order?"

"Nope. Boythorpe 'eard Fagenbush and Ol' Wiggy talkin' and jes took it upon 'iself to keep you out."

It is rare that I am speechless.

"Eh, miss. Close yer mouth. You look right like a codfish, you do."

I closed my mouth and tried to reset my entire worldview. Wigmere had not shut me out. He had not turned me away. Suddenly I felt half a stone lighter.

"Now come on, miss. They're waiting."

Much to my surprise, Will led me past Wigmere's office. "Where are we going?" I asked.

"Level Five," he said.

"Don't you mean Level Six? I've never heard of Level Five."

He just gave me that self-satisfied smile and led me down

the hallway to the small narrow door marked PRIVATE—NO ENTRY. He opened it, and we hurried over to the curtained wall. Will pushed the curtain aside and punched a buzzer.

There was a clunk and a whirring of gears as the lift rose into view. The operator tipped his cap at us. "Where to, mates?"

"Level Five." Will motioned for me to get in first.

"Level Five, coming right up." And then the floor dropped out from under me, and my stomach tried to shoot out the top of my head. Honestly. How did people get used to this?

Will leaned close. "I love that part, don't you, miss?"

"*Love* might not be quite the right word," I muttered.

The lift stopped moving and the door opened. "Level Five," the operator announced.

I stepped out into a room that had spotless linoleum floors and curtained partitions lining the walls. Under the curtains, I could see beds. Rows and rows of beds. I turned to Will. "It's a hospital!"

"The main infirmary, miss. They're waitin' for us in 'ere." He led me past the curtained beds to a small, private room where the magician was resting. Wigmere sat in a chair on the far side of the room. Kimosiri stood in one of the corners, his arms folded and his eyes glued to his master.

"Awi Bubu," I said, and rushed over to his bedside. Slowly

his eyes fluttered open. "Little Miss." His smile was feeble, but welcome nonetheless.

I looked up at Wigmere. His eyes were warm and kind and concerned. "How is he?" I asked.

"Well, he is tougher than he looks. He has four broken ribs, a punctured lung, and a broken collarbone."

Poor Awi Bubu. "Is there anything I can do to help?"

"No," Wigmere said at the exact same time Awi Bubu said, "Yes. Remember your promise."

Wigmere frowned. "That hasn't been decided yet."

Very calmly, Awi Bubu turned his head and studied Wigmere. "Yes, it has. Little Miss has given me her solemn promise."

"But she's a young child. Surely there's another way to—"

"Excuse me, sir. But you yourself have given me similar responsibilities in the past."

Wigmere harrumphed slightly into his mustache, then fell silent.

I took a step closer to Awi Bubu. "But that doesn't matter anyway, does it? Won't you be able to go yourself?"

"It is as Lord Wigmere has told you. I will not be able to travel for a long while."

"Oh. Have you told him *everything?*" I asked Awi.

"Not *everything*, Little Miss. But our similar marks of

Horus do put an interesting twist on our relations. Lord Wigmere and I have been discussing a plan to get your parents to Luxor soon."

"There's barely enough time left in the season to get there and back," Wigmere said. "Which is why we haven't finalized anything." He shot a pointed glare at Awi. The old Egyptian ignored it.

"Actually, I might have an idea," I said.

Both men turned to stare at me.

"I think we've discovered the existence of a temple, Thutmose III's temple, to be exact. It was mentioned in some of the steles and papyruses from Thutmose III's tomb. I haven't had a chance to tell my parents yet, but when I do, it's possible they'd be willing to leave immediately to lay claim to the discovery."

Wigmere leaned forward in his chair, his face set in concerned lines. "And why would you want to do that, Theodosia? Are you so eager to return to Egypt?"

"Well, my last visit was abruptly cut short, if you'll remember. And . . ." I was anxious to return to the land where I was born, to see if I could begin to understand how that had shaped me. I glanced at Awi Bubu, and a look of complete understanding passed between us.

"And as a budding archaeologist, Little Miss has many things to explore in my homeland."

"Exactly."

Wigmere finally sighed. "Very well. If there's one thing I've learned, it's that it's pointless to try to stop you. One might as well try to stop a force of nature. Best to just go along and do everything in my power to see that you are safe. And I will do that much, of that you can be certain." He shot me a ferocious look, as if daring me to argue.

"Very well, sir," I said meekly.

He harrumphed again.

Just then a nurse came bustling in. She went immediately to the side of her patient and gave him a quick examination. She glanced reproachfully at Wigmere. "You've tired him out, sir. He really needs to rest now."

"Very well. We were done anyway." He propped his cane on the floor and rose to his feet. Awi Bubu motioned me closer. I moved toward the head of his bed, and he motioned me closer still. I leaned down and put my ear next to his mouth. "Remember to say nothing to anyone of the things I have told you. Even the wind has ears."

With Awi Bubu's words still echoing in my head, I followed Wigmere out into the hallway, where he began heading back to the lift. "I do not like this, Theodosia. I do not like it at all. The last time you went to Egypt on our behalf, it was because our entire country was in jeopardy."

"But sir, don't you see? If the Serpents of Chaos get their

hands on the tablet and learn where all the really powerful artifacts are, our country—the whole world—will be in even more jeopardy."

"Well, yes, there is that. Speaking of which, you'll be happy to know that we caught all but four of the Serpents of Chaos; only von Braggenschnott and three others got away. It's the largest haul we've ever managed. Needless to say, the Home Office is quite pleased."

"What about Trawley and the Order of the Black Sun?"

"We're keeping Trawley a while longer; the man appears quite unstable. Fortunately for the others, however, they had their ears stuffed with wax for some reason, which kept them from overhearing anything that would compromise us or our organization, so they are free to go. We've given them all a good recommendation and reference to a nice, respectable club. Oh, and here." He thrust a small velvet pouch at me. "The nurse said you weren't wearing the amulet I'd given you."

My cheeks warmed with embarrassment. "I'm terribly sorry, sir. I know it's bad manners to give away a gift, but Henry needed it more than I did."

Wigmere raised one bushy eyebrow. "How's that?"

"He was being haunted by Tetley's *mut*." As Wigmere's eyes widened in shock, I rushed to add, "But everything is all right now, sir. It's taken care of."

A look of intense curiosity crossed Wigmere's face. "And how did you manage that?" he asked.

I gave him a long steady stare. "Do you really want to know?" I would tell him, but I was fairly certain he wouldn't like the answer.

He searched my face a moment longer, then sighed. "No, probably not."

Who said grownups couldn't be taught?